New York Times bestselling author

COLLEEN GLEASON

THREE TOMES BOOKSHOP

CW00552646

STAKES CAKES AND MANDRAKES

Published by Oliver-Heber Books

0 9 8 7 6 5 4 3 2 1

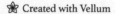 Created with Vellum

CHAPTER 1

In cozy Button Cove, spring pirouetted into May on tiptoes of warm weather, swirling with skirts of soft rains that brought colorful tulips, daffodils, azalea, lilacs, hellebore, and more.

The early farmers' market was in full swing, and there were planter pots of herbs, flowers, and vegetables for sale on tables all along Camellia Court. The street was blocked off from vehicular traffic on Saturday mornings through Memorial Day, after which time the market moved to a larger area during tourist season. There were booths with homemade jellies, honey, and syrups for sale, along with crafty garden decorations like birdhouses and metal stakes, and wreaths woven from dried or silk flowers. Someone was even selling frozen pierogi from an ice cart, and another enterprising soul had set up a table offering homemade jerky and smoked whitefish.

Jacqueline Finch, owner and proprietress of Three Tomes Bookshop, didn't have potted plants or jellies or spreads to offer during the farmers' market, but she had—in her mind—something even better.

Books.

So, during the farmers' market hours, she propped the door to her shop wide open and settled a huge pot of perky red geraniums and spilling purple petunias outside the entrance. Next to the flower pot was a table offering samples of hot tea from the store's tea room upstairs.

Shoppers were enticed to come inside the store when they stopped for the steaming samples—for early mornings in northwestern Michigan in May were still often chilly—and saw the large round table just beyond the doorway. It was filled with a display of beautifully photographed books about gardening, grilling, and farm-to-table cooking. On a different table within eyesight of the casual passerby, Jacqueline had put together a "Beach Read" arrangement that offered everything from Nora Roberts to Hank Philippi Ryan to Harlan Coben to Alyssa Cole and more.

Jacqueline would have preferred to offer coffee samples as well as tea, but Mrs. Hudson—who ran the tea room at Three Tomes and who also happened to be landlady of 221B Baker Street, London—firmly refused.

"This 'ere is a *tea* shop," Mrs. Hudson had told her theoretical boss firmly two days ago when Jacqueline broached the subject yet again. The older woman gestured around the café on the second floor of the bookstore where she reigned supreme. "Not a coffee shop. Plenty o' places to get the demon bean for them who wants it," Mrs. Hudson went on with a forbidding glint in her eyes. "And who wants to cut their belly up with all that strong, nasty brew? When they do, then they're needing to come here for a nice, civilized cuppa, won't they now?"

Jacqueline had mostly given up arguing with Mrs.

Hudson over the tea-versus-coffee issue, so every morning she brought an insulated travel mug downstairs from her apartment on the third floor. It was filled with a brew made from the "demon bean"—coffee, or, in her mind, the Elixir of Life.

Over the last five or so weeks since she'd moved to Button Cove—located on Lake Michigan in the "pinkie" area of the Michigan mitten—from Chicago, Jacqueline had learned to pick her battles when it came to running the bookshop. Especially when it included conflicts with Mrs. Hudson (who really *was* Sherlock's landlady and who had somehow come out of the book and become flesh and blood) or her counterpart and nemesis, Mrs. Danvers—the condescending, sometimes scary, and always dour housekeeper from the gothic novel *Rebecca*.

Literally **from** the gothic novel.

Jacqueline had come to accept the fact that other literary characters popped in and out of books on whims or fancies and made their appearances at or near her store, but it was Danvers and Hudson who were permanent fixtures in the place. In some ways, it was a godsend, for the two women knew everything there was to know about running the store, *and* they worked for free.

Three Tomes Bookshop was housed in a large, square brick house on shady Camellia Court. The bottom two floors, filled with tall, narrow windows and somehow spacious and never-ending rooms despite their Victorian heritage, displayed the wares offered by Jacqueline's store: books—new, vintage, and antiquarian—as well as sundries such as crystals and other New Age accessories, along with the tea room and its offerings. Each room on the first floor showcased a different genre, and on the nonfiction side of the shop, rooms wound into warrens of shelves and alcoves, and more shelves and alcoves. It was amazing how many nooks and crannies could be found by a shopper browsing books, getting lost in a seemingly infinite labyrinth of cozy, tome-crammed spaces—all of which had the space for convenient chairs, benches, or stools on which to sit and peruse.

The second floor was the café, as well as hosting a large children's section and the New Age room. And the third floor was Jacqueline's apartment, where she'd been living surrounded by books—heaven!—for just over a month.

This morning, the third Saturday in May, was such a stunningly gorgeous spring day that Jacqueline had considered offering iced tea instead of hot tea—but she hadn't even suggested the idea to Mrs. Hudson. They obviously hadn't had much in the way of ice back in Victorian England—and she suspected Sherlock Holmes's landlady would have considered cold tea to be sacrilege, and adding lemon to it would be nothing short of blasphemy.

The sky was bright blue, without a cloud to be seen. The blocked-off street had been packed with pedestrians accompanied by toddling children, leashed dogs, baby carriages, the occasional walking aid like a cane, bicycles, and scooters from eight o'clock on. The center of the road was lined with displays of the colorful and aromatic potted plants and other booths, while the sidewalk had remained clear for the merchants to offer tables of their wares.

Across the street from Three Tomes Bookshop was Sweet Devotion—a bakery owned by Jacqueline's friend Suzette Whalley. Several café tables were arranged on the sidewalk, and patrons sipped coffee and enjoyed scones, muffins, pastries, and more from Suzette's gifted baker's hands.

Nadine Bachmoto, owner of the Yoga4Life studio located above the bakery, had set up a small display of colorful caftans and tie-dyed sundresses, yoga mats, and some rustic-looking sandals made from hemp rope. She had lit a few stems of incense and poked them into Suzette's flower pots. Even from across the street, Jacqueline could see the thin tendrils of smoke rising with their scent.

Jacqueline waved to Nadine from across the way, and her energetic friend waved back.

"See you later tonight!" Nadine called, cupping her hands around her mouth so the sound carried. "Mojitos!" She did an enthusiastic fist pump.

Jacqueline gave her a thumbs-up, grinning at the reminder of their Saturday-evening plans. Nadine had recently become enamored with mixology, and had been experimenting with making all sorts of cocktails —which she offered to Jacqueline and Suzette whenever she tried a new recipe. She'd recently acquired a large mint plant and been inspired to mix up all different flavors of mojito. Tonight was to be pineapple.

The three women had become good friends since Jacqueline took over the bookshop more than a month ago. They had a lot in common: a trio of women pushing up against age fifty, each owning and running their own business on Camellia Court—and, at the moment, each of them single and unattached.

It helped that they'd also been joint witnesses to a witch having a temper tantrum, along with the destructive entity that had been possessing a mirror as said destructive entity attempted to destroy Jacqueline's apartment.

And then there was the incident when they'd had

to steal a crocodile tooth from the herpetarium at the zoo...

The three had shared a lot in the last five or so weeks, and Jacqueline was grateful for her new friends because there weren't very many people who would take the mystical, magical elements of Three Tomes Bookshop at face value.

The reminder of temper-tantrum witches had Jacqueline glancing down the street. She heaved a sigh when she saw that the swinging sign was, unfortunately, still there: EGALA'S. She kept hoping either the shop would close just as quickly as it had opened, or at least that the sign would blow away so Jacqueline wouldn't have to be reminded of it every time she looked down the street.

Egala Stone was a witch and distant relation of Jacqueline's, and *she'd* expected to inherit the bookshop. When she didn't, Egala tried several things to chase Jacqueline away and ruin her business, but, fortunately, none of them had stuck.

So, having given up on that tactic, Egala opened her own shop on Camellia Court. Thus far, Jacqueline had not ventured down the block to see precisely what her distant cousin was offering for sale. She was almost afraid to do so, considering that only two weeks ago, Egala had given Jacqueline's friend Wendy a purse that was cursed... and blamed Jacqueline for it.

Jacqueline's phone vibrated quietly in the pocket of the sundress she'd optimistically donned this morning (even though she was wearing a little sweater over it now), and she pulled it out to see a text from Nadine. *Hotness alert,* it read, followed by a flames emoji.

She looked across the street to where Nadine was

watching her and shrugged, miming looking around in confusion even as she grinned at her friend's antics.

Who said high school girls had all the fun?

Nadine held up a hand sideways and jabbed a finger excitedly at its palm, obviously trying to hide the direction in which she was pointing from whomever might be paying attention (not that anyone was paying attention to the antics of two almost-fifty-somethings).

Jacqueline obligingly looked in the direction her friend was not-so-covertly pointing and saw the broad shoulders and strawberry-blond-going-to-white head of Detective Miles Massermey as he strolled down the street. She rolled her eyes at Nadine (even though her friend couldn't actually see her eyes roll from across Camellia, she'd obviously get the point) and, fighting a grin, shook her head—even though she agreed one hundred percent: Miles Massermey was a definite "hotness alert."

But he wasn't alone on this bright and sunny Saturday morning, and when Jacqueline saw the young woman accompanying him, she couldn't control a wince.

The last—and only—time Jacqueline had spoken to Massermey's daughter Mandy was the night of the Great Crocodile Tooth Heist. Mandy, who was a veterinary student at Michigan State, was working at the Button Cove Zoo for the summer, and she'd sort of caught Jacqueline as she was sneaking into the zoo during a horrific thunderstorm.

Now, Jacqueline hesitated between diving into the shop and hoping they wouldn't stop in, and being a badass, owning her "crone-ness" (accepting her crone-ness had been, apparently, the reason she'd had to make the tooth heist), and remaining boldly on the sidewalk to greet them. It wasn't as if she and Massermey actually had anything going on, but there was that potential.

Before she could make a decision (and she was leaning toward ducking inside, to be honest), Massermey held up a hand that gripped a go cup and used it to give her a little wave.

Oh crap. They were definitely headed her way.

Jacqueline smiled at him and tried not to worry whether her Orphan Annie red hair made her look like a schoolgirl. The recent uncontrolled curling of her previously straight hair was the result of facing down—and standing her ground with—the possessed mirror in her apartment. After everything went batshit crazy, Jacqueline had ended up with an eighties-style perm in place of her previously neat French twist...but it didn't look nearly as good on her as it had on Julia Roberts in *Mystic Pizza.*

Now that they were nearer, Jacqueline saw that Massermey's daughter—she must be in her early twenties—was walking a gigantic, shaggy dog the color of an inkblot as she sipped from her own go-cup.

"Hey," said Massermey as they approached. Since the sidewalks on Camellia were shady, his sunglasses were pushed onto the top of his head, and the corners of his light blue eyes crinkled with pleasure as well as age. He filled out a casual button-down shirt with solid shoulders and arms, and a middle that was just beginning to soften and spread. While his close-cropped hair was far more white than strawberry blond, his full beard and mustache still shone like Kris Kringle's, except for two small white patches at the corners of his mouth. "Beautiful day, isn't it?" He was holding two go-cups of, presumably, coffee. "Mand, this is Ms. Finch. You remember my daughter

Amanda, right?" At least he didn't mention the zoo. "And this hairy beast is Cullen. Named, apparently, after someone in a vampire book?" Massermey glanced at his daughter inquiringly. "Or was it a movie?"

"It was both, Dad, and you know it. He watched *Twilight* with me," Mandy said, and Jacqueline watched in fascination as Massermey's cheeks bloomed pink. He was fair-skinned, with a heavy swath of freckles that gave him a ruddy look, but there was a definite blush going on beneath them. "And then he went out and bought the whole DVD set so we could watch the rest of it. With the director's cuts. He was obsessed."

"Geez, Mand, that was supposed to be our secret," he said, giving her a dark look even as his cheeks turned even redder.

"Oh, right," said Mandy, not appearing the least bit ashamed. "Oops." She was laughing even as her father continued to look mortified. "I guess I won't tell her how you were rooting for Jacob, then, hm?"

"I mean... vampires are *not* supposed to sparkle," he said, spreading his cup-laden hands. "And why would Bella want to be with a century-old man, anyway?"

"Excellent point," said Jacqueline. "Plus, I like dogs, and werewolves are the next best thing—er, sort of. Not to mention I've always had a problem with the whole Edward-going-to-high-school thing. Why on *earth* would anyone want to go to high school if he didn't have to? I mean... high school is awful."

"Exactly." Massermey nodded.

"And don't get me started on the plot holes in *Fifty Shades of Grey*," Jacqueline said, ignoring, for the moment, that she'd sold a good number of the series by E.

L. James in the last month and had just reordered three more copies of *Grey*. To each his or her own when it comes to books. As long as people were reading, she was delighted.

"Well, that I won't argue about," said Mandy. She'd transferred her cup to the leash hand so she could bend slightly to pat Cullen, who was sitting patiently next to her. Jacqueline could hardly see his dark, friendly eyes, for they were nearly obscured by the thick, curling hair that fell over them—something to which she could relate. "The *Grey* books were good—deliciously so!—but there were definitely some things about them that made me go *hmmm*."

"Wait... you read *Fifty Shades of Grey*?" Massermey's face was now fire-engine red as he looked at his daughter. "With the—uh... Oooh boy." He didn't seem to know where to look.

"Yep—with the Red Room and everything," Mandy said, smiling gleefully. "It was really *hot*, Dad. You should try them. Unless you already have... "

Massermey's face was now beet red, leaving Jacqueline to wonder if maybe he *had* tried reading the books. Or watching the movie.

Feeling mischievous, she said, "I've got the whole set inside if you're interested, Detective Massermey."

He made a strangling sound, then seemed delighted—and relieved—when he remembered he was holding two cups. "I brought this for you," he said, offering Jacqueline one of them. "A vanilla latte with two-percent and stevia, right?"

Now it was Jacqueline's turn to blush (damn her fair, redhead's skin) as she caught the interested, assessing look from Mandy—who, by the way, did *not* have her father's fair skin or strawberry-blond hair. She had chestnut-brown hair and a light sunburn over her golden tan—probably from working outside at the zoo.

"Right. Wow. Thank you," Jacqueline said, taking the drink. Still feeling the weight of the daughter's attention on her, she lifted the cup and drank too quickly... and scalded the inside of her mouth. Of course. "Yum." She managed to smile while hiding a wince as the roof of her mouth burned. "It's perfect."

"The lady who runs the tea shop upstairs doesn't allow coffee," Massermey explained to his daughter. "She calls it the demon bean. So we—I mean, Jacqueline, has to sneak it in when she can."

"I see," replied Mandy, lifting a brow. "So, Ms. Finch, I'm sure you must have some other steamy books in there... "

Massermey groaned and looked up at the sky. "I thought I'd successfully changed the subject."

"Nice try," Jacqueline said as she and Mandy laughed. "And yes, I certainly do have more books along those lines. I'll be happy to show you."

Mandy gave Cullen's leash to her father. "I'll be right back, okay? You stay with Daddy now, all right, Cully-boy?" she added, bending to look her dog in the eye—a difficult feat, due to the curtain of hair falling from his brow. Nonetheless, Cullen's tongue swiped out to give his mistress a kiss, and he remained politely in a sit. What a good boy he was!

Jacqueline winked at Massermey, who was gritting his teeth, then gestured for Mandy to precede her into the shop... and then realized she'd just gotten herself into a fix. Now she was alone with Massermey's daughter, and it was very possibly going to be *awkward*.

Once inside, before Jacqueline could say anything about steamy books, Mandy stopped and said, "Can we talk? I mean, I'm still interested in the erotica, but I need to talk to you."

Oh crap. Jacqueline managed to keep a smile—albeit a weak one—on her face. Was Mandy going to give her the third degree about her relationship with her father? Or worse, warn her away from him?

Not that there was anything to warn her away from at this point. She and Massermey had only had coffee together a few times, flirted a bit in between, and, just two weeks ago, apprehended a killer.

Well, Massermey had done the apprehending, but Jacqueline had helped clear the way for that.

"Um, sure," she replied. Because what else was she going to say?

"Okay, thanks." Mandy seemed as uncomfortable as Jacqueline was. "Is there somewhere we can—you know—uh"—she gestured to the shop at large, indicating she wanted privacy—"talk?"

Great.

"Sure," Jacqueline said, though her throat had gone dry. Although she'd gotten better at dealing with conflict over the last few weeks—by coming face to face with pissed-off witches, possessed mirrors, angry crocodiles, and dead bodies—she still preferred to avoid it whenever possible.

And she suspected there was going to be some serious conflict coming from Mandy Massermey.

She gestured to the stairs that led from the front area of the shop to the tea room, but just as she started to follow Mandy up the steps, three older women burst into the shop, all in the same sort of cluster of flowing skirts, arms, and legs.

Jacqueline had never been so relieved to see the ZAP Ladies as she was at that moment.

"Good morning, Jacqueline!" sang the shortest,

palest, and roundest of the three as the cluster separated itself into individuals, each of whom was somewhere in the vicinity of eighty years old.

Pietra, the "P" of the ZAP trio, was dressed in a flowing lemon-colored dress that made her pink cheeks look even prettier than usual. She was carrying a small basket, which Jacqueline hoped contained some delectable baked treat.

She loved all of Suzette's offerings at Sweet Devotion—and in fact sold them in the café upstairs—but there was something extra-special about Pietra's glazed blueberry-cream scones. And besides, Petey usually included some catnip biscuits for the two shop cats, Max and Sebastian.

"Hi, Jacqueline," said Andromeda, whose spiky hair was silver with vibrant cornflower-blue tips today. She was lithe and slender, with dark golden skin and an elfin face, and she was already looking around for Sebastian. The cat and the crone had a special affinity for each other, and sure enough, at the sound of Andromeda's voice, the amber-colored feline slinked out seemingly from nowhere. "There's my handsome boy," she said, scooping up the cat.

"Beautiful Saturday, isn't it?" said the third newcomer. Zwyla had to duck when she stepped over the threshold so her blood-red head wrap didn't get bumped askew. An imposing woman dressed in a white peasant blouse and long, tiered denim skirt with sandals that had crisscrossing straps up her calves, she had the features of an African queen and the height of a basketball star.

"Couldn't be more gorgeous," Jacqueline replied with a happy smile.

At first, she'd found Zwyla to be somewhat aloof and even intimidating at times—at least, compared to her gregarious companions. But once she'd gotten to know her better, *and* learned that Paul Bunyan (yes, *the* Paul Bunyan) had an unrequited crush on Zwyla, Jacqueline's reserve had disintegrated and she felt perfectly comfortable with all three of the ZAP Ladies equally. While they were mysterious and secretive in some ways—and annoying at times—they were always a hoot to have around.

"Petey wanted to bring you some scones and catnip for the kitties," Zwyla explained. "And Andromeda has a new tea she wanted you to test out in the tea room—what's in it besides calendula, Andi?"

Andromeda surfaced from where she'd been nuzzling and murmuring to Sebastian. If Jacqueline didn't know better, she'd think the feline and woman were exchanging lovers' secrets. Andromeda's bright blue eyes rose over the cat's fluffy head as she smiled at Jacqueline. "It's got lemon peel and lemon balm, silver sage leaves, raspberry leaves, and dried calendula with a little cinnamon. I think it's perfect for the spring— the sage, you know, for purging. We use silver sage for smudging the house, right? So I thought we ought to consider smudging—so to speak—our own bodily house, you see?"

"I mean, you could *smoke* it if you really meant it to be a smudge for the body," said Pietra.

Andi hushed her with a hand gesture and a roll of the eyes. "The raspberry leaves and lemon balm for feminine health. And the cinnamon for a bit of heat as well as cleansing."

"I'm sure it'll be wonderful," Jacqueline said, successfully hiding her ambivalence. After all, even though she wasn't particularly fond of tea—especially herbal, which didn't have caffeine, so why even bother?—Andromeda's specialty teas sold very well not only through the tea room, but through Three Tomes' online store as well. And the few blends she'd been forced to drink actually had been pretty good... once doctored up with honey or sugar.

"I like it," said Zwyla, her dark eyes gleaming with humor as if she were reading Jacqueline's mind.

"That sounds really good," said Mandy, who'd been waiting politely as Jacqueline greeted the ZAP Ladies.

"It's not really, unless you drown it with honey," said Pietra, leaning close and speaking in a low voice. "But don't tell her I said that."

Mandy giggled. "I'm sure it's still beneficial even with the honey, right?"

"I don't see why not," said Petey. "The Universe wouldn't have given us honey and sugarcane if we weren't meant to enjoy them, now, would she?"

"Definitely not," replied Mandy, still smiling.

Just then, a small surge of people spilled in through the front door. Jacqueline looked around and saw that neither Mrs. Danvers nor Mrs. Hudson were in sight—which was unusual, and, in this case, unfortunate.

Or... maybe not. Delaying whatever it was Mandy Massermey wanted to talk to her about was *fine* with Jacqueline.

"Good morning," she said, greeting the potential customers—one of whom was already approaching the counter with a colorful book about patio container gardening.

"I just *had* to get this," said the customer, a woman in her early forties. She was carrying a pretty summer straw tote bag. Jacqueline noticed the decorative ornate E on the front and couldn't help but wonder if it was from Egala's—a thought that sent a shiver down

COLLEEN GLEASON

her spine for some reason. "The cover caught my eye
from out there on the street—by the way, that tea is
really good! And I'm not even a tea drinker. Anyway,
I've been *dying* do to some container gardening, and
this book just looks so *inspiring!*"

Jacqueline glanced at Mandy, who'd been patiently waiting for her all this time. "I'm sorry—I'll be
right with you."

"Oh, don't worry—take your time. I'll browse a little." Mandy smiled easily. She seemed sincere. Maybe
she wasn't all that eager to talk to Jacqueline about
whatever was on her mind either.

"I don't mind if you bring Cullen inside," said
Jacqueline, even though she winced a little at the
thought of the big dog bumping into stacks of books.
Nevertheless, she had a "dogs welcome" policy at the
shop—as long as they didn't bother the cats—and
Cullen seemed incredibly well behaved. "If your dad
has to leave, I mean."

"That's very nice of you, but Dad won't mind waiting. He's really good about that sort of thing, and he's
got the day off," said Mandy. "I mean, unless someone
ends up dead," she added with a wry smile.

"All right." Jacqueline had already begun to ring
up the container gardening book, but the customer
and her straw tote had wandered away to look at the
Beach Reads table. "Anyway, Mandy, if you want to
check out some of those other books—you know, the
steamy ones?"—she gave her a sly smile—"look on the
red-painted bookshelf in the romance room. I recom-
mend the Sleeping Beauty series by A.N. Roquelaure
—which is a pen name for none other than Anne Rice
—and *Carrie's Story* by Molly Wetherfield. Oh, and
anything by Colette Gale. You'll never think of *The*

Phantom of the Opera in the same way again after you read her take on it," she said with a grin.

"That sounds great," said Mandy, her eyes dancing. "Take your time—it sounds like I'll be plenty busy."

As she took a copy of Cole's *When No One is Watching* from the container-gardening customer, Jacqueline glanced outside to see Massermey standing there patiently with his go-cup and the horse-sized Cullen. He seemed to be enjoying greeting people as they walked past, chatting comfortably with some who stopped to talk or to pet the dog. *What a good guy,* she thought with a little tingle deep in her belly.

"Now, if I can just find my wallet in this thing," said the woman with a laugh as she opened her large straw purse. "It's— Well, what do you know—there it is. Right on top!" She drew out the wallet with triumphant flair. "That's the thing with big purses—you can never find anything in them when you need them."

"Or any size purse. Just ask Stephanie Plum," said Jacqueline with a chuckle. When the customer looked at her in confusion, Jacqueline explained, "She's a character in a really fun mystery series by Janet Evanovich. She's famous for always losing her gun in the bottom of her purse."

"Ooh! Do you have the first book?" asked the customer, her eyes lighting up.

Jacqueline pointed out the book to her—it was conveniently on the Beach Reads display—and happily rang it up.

"I wish you all the best with your container gardening," she said, slipping the three books into a bright blue Three Tomes Bookshop bag. "If you're local, you should stop back in and show me some pictures of your patio garden."

"Oh, that would be nice—and that's an incentive for me to actually *do* it," said the customer, whose name, Jacqueline had seen from the credit card, was Harriet Wellburg. "Plant things, I mean. Girls, did you find anything?" she said, turning to the two other women who'd surged in with her a few minutes ago. "I hit the jackpot!"

Over the next twenty minutes, Jacqueline got caught up in a flurry of helping customers find books, buy books, and order books. She lost track of the ZAP Ladies as well as Mandy, but every time she glanced up, she could see the detective still standing on the street with the ever-patient Cullen. And every time she saw him, her heart did an extra little bump that she tried to ignore.

What are you, sixteen? she asked herself.

"Thank you," said the last of the flurry of customers, who'd purchased three Piers Anthony books solely on Jacqueline's recommendation.

She was just about to poke her head outside and invite Massermey and the dog in when she remembered she'd meant to put out some water for any canines walking by. By the time she got the heavy pottery dish filled and brought it down from the café, another rush of customers had filtered in.

But by now, Danvers had materialized from somewhere in the depths of the shop and taken up the position behind the sales counter, looking like a grumpy black crow. Nonetheless, she was efficient at ringing up the customers—and *almost* pleasant at times—so that gave Jacqueline the opportunity to slip outside with the sloshing dish of water.

"Here you go, boy," she said, setting the water

down in front of Cullen, who slurped gratefully.
"Sorry about keeping you," she said to Massermey as
she rose. "I just got swamped, and Mandy is still
browsing."

"It's not a problem," he replied. "It's a beautiful
day, and I don't have to be anywhere but here." The
way his eyes lingered on her for a moment made
Jacqueline's stomach flutter a little.

"Oh, *there* you are! Detective Massermey!" came a
shrill voice. "I've been trying to reach you all morning.
You weren't in the office!"

Jacqueline felt the man next to her stiffen and
heard him smother a sigh as he turned and smiled.

"Mrs. Kilmeade. How are you today?" he said.

"Why, I'm just fine, but I'll be much better if you'll
give me an update on the investigation." The woman,
who was probably in her late sixties, was so thin that
she would have blown away in a strong wind. Her skin
was dead white and surprisingly smooth for her age,
with just the slightest of sag at her jaw. Iron-gray hair
was pulled back in a high, fifties-cheerleader-style
ponytail and held in place with a sparkly pink
scrunchy. Chandelier earrings of real turquoise and
silver dangled from her ears. She wore capri-style
jeans and what appeared to be an original Led Zep-
pelin t-shirt over her bony shoulders and boyish figure. Though it wasn't forecast to rain, she was carrying
an umbrella.

"We're following all relevant leads," replied
Massermey in a tone Jacqueline had never heard before. It was a combination of well-suppressed aggrava-
tion and perfectly correct politeness, with just a hint
of "not this again"—or maybe it was "get off my back."
"As soon as we have any information, I'll be in touch."

"I tried you at your office this morning," said Mrs.

Kilmeade. "But apparently you weren't *in*." She eyed
Cullen accusingly.

"I have the day off, ma'am," said Massermey in a
very polite voice. "And I'm spending it with my daughter." He absently shifted the leash in his hand, and
Cullen looked up, tongue lolling happily from the side
of his mouth.

Mrs. Kilmeade blanched, her eyes wide, and
looked from Cullen to Massermey and back to Cullen
again. Jacqueline suppressed a chuckle. Did the
woman really think Massermey's daughter was a big
black dog?

Then all vestiges of humor disintegrated because,
after all, Jacqueline *did* live on Camellia Court, and
she *did* have people coming out of books, and witches
living down the street, and possessed mirrors and who
knew what else... it certainly wasn't out of the realm of
possibility that there could be a shapeshifter in the
area.

Good grief. She shut that thought down *immediately*. The last thing she needed—the very last thing—
was a character from a Nalini Singh or Ilona Andrews
book showing up. Not that she would mind if Bones
from Jeaniene Frost's books happened to show up...

"She's inside," said Massermey. "My daughter is
inside the bookshop."

"Oh," said Mrs. Kilmeade, visibly relieved. "I see."
She peered at the window, which had Three Tomes
Bookshop painted in its signature bright blue lettering
arching over the top of the window pane so as to leave
the book displays inside visible and framed by the
words.

"Why don't you go on inside and take a look
around?" Jacqueline said.

"Oh. I don't know... this is *that* bookshop, isn't it?"

Mrs. Kilmeade pursed her lips and lifted her nose as if something reeked. "I've heard *all* about it. All the *talk*. Maybe you ought to start investigating what goes on in *there*, too, Detective." She sniffed and reached up to tighten her ponytail even as she peered inside.

"I'm Jacqueline Finch, the owner. Go ahead—you can look around and see for yourself," Jacqueline said, trying to remain friendly and nonchalant.

Mrs. Kilmeade eyed her with great skepticism, then, reluctantly—as if she were about to beard a lion in its den—she stepped across the threshold into the shop.

Jacqueline and Massermey exchanged amused glances as Mrs. Kilmeade stood there, looking around, then stepped back outside almost immediately. "It's fine. But I don't need any *books* right now." She gave Jacqueline another suspicious look. "As if that's the only thing they sell there, isn't it?"

Jacqueline had had enough. Time to nip this in the bud. "Oh, look—they're giving away free cake samples at Sweet Devotion!"

"They are? Where? But they never do that! And their muffins are always too dry," said Mrs. Kilmeade even as she eyed the bakery with interest. She popped open her umbrella. "Well, I'd better be getting on, Detective. You remember what I said, now, all right?"

"Yes, of course," replied Massermey in a more relaxed voice—probably because the woman was leaving.

"What investigation?" Jacqueline demanded as soon as the crotchety old bat was out of earshot.

"Oh, it's nothing," he said, flapping a hand. "She's got herself all worked up because it looked like someone dug up a grave in the cemetery and knocked over a gravestone."

"That sounds kind of serious," Jacqueline replied. "Vandalism at the very least."

"Oh, we take that sort of thing very seriously," he replied in a sober manner, as if realizing he might have sounded cavalier. "But it turned out someone had just dug up some old black-eyed Susans and a few prickly clovers and accidentally knocked into the stone. It was an old one from the Renfield family, and it fell over. I explained all of that to her, and that the stone is being fixed, but she wasn't satisfied. She lives next to the cemetery," he said with a sigh. "And she keeps the department informed when any kids are so much as putting a toe on the grass in the graveyard."

"Oh, I see," replied Jacqueline, remembering the days when she had been a nerdy preteen and how she'd pretended to be Nancy Drew while walking through a twilit cemetery with its long, dark shadows and utter stillness. "There's nothing wrong with walking through a cemetery, as long as you're respectful."

"Exactly." Massermey smiled at her. "I find them not only very peaceful, but also really interesting... and sad, too. The number of children buried there in the eighteen-hundreds is awful. So," he said, his smile turning into something a little more dangerous, "what's all this so-called *talk* about the bookshop? What exactly should I be investigating?"

Jacqueline felt her cheeks heat because there was a *lot* to read between the lines of those words. "I have no idea what she was talking about," she replied blithely, even though her heart was thudding hard and she actually *did* know what Mrs. Kilmeade had been talking about.

"Maybe I ought to do some checking things out,"

he said, that smirk still quirking behind his beard and mustache. "After hours, of course."

"Well, Detective," she said, "I'm not one to stand in the way of the authorities doing their job. So just let me know when you want to, um, open the investigation." She hoped her cheeks weren't as red as they felt, but knew that was probably a vain hope.

"As a matter of fact, I'm free tonight," he replied. "Apparently, Mandy's got dinner plans and forgot I had the day off." He sighed. "I'm not sure if I should be happy or sad that I'm not going to have to start the second season of *Bridgerton* tonight. It'll keep me watching all night."

"Oh, crap," Jacqueline replied, definitely feeling a little wave of disappointment. But not enough that she'd blow off her friends for a guy. "I've got plans to taste Nadine's take on pineapple mojitos tonight. Can we plan for that investigation another time?"

He looked a little disappointed too, but replied, "Well, since I know the three of you usually have pizza night on Sundays, I guess we're talking Monday? If you're free, *and* if a dead body or something else doesn't come up."

"Actually, I'm free tomorrow night because we're getting together tonight instead. For the mojitos. So Sunday would be perfect," Jacqueline replied, then suddenly realized she'd just agreed to what amounted to a *date*. "Um... would you like to start the investigation in my kitchen? I make a pretty good chicken piccata."

"One of my favorites," he said. "I'll bring the wine."

They smiled at each other for a moment before Cullen, who must have been trained to ruin the moment, whined and butted his head against Massermey's leg.

"I think he's getting bored," said Massermey. "I'll walk him down the street and let him sniff around a bit."

"I'll tell Mandy," said Jacqueline, suddenly feeling guilty that she'd been out here flirting with the young woman's father while the woman was waiting inside for her.

She guessed it was time to put on her game face and find out what Mandy wanted to talk to her about.

She just hoped the gal didn't have a problem with her maybe, sort of dating her father, because that ship, in the form of chicken piccata, was now firmly on the horizon and heading in to port.

JACQUELINE FOUND Mandy snuggled in the big red velvet chair in the romance room. She had a stack of erotic novels next to her, including *Bared to You* and *Wicked Ties*, and was paging through *The Claiming of Sleeping Beauty*, which had been Jacqueline's own introduction to erotica written for women.

"Wow," said Mandy, looking up with clear, bright eyes. "This is intense. You ought to sell vibrators here to go with them!"

Jacqueline choked on a laugh. "Um... probably not. Anyway, Anne Rice sure knew how to write, whether it was vampires or sex, hmm?" she said with a grin. "Speaking of the undead—your dad took Cullen for a walk down the street. He said he'd be back in a minute. Did you want to talk now?"

"Yeah." Mandy didn't sound very enthusiastic, but she closed the book and looked around. "I guess we can talk here, since no one is around."

"Only Mrs. Danvers out in the front room for the moment," replied Jacqueline.

"So. I need your help."

Jacqueline's heart froze in her chest. The last time someone had spoken those words to her in this bookstore, it was a teenaged girl who wanted a love potion.

And then there'd been the woman who wanted a protection amulet because her husband was trying to kill her.

And another woman had approached and said she needed "help," but they'd been interrupted, and, fortunately, Jacqueline hadn't seen her since.

That sort of thing was the "talk" Mrs. Kilmeade had probably been referring to. Somehow, someway, Three Tomes had acquired the reputation of being a sort of... witchcraftery place where women could come and get charms or spells or amulets or potions to help with their problems. They all seemed to think Jacqueline could—and would—assist them with their problems.

"What sort of help do you need?" she asked gamely.

"It's about my dad."

Jacqueline felt the color drain from her face. Damn. "Yes?"

"Well, it seems like you are sort of... close—"

"Not really," Jacqueline said quickly. "We've met for coffee a few times, but that's about it—"

"He said you helped him when that man died up at Big Bay Winery," Mandy said.

"He did?" Jacqueline wasn't sure whether to be pleased or worried that Massermey acknowledged how she'd gotten involved, since her involvement had included a bit of... feminine energy.

Not magic.

Not witchcraft.

Feminine energy.

"Anyway, so... I need your help. I've been sort of seeing someone," Mandy said. "And I don't think Dad's going to... like it."

A rush of relief swept over Jacqueline so strongly that she felt lightheaded. This wasn't about her and Massermey after all. *And* it didn't seem like it was going to be about feminine energy either.

"You don't think your dad is going to like the ma— the person you've been seeing?" She swiftly corrected herself from the assumption that Mandy was talking about a man. Maybe she liked women and was worried her father wouldn't understand. "Why not?"

"Well, he's... older than me. Quite a bit." Mandy's smile was pained and a little crooked. "Honestly, I think he's going to blow a gasket when he meets him. Dad, I mean. Blow a gasket." She huffed a sigh. "Luke won't mind; it'll be Dad. It's because he's a cop, you know. He's always thinking the worst about everyone."

"How much older is this Luke than you?" asked Jacqueline. She figured Mandy was twenty-two or twenty-three if she was a year or so into veterinary school.

"He's forty... five."

Jacqueline swallowed a gasp. Massermey, who was probably about fifty himself, was definitely going to hit the roof. "Yeah," was all she allowed herself to say —though she was thinking plenty.

Mandy was looking at her with pleading, hopeful hazel eyes. "I was hoping maybe you could, sort of, I don't know... help him get used to the idea?"

"Get used to the idea that his daughter is dating someone more than twice her age?" Jacqueline said, working hard to keep her voice mild. She was pretty sure she succeeded. "I don't think there's much anyone can do to help him get used to it. Um... how long have you been seeing—uh, Luke? Is that his name?"

"Only a few weeks. He came into the zoo and we started talking—it was by the bat house." Mandy's cheeks flushed a little, and her eyes went dreamy. "He thought they were so cute, and I started by teasing him that maybe he was a 'bat man,' and it just kind of went from there." The glow faded from her eyes. "I know I don't even know you, but I know my dad thinks you're really cool, and if you like him even a little bit, you'd probably want to help him get through this, you know?"

Again, Jacqueline had to bite her tongue. She had *so many* things she wanted to say. And, for one crazy moment, she had the insane idea of making an anti-love potion to help Mandy extricate herself from what had to be—*had* to be—a really messed-up relationship. Why, *why* would a twenty-three-year-old woman want to be with a man her father's age?

Unless maybe he was rich... ? Even as she had that thought, Jacqueline hoped that Mandy Massermey wasn't as superficial as all that.

And Massermey had told his daughter that she, Jacqueline, was *cool*? Her tummy warmed pleasantly.

"So, uh, tell me about Luke," she said. "What does he do? Does he live near here?"

Mandy's eyes lit up again. "I knew you'd help! He's only been here in Button Cove for a few weeks. In fact, we met his very first day here. He's running the funeral home over the summer while the owner's gone, and it's—"

Thud.

The sound—a familiar one to a person who worked and lived around lots of books—somehow went straight to Jacqueline's ears, even though it came from another room. Every hair on her body stood on end and she lost the rest of what Mandy was saying.

Because she knew what that sound was.

She knew what it meant.

A book had fallen from the shelf in the other room. Not because a customer had dropped it. Not because one of the cats had knocked it over.

Because someone was coming out of a book.

And that meant Jacqueline's life was about to become even crazier.

CHAPTER 2

"Excuse me for a minute," Jacqueline said, starting out of the room without waiting for Mandy to respond.

She hurried across the hall into the general fiction section, which also housed an entire collection of vintage volumes.

The area was silent and empty, but there was one book on the floor, right in the middle of the rug. It was old and worn, and it was open—which definitely portended the imminent arrival of some literary character from...

Jacqueline picked up the book, and her heart sank.
Crap.
Dracula by Bram Stoker.

Why oh *why* couldn't it have been *Little Women*? Or *Anne of Green Gables*? Or *Winnie the Pooh*?

Trying to talk herself out of freaking out—the last thing she needed was the eponymous vampire showing up around here and enthralling (and killing) all the young men and women—Jacqueline closed the book and slipped it back into its place on the shelf.

Maybe she'd get lucky. Maybe Mina Harker would

show up instead. She was a reasonable character who probably wouldn't stir up too much trouble.

But the problem was, Jacqueline knew that who-ever was coming out of the book had some sort of role to play in the real world. Which meant disrup-tion, confusion, and, most likely, danger and craziness.

Please don't let it be Renfield, she thought, putting her hand on the aged spine of the book and closing her eyes to beg the Universe to keep that from happening.

She actually didn't know which would be worse—having Count Dracula, the seductive, evil, and violent vampire, or Renfield, the insane, larvae-eating pris-oner, make an appearance.

Or the three female vampires who attempted to seduce and feed upon Jonathan Harker, Mina's hus-band, and anyone else who crossed their path.

Oh shit. She remembered, suddenly, that Massermey had mentioned the name on the grave Mrs. Kilmeade had been complaining about was Renfield.

It was probably a coincidence.

She hoped it was a coincidence.

And she thrust away the reminder that Sherlock Holmes always professed that there was no such thing as coincidence.

With a sigh, she opened her eyes and glared at the ragged, faded, mustard-colored spine of the book with its blood-red titling. "Actually, it would be best if *no one* came out of you," she said, because there were re-ally no characters from that book that she could see fitting in here in Button Cove.

But the fact was, Jacqueline had no control over whom—or what—emerged from these old books, or

when, or how... and when they returned to the pages
—and stayed there.

Still glaring at the deceitfully innocent-looking
tome, she wondered what would happen if she destroyed the book. Burned it. Tore it apart. Threw it into
the lake. Hid it.

"What is going on in here?"

Jacqueline spun to see Mrs. Danvers in the doorway. The woman, whose age was indeterminate but
probably not too far from Jacqueline's own forty-eight,
had her dark hair scraped into a no-nonsense knot at
the back of her head. She wore a forties-style dress of
blue so dark it appeared black except in bright light,
along with completely out-of-fashion thick wool
stockings and chunky black shoes. A ring of keys hung
from her belt, but for some reason never jingled to
foreshadow her presence.

Jacqueline lifted a brow and gave the woman an
imperious look—which was very out of her nature, in
general, but was a tactic she'd discovered was the best
way to take Mrs. Danvers down a notch.

It worked, for the crotchety old crow inclined her
head just enough to not be considered impertinent
and said, "Are you in need of assistance, ma'am?"

"*Dracula* just fell off the shelf," Jacqueline said.
"Do you know why? Or whom to expect?"

"Of course not, ma'am," replied the housekeeper,
who may or may not have been the person who'd set
Manderley on fire in *Rebecca*, but who was certainly
not above that sort of machination. She drew herself
up even more ramrod straight than usual and sniffed
audibly through her blade-sharp nose. "That is certainly not my concern. Ma'am."

Jacqueline barely managed to control a retort, for
on any other day, Danvers assumed *everything* was her

concern. "Very well. Thank you. Do you need me up front?"

"No, ma'am. I heard a... disturbance." Her cold, dark gaze fixed on Jacqueline as if she had been the one creating the disturbance.

But she had only been freaking out in her head... hadn't she?

"I'll be out to help with the customers in a minute," Jacqueline said in what she hoped Danvers would recognize was a dismissal.

With a sigh, she left the general fiction room and returned to where she'd left Mandy. But to her surprise, the young woman was gone. The stack of erotic novels was still next to her chair, but Jacqueline noticed that Roquelaure's *The Claiming of Sleeping Beauty* and Gale's *Unmasqued* were missing. She smiled to herself as she re-shelved the ones left behind. If nothing else, Mandy would have some steamy reads ahead of her.

Then she sighed again, even more stridently. Mandy had asked for her help, but Jacqueline wasn't sure she should be interfering. Besides, what was Jacqueline going to say to Massermey when she herself had serious concerns about the relationship between his daughter and her boyfriend?

Maybe she should try to find out who this Luke was and check him out. Mandy had left before she told her much at all, but between Suzette, Nadine, and the ZAP Ladies, Jacqueline suspected they could figure out who this new guy was if he owned a business and had only moved here a few weeks ago.

Just then, a trio of women filtered into the room.

"We're looking for the latest Kate Claybourn," said one of them.

Jacqueline happily showed them the books, then

slipped into a discussion about the differences between Amanda Quick, Jayne Ann Krentz, and Jayne
Castle (which was that they were all the same author,
but each pen name wrote a different type of romance:
historical, contemporary, and futuristic).

By the time she finished there, another customer
hailed her in the sci-fi-fantasy room. Next, she assisted
another shopper to find a book about code-breaking...
and then also sold them a volume about Elisabeth
Smith Friedman and her cryptanalyst work during the
world wars.

The rest of the day went by in very much the same
way. Every time Jacqueline thought about making her
way to the front counter, she would happily get way-
laid to talk to someone else about their book choice,
or to make a recommendation. She barely had time to
scoot upstairs to her apartment to grab the tuna sandwich she'd made last night, wolf it down with some
iced tea (for some reason, she didn't have an aversion
to iced tea like she did to hot tea), and get back downstairs to the steady stream of customers.

She supposed it was a good thing Danvers and
Hudson didn't need lunch breaks. At least, she assumed they didn't.

When she made it back downstairs after her quick
lunch, Jacqueline found a trio of stylish young women
chatting around a table in the tea room. She remembered them, for they'd been hovering outside the front
door, looking in the window as they sipped their tea
samples until she urged them to come inside with the
promise of more tea upstairs. The fact that they had
several Three Tomes shopping bags sitting on the
table indicated she'd definitely profited from inviting
them in.

Even as she smiled at the three of them, she

scanned the room for any sign of an interloping *Dracula* character making his or her appearance.

To her relief, no one appeared out of place—except for Mrs. Hudson, in her high-necked Victorian frock.

"...*so* very handsome. And elegant," one of the women was saying, fanning herself enthusiastically, as Jacqueline walked by. But the following phrase had her stumbling to a halt: "His name is Luke Blackstone, and it's just such a shame that—"

"And what can I get for ye, ma'am?" Mrs. Hudson bustled up to Jacqueline at that moment. "You really oughter be trying that new tea from Andromeda. It's got those yellow flower leaves in it—can't remember the name. Cally something. How about I make you a nice, strong—"

"Shh!" Jacqueline hissed, trying to hear what else the woman was saying. When Mrs. Hudson gave her a shocked, affronted look, Jacqueline sighed and said, "Yes, yes, a nice strong cuppa with lots of honey—and some oat milk—would be very nice. Thank you, Mrs. Hudson."

Just as she'd learned how to deal with Mrs. Danvers—sort of—she'd learned how to deal with Mrs. Hudson, who, despite her often tart dialogue, could be easily offended if one wasn't careful.

"Good afternoon," said Jacqueline, approaching the group of three women. "I hope you're enjoying yourselves."

They all looked at her with friendly smiles. "You're the owner here, aren't you?" said one of them. "They said you're new here, too?"

"Yes. Jacqueline Finch. Thank you so much for coming in."

"It's such a nice day—and with all the windows

open up here, it feels like we're up in a treehouse or something," said a second woman.

"I couldn't help but overhear you mention Luke Blackstone," said Jacqueline. "Isn't he new in town?" She gave a little laugh. "I haven't been here that long myself, so I'm just trying to get to know all the other business owners... but I haven't met him yet."

"Oh, you're in for a treat," said the third member of the group with a wicked smile. She, like her friends, was probably in her early thirties and was dressed in a yellow and white sundress with a crocheted vest over it—an ensemble that looked like it was straight out of *Sundance Catalog*, which was usually too pricy for Jacqueline's budget but carried gorgeous items. "He's very soothing and friendly, and *very* nice-looking."

"Very appropriate for an undertaker," said the first woman, who had long *Daisy Jones and the Six* brown hair. "I mean, you want the man who's going to embalm your grandma or great-uncle to be smooth and calm and very polite. He can help me through my grief any time," she added with a grin.

Jacqueline, who'd winced at the usage of the word "undertaker," blinked when she realized that Mandy Massermey seemed to be dating the new mortician in town... who was apparently very popular with the ladies. Or at least had attracted some interest.

"Right. I remember reading about it. He took over Brittany Funeral Home, didn't he?" she said, feeling a little uncomfortable over the jokes related to embalming and grief. Losing a loved one was not a laughing matter, even if they had lived a long life.

"That's right." The woman in the Sundance-style sundress leaned forward. "By the way, I'm so glad you stopped off to say hi, Miss Finch. We've heard *all* about your place." She gave her an exaggerated wink.

"I'm Staci—with an i—and I have a feeling I'm going to be needing your help in the near future. So don't be going anywhere, now, all right? We're here for the summer, so we'll be in regularly." She and her companions giggled, and Jacqueline decided it was time to make her exit.

She didn't want to be asked about love potions or charms or spells or anything. Especially if they were all interested in this Luke Blackstone.

"Here you are, then, dearie," said Mrs. Hudson, unwittingly coming to the rescue with a delicate china cup of tea.

Jacqueline took it and excused herself from the gaggle of women. "Did you put oat milk in it?" she asked Mrs. Hudson, peering at the pale gold brew that was far too translucent to have had any sort of milk added to it.

The derisive snort from Sherlock's landlady told her all she needed to know, but Mrs. Hudson wasn't satisfied with that. "Fake milk in your tea? You'll have the real cow's milk or none, dearie, trust me on that. Now drink it up—I did put some honey in, as I know how sweet you like it."

Good thing Jacqueline wasn't lactose intolerant.

The tea wasn't half bad, mainly because of the honey. She wondered if it was actually going to cleanse—or "smudge" her—from the inside. Jacqueline carried the delicate cup downstairs with her and found a smattering of customers in the front room waiting in a short line to be rung up by Mrs. Danvers.

Since the housekeeper had everything well under control, that gave Jacqueline the chance to step outside. It was nearly four o'clock by now, and the farmers' market crowd had waned hours ago. The last few tables in the street were being removed, and soon the court would be open again to vehicular traffic.

"What an interesting plant," Jacqueline said, noticing a little pot within a cluster of other pots of petunias, begonias, primrose, and impatiens, along with some unusual orchids and succulents. She had always enjoyed her little garden back in Chicago, and was well versed in the plants usually offered for Midwest gardeners, but she didn't recognize the plant growing in a five-inch terracotta pot.

The specimen had bumpy green leaves that resembled those of a primrose, but they were longer and darker and more pointed than those of the pretty yellow, purple, and pink perennial. The flowers, which had no stems to speak of and nestled right among the leaves, were pale lavender with starlike, pointy petals.

The stocky woman to whom she'd been speaking smiled and paused in the process of packing up a myriad of pots into her wagon. She'd been one of the vendors and was obviously ready to close up shop.

"That's a mandrake," she said, pushing a string of curling gray hair out of her face. "Hard to come by, and a dangerous species. I couldn't believe it when I saw one here at the market, so I snatched it up. Usually I have the most unique plants for sale, but not today.

"You see, I'm a plant collector and have a small nursery, so I'm always intrigued when I see something unusual. The flowers will turn into small fruits. Mandrake isn't native to Michigan, so I'll have to baby it and maybe keep it in a pot." She smiled. "A larger one."

Jacqueline grinned back. "It probably won't scream when you pull it out of the pot to replant it," she said, referencing the Baby Mandrakes that had become famous thanks to Harry Potter.

"Well, I'm not going to take the chance," the woman replied with a chuckle. "Folklore says you tie a string or rope to the plant and then tie the other end to a black dog—I hear it has to be a black dog—and make him pull it out. Under the moon, of course. Not sure if it has to be full or not... I'll have to do some research."

"Of course," Jacqueline said gravely, even though she knew her eyes were dancing with the same humor in the other woman's. She introduced herself and added, "I wish you luck with the mandrake."

"Thank you. My name is Lucy Frontera, and I live outside of town, out on Hallibard Hill. Nice to meet you, Jacqueline. I hope you'll stop by my nursery some day."

Jacqueline assured her she would definitely do that.

After Lucy left—Jacqueline tried not to think about the fact that there was a Lucy in *Dracula*, because that Lucy had turned into a vampire and had to be killed—she walked into the shop to find it mostly cleared out of customers. Mrs. Danvers was helping a burly man who was buying a stack of the gorgeous fairytale picture books that had been illustrated by Darby Wright. Jacqueline had met Darby at a library event when she still worked in Chicago, and had arranged for a large order of signed editions for the bookshop of the stunning volumes of *Sleeping Beauty*, *Cinderella*, *The Twelve Dancing Princesses*, and *Jack and the Beanstalk*.

She wandered back through the store to discover that the rest of the rooms were empty of customers and, thankfully, people popping out of books. It was quiet and peaceful, a welcome moment after the busy-ness of the morning.

Jacqueline took the opportunity to slip out the back door of the shop. There was a large cedar tree that grew right next to the building; in fact, it was so close to the old Victorian house that its roots and part of the trunk were visible in the cellar. The walls had been built around it, purposely and probably at least a century ago, by Jacqueline's relative, Cuddy Stone.

Outside the back door, the cedar sat in one corner of a garden that was in a tiny step-down courtyard, enclosed by low brick walls with a little, waist-high wrought-iron gate. Jacqueline couldn't wait to get some perennials and annuals in the ground in that space, and she planned to add a small café table and chairs for shoppers who might want to sip their tea outside. The garden would get plenty of sun in the afternoon, but in the morning would be cool and shady.

Right now, the area was strewn with fallen leaves, old stems and twigs, and tiny, spiky branches from the cedar. There were a few patches of grass starting to peek through, along with a rosebush that had begun to green out, along with the very first hints of salvia and lavender waking up from the winter. She saw Shasta daisy leaves and iris spikes and the last straggling blooms from a clump of daffodil.

I'll do some spiderwort, she thought, looking around the little sunken area. *Right next to the cedar.*

The little bluish-purple flowers of the spiderwort plant perked up and opened in the shade and would come back every year.

Morning glory to climb on a trellis over there...

Jacqueline was humming along, planning her garden plot, when she noticed something new. She'd been out here many times over the last few weeks, but hadn't done much but a little weeding, since she'd been busy with the reopening of the shop and moving into her apartment... and it had been too cold and the weather too unpredictable to start gardening quite yet.

But she knew every inch of the garden and had been checking daily to see what new delight was springing up from beneath the winter's blanket of leaves and dead grass... and this plant was new.

At first she thought it was a primrose, coming back after the winter. But it was a little late for that, and when she took a closer look, she realized she was wrong... which never would have happened if she hadn't just met Lucy Frontera.

It was a *mandrake* plant.

Just sitting there in the ground, pretty as you please, right in the sunniest corner of the garden.

"Where the heck did you come from?" Jacqueline crouched next to the dark green leaves. She was in the habit of talking to the plants in her garden, although usually she spoke more softly and encouragingly to them. Especially when they were just waking up from winter.

"You're not native to Michigan," she went on, reaching to touch the bumpy, dark green leaves. "How did you manage to make it through the winter and show up here?"

She suddenly looked up and around, then focused her attention on the cedar, which, according to the indigenous people who'd lived here in northwestern Michigan, was a sacred, powerful entity.

"All right," she said, speaking to the tree and the space at large. "I realize this is a very unique location, so that must be the reason a *mandrake* is growing here." She'd learned from the ZAP Ladies that Three Tomes Bookshop was situated on the junction of several powerful ley lines, which at least partially ex-plained all of the mystical and unusual happenings there.

And could explain why a non-native plant that couldn't overwinter in Michigan was popping up. Maybe.

She was also aware that Andromeda's garden at the house the ZAP Ladies shared was filled with plants that thrived year-round—even non-native ones.

"Simple explanation," she said. But she couldn't dismiss the coincidence that only a few minutes ago she'd met someone with the rare mandrake plant... and now she'd come back here to find one growing in her own garden.

Coincidence?

Jacqueline scoffed. She'd only been living here for a few weeks, but she'd learned there was no such thing as coincidence on Camellia Court.

CHAPTER 3

"**G**irl, your mixology skills are really getting good," said Suzette.

"Thank you, thank you... thank you very much," Nadine replied in a poor impersonation of Elvis. But she was grinning as she used a long wooden dowel to muddle some fresh mint leaves along with a few chunks of pineapple in her cocktail shaker. "You ready for a second one, Jacqueline?"

"Sure, why not? I only have to walk across the street to get home." Jacqueline held out her glass from where she sat in a lounge chair on the postage-stamp-sized balcony outside Nadine's second-floor apartment. The yoga studio took up half of the second floor, and Nadine's living quarters the other side.

Suzette sighed, pushing her thick, wiry hair out of her face. It was dark and liberally threaded with gray. "I really need to move closer. It's a pain when I have to drive home outside of town, and you two only have to walk across the street from each other."

"You can always call Gerry Dawdle," said Nadine, referring to the doctor who'd moved to Button Cove after he retired, and now drove the only rideshare in town—which happened to be a hearse.

Only in Button Cove, Jacqueline thought with a grin. *God, I love this town.*

"Or you can always crash at my place," she said. "There's an extra room I'm going to set up as an office —though I don't know why I need another one besides the one downstairs. Either way, it's got a sofa bed in it now, and it's all yours."

"Thanks," said Suzette. "If I have many more of these, I might have to take you up on that." She lifted her glass in a toast. "What a gorgeous night!"

"It's so nice to be able to sit outside—and smell the lilacs!" Jacqueline lifted her nose to sniff the faint scent of one of her favorite flowers. That brought to mind the fact that she hadn't been thinking about the garden outside the bookshop... and the mysterious appearance of the mandrake interloper therein.

"So," said Nadine, looking up at her from where she now sat on a big pouf pillow. She'd gracefully folded her round, curvy body into some sort of lotus pose that Jacqueline could only dream of attaining. "Any books fall off the shelf lately? You look a little stressed."

"And here I thought the first mojito took away all the signs," Jacqueline replied.

"Nope. Why do you think I offered you a second one?" said Nadine.

They all laughed, and Jacqueline reached out to scoop a tortilla chip through a bowl of salsa. No one had been in the mood to cook, so they were munching on chips, salsa, guacamole, and whatever chunks of pineapple weren't being macerated for the mojitos... which numbered about three.

"Well, a book did fall today, but I haven't seen any sign of one of its residents," Jacqueline said.

"Which book?" demanded Nadine, pouring fresh mojitos into all three glasses from where she sat.

"*Dracula*."

"Ooooh," said Suzette. "And *yikes*."

"Yeah, no kidding," Jacqueline replied, looking out into the growing darkness. She shivered a little and hoped the undead had stayed inside Bram Stoker's book. It was one thing to read about vampires in *Twilight* or the Black Dagger Brotherhood, but she did *not* want to come face to face with one in real life—even if it was a sexy guy like Wrath.

"All right, so I have to admit semi-ignorance," said Nadine, peering at the nearly decimated bowl of guacamole. "Geez. I think we're going to have to order something in, because I'm a lot still hungry and this is almost gone. You two are piggies."

"We worked hard today," said Jacqueline. "We deserved it."

"We can order Lupe's. Will your boyfriend Gerry bring it over to us, like Uber Eats?" asked Suzette.

Nadine's cheeks turned a little pink. "Depends whether he's on a run, and let's not put a label on our *friendship*. We're just talking a little."

"Mmhmm," Jacqueline said, waggling her brows. "That's what Suzette said about the architect. Not sure I buy it." Wow... the mojitos had really gone to her head if she was teasing her friends about men.

"Who, by the way, I'm no longer 'talking to'," said Suzette grimly, swiping up the last bit of guac. "Nice guy, but there was no spark. Now, the new guy at Brittan—"

"*Anyway*, as I was saying," Nadine said. "About my ignorance—"

"Wait—we should order food first before we get into all that. It's Saturday, and Lupe's will be busy, and it'll take forever," said Jacqueline.

"Right," said Suzette, already pulling out her phone to do the ordering. "And it's not even after Memorial Day yet. Just wait till all the tourists descend. You want your usual, Jacqueline?"

"Yep, enchiladas suizas, and why don't you have them throw in a big side of guac?"

Once they got the order sent in and Gerry Dawdle agreed by text to play food delivery person, Jacqueline and Suzette turned their attention to Nadine.

"All right—ignorance? What on earth are you talking about?" said Jacqueline.

Nadine sighed. "It's kind of embarrassing, but... *Dracula.* I don't really know a darn thing about the book other than there's a vampire, and I really think you ought to fill me in if there are going to possibly be bloodsucking fiends wandering around town. I think I saw the movie with Keanu Reeves, but I fell asleep halfway through it."

"Ahh... Keanu," sighed Suzette. "Pretty much one of the most perfect males whoever walked the face of the earth. Not that I'd actually know, but, you know, from watching from afar." She grinned, her eyes a little glassy. Jacqueline wasn't surprised, knowing that her friend had been up since four that morning working in the bakery. She'd make sure Suzette crashed in her extra bedroom, because her friend had to get up early tomorrow even though the bakery was closed on Mondays.

"All right, here's the Jacqueline's Notes version of *Dracula* for those of you who don't know the story. Main character: Jonathan Harker, who meets Count Dracula in a castle in Transylvania, along with three murderous female vampires who try to seduce and feed on him. Jonathan barely escapes, and he goes back to London.

"Then there's Mina Harker, his fiancée and then wife during the book. She's got her head on straight and helps them destroy the vampires, even though Dracula—who follows Jonathan to London—feeds on her, and she drinks his blood and is going to turn into a vampire unless he is killed."

"Wait, so that's how it works? The vampire drinks the blood and then the victim drinks his?" said Nadine. "Did it work that way in *Twilight*? I cannot remember. I probably slept through that movie too. That's when the girls were little. It was all a blur."

"Either the vampire drains the blood and the person dies, or if the vampire wants to make the person into an undead, the person has to drink the vampire's blood," said Jacqueline. "That's fairly common in vampire mythology, though not always the case. I think Anne Rice does it a little differently."

"Wasn't there an old doctor in *Dracula* who knew all about vampires?" asked Suzette. "Van Der Something? I didn't sleep through the movie, but it was a long time ago. I don't like to read scary books, so I haven't read any vampire novels."

"Oh, you're missing out," said Jacqueline. "There are some really good ones. In fact, I think I might set up a display of only vampire books," she said thoughtfully. "They make great beach reads."

"Sure—why not keep with the theme?" teased Nadine.

Jacqueline grimaced. "Hm. Maybe not. Anyway, it was Abraham Van Helsing who was the professor, and he was the only one who really knew how to kill vampires—at least in *Dracula*. And then there was

Lucy Westenra, the beautiful young innocent who was seduced by Count Dracula and turned into a vampire when he *pierced* her with his fangs? Get it?... oh, yes, the sexual undertones and *over*tones are rampant in this book," she added with a bit of relish. "I could go on for hours about all of that, but I won't."

The other two laughed with obvious relief.

"Those are the main characters, but there's also a Dr. Seward and Lucy's suitor named Quincy and— ugh—Renfield. Besides Dracula and the three female vampires, Renfield is the one we *do not* want to show up. Trust me." Jacqueline shuddered and tossed back the last of her drink. "Basically, Dracula wreaks havoc seducing and killing people, and Van Helsing, Jonathan, and the others—especially Mina Harker— all work together to kill him."

"Great," said Suzette without enthusiasm. "So we could have any number of undead wandering about Camellia Court. Maybe I *will* go home tonight. It's probably safer over by the cemetery than it is here with people coming out of books and all."

"Maybe I should get some garlic and a stake," said Nadine.

"We just ordered from Lupe's," said Suzette. "And it takes forever for your grill to heat up."

Jacqueline and Nadine burst out laughing, their hilarity egged on by the amount of mojito they'd imbibed.

"She meant a wooden stake to stab vampires with," said a giggling Jacqueline, not even caring that she ended her sentence with a preposition. Not only would Nadine and Suzette not judge her, but she was too tipsy to care even if they did. "And garlic to repel them."

"Oh, ha!" Suzette lost it and fell into gales of laughter.

They were still giggling when Nadine's phone chimed. "That's Gerry with our food," she said.

"Tell him to come on up," said Suzette. "We can get all the details from him about your *relationship*."

"Good God, no you *won't*," said Nadine. Her face was pink, and not from the exertion of pulling out of a yoga asana and to her feet. "I'll meet him down—"

"Hellooooooo!" came a masculine voice through the open screen door downstairs. "You left your door un-locked, Nadine." There was heavy clomping on the stairs as Gerry made his way up.

Moments later he appeared, accompanied by the delicious smells of authentic Mexican from Lupe's. He was a tall man, well over six feet, with gangly limbs and knobby knuckles, and he had to stoop a little to get through the door when he came out onto the bal-cony. His gray-brown hair, thinning just a little on top, was pulled back into a short ponytail that actually looked good on him, and not like he was trying to harken back to his youth.

"Looks like you're having a good time here. You text me if you need a ride home, Suzette," he said, pointing a gentle finger at her. "I spent forty years trying to keep people alive in the ER; now I just try to keep them from getting there."

"I will, but only if we can go past Brittany Funeral Home," said Suzette. "I wanna see if I can get a glimpse of the new guy there. He's kind of *hawt*. Even though I'm glad to be single, there are days when a gal wants to get laid. You know?" Her words were a little slurred.

Jacqueline paused in the process of disseminating

their carryout order onto the table. "You've met him? Luke Blackstone, right?"

"Just briefly."

"Little bit of an odd duck, I've heard," said Gerry. He seemed to be in no hurry to leave and was standing, leaning against the side of the building, arms folded. The balcony was so small that there wasn't room for another chair.

"Oh?" replied Jacqueline. "Tell us more, and have some chips and guac if you want."

"You hear things, driving people around," said Gerry, eyeing the spread of food. "I feel like a servant from back in the *Downton Abbey* days. People talk in front of you and don't even realize what they're saying."

"Well, give us the tea!" said Nadine. "What's up with this guy?"

Gerry shrugged. "Just a lot of women buzzing about him. That he's new, single, and definitely of interest to many a female in town. And probably some males too, to be fair."

"That doesn't seem so odd," said Suzette.

"It seems he doesn't like to socialize much. Never accepts invitations—at least, from what I overheard. No one's ever seen him except at the funeral home—where he works."

"I've got more tea," said Jacqueline, cutting into her enchilada. "Big scoop. Which might explain why he's not very social. Apparently, Luke Blackstone is dating Massermey's daughter."

The reactions from her friends and Gerry were exactly what she'd expected: shock and awe.

"Massermey's gonna kill him," said Nadine, her eyes wide, when all the *oohs!* died down.

"True dat," said Jacqueline.

"Why do older guys always date much younger women?" moaned Suzette. "Not that I really care, because I don't want a man, but... "

"I don't," said Gerry. "Date much younger women."

No one looked at Nadine, but from the corner of her eye, Jacqueline could see her cheeks flushing darker. Hm. That was interesting.

A little awkward silence hung there for a minute, then Jacqueline said, "Weird thing happened today at the shop."

"When doesn't something weird happen at the bookshop?" said Nadine, whose blush had faded.

Jacqueline laughed. "I know, right?"

"So... what happened?"

"A mandrake plant—which isn't native to this area and can't overwinter here—showed up in the little garden courtyard behind the shop."

"Wait... a mandrake plant? Like the babies in the pots in Harry Potter?" said Nadine. "I didn't sleep through *those* movies. Maggie Smith was in them."

"And Emma Thompson," Jacqueline reminded her.

"They're both goddesses," Nadine said with feeling.

"Mandrake's poisonous," said Gerry. "Especially the roots."

Jacqueline nodded. "I know. And it's native to Europe, so I don't know how it managed to show up here in my garden. There was a woman cleaning up from the farmers' market who bought a mandrake plant from someone. At least, that was the impression she gave me—that she'd bought it at the farmers' market."

"Well, you know who'd know," said Nadine. "Andromeda."

"Exactly. I will definitely be talking to her. And doing more research about it."

"Not really something you want just growing willy-nilly around," said Gerry, just as his phone chimed.

"I agree," replied Jacqueline.

"Well, that's my cue to get on my way," said Gerry, tucking his phone back into his pocket. "I've got a pick-up. See you all later." He gave a little wave and slipped out the door.

"All right, so what's the deal with you and the hearse driver?" Suzette demanded of Nadine. "It seemed a little... awkward."

"Nothing. Really, it's nothing. We've just talked a few times, and then I kind of... backed off. I got cold feet, all right?" Nadine said. "I just don't know if I want to be with another doctor, you know?"

Suzette gaped at her. "Gerry Dawdle might have a medical degree, but he is about as different from Noah as a man can be." Noah was a surgeon, and he and Nadine had gotten divorced several years ago.

"I know, I know." Nadine looked a little miserable, and her big hazel eyes glistened with emotion. "I know I talk a big game, but it's scary... you know... getting back out there."

Jacqueline patted her hand. "Never been married, but I can tell you it's *always* scary out there. Take your time. No rush."

"Speaking of no rush... how's it going with you and Detective Get-His-Massive-Hands-On-Me?" said Nadine, obviously willing to divert attention from herself.

"He's coming to dinner tomorrow night," Jacqueline replied, and her cheeks heated when her friends gave little appreciative "mm-hmms." "Mandy—his daughter—wants me to help pave the way with him that she's dating an older man."

"Um... good luck with that," said Suzette. Now that she'd dug into her tacos carnitas, the glassiness in her eyes had faded a little.

"Why did she ask you?" said Nadine.

"I think she thinks I know Massermey better than I do. At least she didn't want a love potion or anything like that." Jacqueline shuddered. "There was a trio of women in the tea room today who were giving me looks like they were about to ask me for a charm or spell or something. And they promised to be back." She sighed. "Oh, and a Mrs. Kilmeade was complaining to Massermey about some kids vandalizing the graveyard. I guess the one over by you, Suzette?"

"Yes. A headstone was knocked over, and there was some loose dirt, but I heard it was just an accident when someone went to dig up a flower bush or something. Some of those gravestones are so old."

"That's what Massermey said, but apparently Mrs. Kilmeade didn't think he'd investigated enough."

"Dory Kilmeade is a high-maintenance busybody, though, so, *pffft*," said Suzette. "She's only been there for a few weeks, but already I'm fed up."

"Well, I just have to say this, even though I'm sure it means nothing, but... " Jacqueline took the last gulp of her mojito for support. "Some vampire mythology says the undead need soil from either graveyards or their own burial plot in order to sleep and be safe... " She bared her teeth in a humorless smile. "Surely it's a coincidence that *Dracula* falls off the shelf on the day I learn about a cemetery with disrupted soil... right? *Tell* me it's a coincidence."

Nadine tsked. "You know what Sherlock Holmes always said—and I know this only from Mrs. Hudson, who would *know*—there is no such thing as a coincidence."

"Gee. Thanks a lot for the reminder," said Jacqueline grumpily. "And I'm sure it's another *not*-coincidence that the name of the headstone that got knocked over was Renfield. Like the creepy-crazy character in *Dracula* who eats larvae in order to absorb its life force." Now her smile was more sickly than simply without humor. "I *really* don't want there to be a connection."

"Well, when you put it that way," said Nadine. "I'm *sure* it's a coincidence."

"It has to be," said Suzette with a discreet little hiccup. Now she was looking sleepy, not loopy. "The graveyard stuff happened last week, and the book just fell today, right? Thus the character didn't come out before today. So you're good. It's not Dracula or his three vampiresses digging up the cemetery."

"Okay. Whew. That's completely logical, and I feel much better. Now we just have to wait and see who shows up," said Jacqueline.

"It's the 'we' part I hate," moaned Nadine.

"Hey, that's just one of the benefits of having me as a friend," said Jacqueline. "One of the many. Another is my extra bed. You ready, Suzette?"

"Yes. I've been up since four and I have to get up in"—Suzette checked her phone—"less than seven hours. God knows I need my beauty sleep!"

"You mean you can get more than seven hours of sleep?" asked Nadine, awed. "In one night? I'm lucky if I get five, with night sweats and not being able to go back to sleep if I wake up."

"I hear you," said Jacqueline with feeling. "And now I'm very jealous of Suzette and her seven hours of sleep!"

Suzette just grinned and fluffed her frizzy hair.

They all brought in the dishes and loaded the

dishwasher, then Suzette and Jacqueline said good-night to Nadine, who was yawning by this time too.

"See you tomorrow."

They crossed a silent, empty Camilla Street, and Jacqueline was unlocking the back door to Three Tomes, which had a staircase that led directly to her third-floor apartment, when she realized she'd left her purse at Nadine's.

"I don't know why I even brought it with me," she said in disgust. "I was only going across the street. Go on up, Suze, and get to bed. There's an extra tooth-brush in a package in the bathroom. I'll dash back over and get it."

Suzette yawned. "I'm a little more toasted than I seem, so, yeah, I'll take you up on it."

"There's also ibuprofen in the cabinet in the bath-room. Take three with a big glass of water. I'll be right back," Jacqueline said, opening the door for her friend to go inside.

When she came back around to the front of Three Tomes, Jacqueline glanced down toward Camellia House, where the ZAP Ladies lived at the end of the court. There were lights on inside, and she smiled, wondering what mischief the three women were cooking up on this Saturday night. She hadn't had a chance to talk to any of them when they came by this morning, but tomorrow she would ask Andromeda what she knew about mandrakes.

Jacqueline drew in a deep breath of air scented with lilacs and walked across the street as she called Nadine to let her know she was coming.

"I was just about to text," said Nadine as soon as she answered. "Thanks for catching me before I got in bed. I just put my jammies on! It's getting chilly." It was mid-May in Michigan, which meant that no matter how warm the days might be, the nights could get into the forties.

Jacqueline laughed. "I've seen you in your jammies, and you look cute and comfy."

She got her purse, got to see Nadine in her cozy pajamas, and got to give her a hug. "Thanks for the hospitality and the mojitos. And don't worry about Gerry Dawdle. I think he likes you, and you can just take your time deciding if you like him—and his copilot ghosts—too. It's not a race."

Nadine hugged her back, and Jacqueline was surprised to hear a little sniffle. "I don't know what's wrong with me. I've been so up and down lately."

"It's probably hormones," said Jacqueline. "We just can't get away from them, no matter what."

"He's a nice guy—even if he does drive a hearse around with ghosts," said Nadine, wiping the single tear from her eye. "Man, I'm such a waterworks lately."

"Don't worry about it, sweetie. Life's really tough sometimes," said Jacqueline. She gave her friend a kiss on the cheek and said goodnight.

As she was crossing back over Camellia, she couldn't help but look toward Egala's shop... and the next thing she knew, her feet had turned and were taking her up the block toward it.

Jacqueline didn't want to be seen gawping in the windows or displaying any sort of curiosity that Egala might see, so she'd avoided going by on that side of the street during the day. And she certainly hadn't even considered going *inside*. But after ten o'clock at night, the shop would be closed and no one would be around to notice if she peeked in the windows. It was the perfect opportunity to assuage her curiosity.

The street was deserted and quiet. A chill breeze

coming in from the lake several blocks away made Jacqueline wish she had a windbreaker, but she didn't turn back. There was a blaze of stars in the sky, along with a half-moon lighting her way down the empty swath of road, and the only sound was the distant barking of a dog.

Maybe it's a black dog tied to a mandrake to pull it from the ground, she thought wildly, and gave a quiet little laugh, thinking of Cullen, Mandy's dog.

Jacqueline had her mobile phone with her, but she didn't need its flashlight, for a street lamp shone almost directly into the front window of Egala's shop.

Unlike Three Tomes' large, square Victorian, Egala's took up only a narrow sliver of a staid brick building. The storefront was barely fifteen feet wide, but the bow window certainly attracted one's attention.

Little, dancing, glittery lights of pink, red, and orange decorated the display inside, and Jacqueline suspected they weren't your run-of-the-mill plug-in kind of lights. They were probably, knowing Egala, charmed to be alluring and draw in customers. And to run on something other than electricity or battery.

At least I don't need a spell to get customers inside my shop, she thought, even as she found herself gazing at the window display and then deeper into the shop— the interior of which was lit with low but effective night lights. There were purses and handbags and pocketbooks and wallets and totes... everything a woman might need to carry her stuff around in. Each one of them had a clasp or a metal medallion with an ornate E stamped on it—just like the fabulous straw tote Henrietta Wellburg had been carrying when she bought books earlier today.

Jacqueline shuddered a little, remembering the

special purse her friend Wendy had acquired from Egala a few weeks ago. It had been cursed, and it caused Wendy to do and say all sorts of awful things before everything got straightened out.

Jacqueline didn't believe Egala would be selling cursed purses—it certainly wouldn't be a way to stay in business very long—but she didn't fully trust the other woman to be as innocent as the shop might make her seem. Still, the stylish tote Harriet had carried seemed as benign as any other summer bag, so Jacqueline told herself it was none of her concern.

She was just about to turn and walk back home when she heard voices. A man and woman came from around the corner, walking along the sidewalk.

With a start, Jacqueline recognized the woman as Mandy Massermey.

And that must be Luke Blackstone she's with.

Curiosity propelled her forward, and she waved. "Mandy! Is that you?" She figured if Mandy had had the nerve to ask for her help with her father, then Jacqueline had the right to interrupt her date.

"Oh, hi, Ms. Finch," said Mandy. She didn't sound the least bit upset about being interrupted. "What are you doing out so late?"

Jacqueline declined to mention that it wasn't even eleven o'clock, and that she might be pushing fifty, but she didn't exactly turn comatose at eleven.

It was more like eleven thirty.

"I was just coming home from a friend's house. And you must be Luke," she said, smiling at the man she could only think of as the Infamous Luke Blackstone, Mortician.

"I am," he replied in a deep voice.

Jacqueline looked up at him and felt a sudden, not-unpleasant shiver shimmy through her body. He was tall and slender, with an almost military bearing, and a sense of classic formality about him. He was clean-shaven and had very dark hair. In the moonlight, his face looked almost pearlescent.

"It's a beautiful night for a walk," Jacqueline said, unable to take her eyes away from his. They were dark and compelling, and she felt that little shiver again. He was *very* handsome, and seemed excruciatingly polite and gentlemanly. She could see why all the women had been chattering about him.

"We had a wonderful dinner at Roots and Range," he said. "Then decided to take a little walk under the stars. My office is just over there." He looked down at his date and gave her a sweet smile.

"Very romantic," Jacqueline said.

"It is," said Mandy, leaning into Luke's arm comfortably. "But I do have to work early in the morning —someone's got to feed the hippo—so we'll have to call it a night soon."

"I understand," replied Luke, still smiling. "It's very nice to meet you—but I didn't even get your name," he added to Jacqueline, in an obvious attempt to end the conversation.

"Jacqueline Finch. I own Three Tomes Bookshop." She gestured vaguely down the block. "Feel free to stop in for a tea some morning. We can kick-start your day with a different type of caffeine... plus there are scones and cupcakes from Sweet Devotion." She grinned up at him, and realized she was on the verge of *flirting*... which was *so* not cool for many reasons.

What the hell was wrong with her? Too many mojitos.

He chuckled. "Oh, I don't do mornings. I'm a serious night owl. When Mandy here goes home to sleep, I stay up and work. Then I sleep most of the day unless I have an appointment."

"You're at Brittany Funeral Home, right?" said Jacqueline, suddenly reluctant to let him walk away. She wanted to know more about him. "That's just over on Tulip Street, right?"

"Yes. I'm here semi-temporarily," he replied. "And Mr. Brittany is going to Europe for a month—it's a big wedding anniversary for him—so I'm covering everything while he's vacationing. Hope we don't have too many people passing on while he's gone!" Luke added with a wry smile that somehow charmed her even though it was a little in poor taste.

"Goodnight, Ms. Finch," said Mandy in a firm manner that indicated she wanted her man to herself and that Jacqueline should be on her way.

"Enjoy the rest of your evening," Jacqueline said. She couldn't help but watch as they walked off, arm in arm. Something about the man compelled her interest.

Then, almost as if he felt her looking, Luke Blackstone glanced back at her as they turned the corner. He gave a brief smile... and Jacqueline swore she saw his eyes gleam red from the lights in Egala's shop window.

It gave him an eerie look, and left her feeling a little unsettled.

CHAPTER 4

The next morning was Sunday, and Jacqueline made her way downstairs from the third-floor apartment, an insulated coffee cup in hand. She had the mildest of headaches, which would soon be eradicated by the ibuprofen she'd swallowed and the dried-peach scone she had swiped from the tea room on her way down. Mrs. Hudson wasn't around yet, so she didn't have to hide her contraband coffee, either.

Suzette had risen early and slipped out and over to the bakery without making a sound—something Jacqueline appreciated, since she didn't usually sleep well (thank you, perimenopause).

The shop didn't open until ten on Sundays, and closed early, so it was a short day for Jacqueline that often ended with pizza at Nadine's. Since the store was closed on Mondays, this was almost like the beginning of her weekend.

No pizza tonight—but it was her first official date with Miles Massermey. Jacqueline smiled even as her tummy did a weird little squish. She hadn't even *tried* to date for years. Her relationship with Len, her plus-one and occasional friend-with-benefits back in

Chicago, could never have been described as "dating."

"Good morning," she said to Max, who was sprawled in the front window, basking in a circle of sunshine. She was mildly surprised to see him in such a public place; Sebastian was the attention hound (or cat, as the case may be), and Max usually limited himself to perching high on a shelf and glowering suspiciously down at people. She gave his ink-black fur a long, gentle stroke and was rewarded with only a mild glare, so she gave him a little scratch between the ears too, which he accepted arrogantly.

Sebastian wandered in, obviously aware that petting and attention were on the agenda, and wove through Jacqueline's feet until she bent to pat him too.

It wasn't until she went behind the counter to boot up the computer for the day that she checked her phone, which had been on silent for the night.

When she saw the rows of texts and missed calls from Suzette and Nadine, she felt her stomach drop.

It took her two interminable seconds to open them, and when she saw the first one—which was from Nadine—her stomach did more than drop.

Someone found a dead body!!!

Then Suzette had replied: *In the graveyard!! By my house!!!!!* followed by a *The Scream* emoji.

Jacqueline fumbled with her phone as even more texts came in. She managed an *OMG* reply, then *Who is it?*

But by then she'd scanned through the rest of the previous texts and gotten the information.

The body of a young woman had been found in the graveyard next to Mrs. Kilmeade's house. Cause of death undetermined, though there'd been lots of blood.

You wont beleive this! Suzette had typed—with lots of typos, due, obviously, to her state of mind and poor autocorrect. *She had 2 puncture wounds! Onher neck! ZOMG ZOMG*

Jacqueline stared at her phone, at that text, and felt all of the blood drain from her face. *Good God...*

She was still staring at the screen, wondering if she —and Button Cove—could be so unlucky that Count Dracula or his vampiresses had come to town, when Mrs. Danvers stalked into the room.

"*There* you are. There is an *individual* who wishes to speak to you," she said. For once, there was actually a bit of color in her cheeks—two pink splotches that appeared almost clownish in her porcelain skin. "Ma'am," she added.

Jacqueline bit back an annoyed retort—surely she had better things to do than talk to a customer when there was very possibly a *vampire* in town, killing people. But she quickly dismissed her irritation. There could be many explanations for the woman with two puncture wounds on her neck— including exaggerated or bad information, a.k.a. gossip.

"Where is this person?" Jacqueline replied. The store wasn't even open yet, and she hadn't heard anyone come in.

"Up there, ma'am." Danvers's expression became even more prune-like and haughty as she gestured to the tea room on the floor above them. "That Hudson woman seems to be quite enamored with him. To the detriment of her work. I'm certain you'll soon set it all to rights, ma'am." Despite the positive words, her tone indicated serious skepticism.

But Jacqueline was used to Danvers's sly arrogance, and she fixed the woman with a cool, Lady of the Manor stare. "I shall indeed. And *you* may return to whatever it was you were doing."

"Yes, ma'am," replied the housekeeper, as demurely as she'd ever done—which wasn't all that demure in the first place. But the Lady of the Manor technique usually worked to take Danvers down a notch and remind her who was in charge. Ostensibly, anyway. "I was dusting the nonfiction rooms, ma'am. And wondered if you wanted me to set a fire in any of the hearths."

"Not today, I don't think," replied Jacqueline as she started to the sweep of stairs that led to the café. "It's going to be warm."

"Very well, ma'am." Danvers shot one more glare at the ceiling—Jacqueline wasn't certain whether the target was Mrs. Hudson, the newcomer, or the entire situation—then turned neatly and headed down the hall.

By the time Mrs. Danvers was out of sight, Jacqueline was at the top of the stairs.

"And there ye are, now," Mrs. Hudson was saying. "Sweetened it up with a big spoon of honey for you, then, since you've come a long way, now, haven't you, dearie?"

"*Ja*," replied the man sitting on the stool in front of the counter. He looked at the sturdy pottery mug she set in front of him. "Das is goot, madame. *Danke*."

Jacqueline's first impression of the man was of solidness and a sort of square shape. He had broad shoulders and a sturdy neck, and a head that sat perfectly on top of it. His blond hair was combed back from a pale, clean-shaven face with a broad nose and square chin. As she came into view, he turned to look at her with calm blue eyes that gleamed with intelligence. She estimated his age to be rather close to hers

—in his late forties—and he was quite a bit younger than Mrs. Hudson.

Even though, sadly, the man didn't look anything like Hugh Jackman, she knew who he was. "Professor Van Helsing, I presume?"

"*Ja, natürlich*," replied the famed vampire hunter from *Dracula*. "And who are you?"

"Jacqueline Finch," she replied. "This is my book-shop and café." For the first time, she got a good look at Mrs. Hudson. The only way to describe the expression on Sherlock's landlady's expression was shell-shocked... and not because she was horrified. No, the woman appeared besotted, and she didn't seem to even notice Jacqueline's presence.

"And how about we have us a nice strawberry cup-cake now, too, dearie," said Mrs. Hudson, setting down a plate on which sat a pretty pink cupcake with a tall swirl of pale rose frosting and sprinkles. Obviously from Sweet Devotion. "Big, strapping man like you needs his energy, now, don't he?"

"I'm told you wanted to speak with me," Jacqueline said to the professor. She decided it was probably just as well that Mrs. Hudson didn't seem to notice her in the presence of the attraction of Abraham Van Hels-ing. "What can I do for you?"

"*Ja,*" he replied before slurping his tea. Mrs. Hudson didn't so much as wince. Instead, she gazed fondly upon him as she spent several minutes ab-sently drying a teacup. "Das ist a pleasure to meet you, Frau Finch."

From the book, she knew that Van Helsing was Dutch, but that he also spoke with a German accent.

"Do you know why you're here?" Jacqueline asked. "And it's Fräulein Finch."

Van Helsing's eyebrows rose. "Das ist true? There

is no Herr Finch? Vor such a handsome woman like you?"

Jacqueline leveled an irritated look at him. "No, not that it's any business of yours. Do you know why you're here? Why you came out of the book?"

Please don't say, "Because there's a vampire around," she thought desperately. *Please.*

"Good heavens," said Mrs. Hudson, tearing her admiring gaze from Van Helsing and turning it toward Jacqueline. "That's not really a polite question, is it now, dearie?"

Jacqueline gave her a narrow-eyed look. She and Mrs. Hudson had gone a few rounds in the past when Jacqueline had asked questions about how the characters came out of the books, and why, and when they went back... and more. Each time the conversation ended with Jacqueline learning absolutely nothing and Mrs. Hudson being affronted that she should dare to ask.

"I think it's only fair to ask what brought him here," she replied evenly. "Professor?"

"Vhy, I don't precisely know that," he said, and slurped the tea again. "I chust voke up and I vas here."

Jacqueline grimaced. Why was it the characters never seemed to know what they were doing here— or at least, *pretended* not to know? "There was a woman found dead in the graveyard this morning. She had two puncture wounds on her neck," she told him.

Mrs. Hudson gasped and raised a hand to the high ruffled collar of her equally ruffled bodice and apron. "Surely not. How terrible."

"Two puncture vounds, you say?" Van Helsing's accent was thick and annoying, but that was how Bram Stoker had written the character, so Jacqueline had no choice but to deal with it. "It could be the vork of zee Un-Dead, you know."

"Yes, I know that. I suppose if that's the case, that might be why you're here," Jacqueline replied firmly.

Van Helsing raised bushy eyebrows. "Vell, it is true zat I did help vith the dispensation of zee Count Dracula and his Un-Dead brides. But I haff many ozzer skills and much learning and—"

"And it's far too dangerous," said Mrs. Hudson flatly. "Hunting up those creatures. You just sit right here and enjoy your tea and that delicious cupcake and put that worry right out of your head, Professor. I'm certain the inspector—er, I mean the detective—will see to the problem." She gave Jacqueline a dark look, as if *she*, Jacqueline, had conjured a vampire—a.k.a. the problem—out of thin air and called Van Helsing from the pages of his book.

"If it turns out that there is an undead wandering about Button Cove," Jacqueline said, ignoring Mrs. Hudson's comment, "then I will certainly be consulting with you, Professor Van Helsing."

"But surely there are *other* vampire hunters," said Mrs. Hudson, giving her a mutinous look. "Others who can assist with the problem. The professor has already done his due, and, well, it's a job for a younger man, isn't it, dear?" The "dear" was directed at Van Helsing.

"But the professor is here, and none of the other vampire hunters are," replied Jacqueline, wondering why she was bothering to argue.

"There was a girl hunted those undeads," said Mrs. Hudson, frowning as she wrinkled her nose as if to assist in retrieving the memory. "I'm sure of it. It's only a vague recollection, but I'm quite certain Mr. Holmes knew her—"

"A *girl* hunting vampires? Vhy, zat is *preposterous*," said Van Helsing, obviously affronted by the very thought. "Zome little girl hass no knowledge or zee strength to do such a dangerous task!"

"Clearly you've never met Buffy," said Jacqueline with much snark. She was also thinking of Anita Blake and Victoria Gardella—badass women (not girls, by the way) who hunted vampires, but on the pages of books instead of on screen. Victoria Gardella had even worn a *Bridgerton*-style dress and ditched her chaperones while doing so.

Abraham Van Helsing had no idea what more modern literature had done for feminism.

"Buffy?" Mrs. Hudson pursed her lips. "Sounds like someone who likes polishing shoes, you ask me, dearie."

"Well, Buffy is the name of, arguably, the most famous female vampire hunter," replied Jacqueline.

"Ridiculous," said Van Helsing before taking a final slurp of tea. "No little girl iss going to hunt down zee Un-Dead. Even Mina Harker, who vas hypnotize and connected to zee count after he *fed* on her, could not haff done it vissout *my* help." He set his mug on the counter with a solid thud. "And so, *ja*, if I am needed, I vill help to capture zees Un-Dead and dispatch zhem."

"I'm delighted to hear this," said Jacqueline, ignoring Mrs. Hudson's fuming—which had taken the form of loud clattering of mugs and tea canisters. She hoped the landlady wouldn't break something.

The shop door rattled below, and Jacqueline sighed. It was just before nine thirty, and the closed sign would remain in place for another thirty minutes. But still, someone thought they needed to come in, and she would be a good entrepreneur and go down to find out who and why.

Her internal griping dissipated, however, when she trotted down the stairs and discovered Nadine and Suzette were the culprits.

"Can you *believe* it?" cried Nadine as soon as the door opened. She burst over the threshold, her layered, medium-length hair caught up in a short ponytail. She was wearing yoga gear, as usual, even though Jacqueline knew she didn't have a class until noon on Sundays.

"Talk about *timing*," Suzette said, shoving in behind Nadine. "That book falls off the shelf, and *boom!* we have a vampire show up. Do you think it's Count Dracula?"

"I don't know. If so, that would mean two characters came out of the book at one time, which hasn't happened before," replied Jacqueline. "Not that there's a rule against more than one character coming out— at least, who the hell knows if there's a rule. No one will tell me what the rules actually *are*."

"Except that a real person can't go into a book," said Nadine. "Or, at least, *shouldn't*."

"Well, I came out unscathed," said Jacqueline, referring to her unscheduled and unwanted foray into *Cinderella* a few weeks earlier. "I feel like it's a complete free-for-all, to be honest. And Danvers and Hudson refuse to answer any of my questions about anything."

"So you're saying someone else came out of *Dracula*," said Suzette, drawing Jacqueline's attention back to the matter at hand.

"Technically, I don't know if it's someone *else*, meaning a second person who came out. Because we don't really know if there's a vampire loose, do we?

Those puncture marks could have a number of other explanations. Anyway, regarding the book—Professor Van Helsing has appeared. He's upstairs being cooed at by Mrs. Hudson," said Jacqueline with a little roll of her eyes.

"But what else could it be if not a vampire?" demanded Nadine. "The woman was dead, had lost a lot of blood, and there were puncture marks on her neck. And she was found in the graveyard. Of *course* it's a vampire."

Jacqueline sighed. "Then maybe they came from somewhere else—the vampire, I mean. Not from a book." When her friends both gave her strange looks, she shrugged. "Look, we've got witches and we've had curses and possessed mirrors, and we've got characters coming out of books... who says we can't have vampires or—or werewolves or whatever just living here in Button Cove? Like I said: *Free. For. All.* It's like a freaking Sookie Stackhouse book." She was exhausted thinking about it all, and it wasn't even ten a.m.

"You need to find out what you can from Massermey," said Nadine. "About the dead woman. Who she is, what the wounds were like—and what *they* think it was."

Since Jacqueline had already come to the same conclusion, she nodded, then said, "There is *no way* Massermey is going to believe there's a vampire running around town."

"Well," said Suzette, "he's not going to have a choice if that's what it turns out to be."

"True." Jacqueline looked at the clock and saw that it was nearly time to open the shop. "All right. If you find out anything else, text or call. I've got to get some work done."

"I thought that's why you had Danvers and Hudson," teased Nadine.

Jacqueline gave her a dirty look. "There are days..." was all she said—mainly because Danvers was usually lurking about somewhere, listening.

Once her friends left, Jacqueline had less than ten minutes to boot up the computer and get ready to open. She flipped the CLOSED sign to OPEN two minutes before ten, then strolled down the hall to the back of the shop to unlock the back door.

She stepped outside and got a whiff of lilac in the air, and stood enjoying it for a moment. Then she looked over at the little courtyard garden that was just waiting for her to fill it with annuals, and to round out whatever perennials came up. She was hoping to have—

What the hell... ?

Letting the door close behind her, she rushed out to the courtyard.

No, her eyes were not deceiving her.

Where yesterday there had, inexplicably, been a mandrake plant growing in a corner of the courtyard... there were now *three* mandrake plants.

How was that possible?

Were they *mating*?

She looked more closely, just to make certain all three were really mandrakes.

They were.

As Jacqueline stared down at them, she noticed a thin trail of soil that ran from one of the plants over the knee-high brick wall that enclosed the courtyard.

Had someone planted the mandrakes and left a trail of dirt? That was the only explanation—and one she didn't particularly care for.

Unless...

The tension in her shoulders eased as she remembered her thoughts from last night. "Andromeda had to have planted them," she said aloud. "All of them." The three crones had come over yesterday during the farmers' market, but Jacqueline hadn't really had the chance to talk to them. Maybe Andromeda meant to tell her about it then.

That made a lot of sense.

Feeling far better about the mandrake situation, but still uncomfortably aware of the vampire conundrum, Jacqueline went back inside the shop to wait on the customers she could already hear had come in the front door. She had to smile about that; she was so very fortunate to have such an active, profitable bookshop.

Although people had come in for tea, pastries, and books, there were plenty who came in to gossip as well. Everyone was abuzz over the poor woman who'd been found in the graveyard.

"I simply can't believe it," said a well-dressed woman in her sixties who'd probably just come from church. She placed the fourth, fifth, and sixth Eve Dallas books on the counter and shook her head as Jacqueline rang them up. "Here in Button Cove! I heard she had *bite marks* on her neck," she whispered. "But that's *got* to be a rumor. Now, where is my—oh, there you are."

She smiled in surprise as she pulled her wallet from the large, pale pink purse she was carrying. It had a smattering of white flowers cut out of leather and attached with little coppery-pink studs that acted as the center of the daisies. Jacqueline noted with a little grimace that the bag had the same ornate E on its metal clasp as Henrietta Wellburg's. "Right on top!

This purse is about as big as a cruise ship, and I can still find my wallet. What a miracle."

"It's a great purse," Jacqueline said as she slid the books into a Three Tomes shopping bag. She hoped she didn't sound as snarky as she felt.

"It's from Egala's, as you might have guessed. The E, you know. I walked by and saw it in the window, and the next thing I knew, my feet were taking me right inside because I *had* to have it."

Jacqueline could only imagine. She wondered what sort of charm Egala had put on her shop, or the bags inside it. *At least I don't have to resort to such nonsense,* she thought—then pushed away the niggling suspicion that maybe Cuddy Stone, the previous owner, had taken advantage of the crisscross of energy and ley lines here on Camellia Court and incorporated her own sort of nonsense. After all, the shop was almost always busy, and the sales both online and in person were robust. No matter what a customer wanted when they walked in, it was somehow always there.

Even if Cuddy Stone had done something like that, Jacqueline herself was innocent of such tampering—and she wanted to stay that way. And she steadfastly did *not* glance over at the old, locked bookshelf under the stairs that held many antiquarian books... including the brick-shaped one where she'd found a recipe to make a protection amulet a few weeks ago.

"*Pink* patent leather—how could I resist? And with these pretty white leather flowers on it. I just *adore* it." The woman was still waxing rhapsodic over her bag. Just then, the riff from George Thorogood's "Bad to the Bone" began to play from the depths of the purse. "Oh dear, that's my girlfriend," the customer said, opening the massive purse to peer inside. "Where is my phone— Oh. *There* you are. Right on top again!" She fumbled out the phone as she took the bag of books from Jacqueline. "Thank you!" She waved gaily as she tapped the screen to answer, then swept out the door as she spoke into the phone.

Jacqueline smiled after her, mostly amused by a best friend whose ringtone was "Bad to the Bone." That sounded like someone she'd enjoy meeting... especially if she was a sixty-year-old woman.

Just then, her own phone chimed with a text message and her heart did a little skip when she saw that it was from Massermey. She hoped he wasn't going to cancel for tonight—but she'd understand if he did.

Gonna have to take a rain check, said the text. *Or be really late. Have a situation here.*

She replied: *I heard. Very sorry about that. It's awful. No problem to reschedule. I'm not going anywhere.*

There was a pause, then a new message popped up. *Thanks for understanding.*

But a cop has to eat, she replied after a moment of contemplation. She wanted to see him, true, but she also wanted to pick his brain about the dead woman. *Have time to just swing by for a sandwich? Or a to-go container?*

Maybe. Hope so. Thanks. Will lyk.

She replied with a smiley emoji and decided to let it go at that. She was in the mood for chicken piccata, so she'd make it anyway. If he came by, she could have something packed up for him to take with him.

In the meantime, she had customers to attend to.

"Excuse me," said one of them, catching Jacqueline with a smile. She, too, was carrying an Egala bag —this one was sunny yellow, with a faux-crocodile texture overlaid with gold and amber. "I'm looking for those fairytale books that have the gorgeous illustrations—I guess they're by a local artist?"

"Semi-local. She lives in Chicago, but I heard she's going to be moving not too far from here to Wicks Hollow," said Jacqueline, gesturing for the customer to follow her up the stairs. "The children's section is up here. The artist's name is Darby Wright, and I've never seen such stunning illustrations. My favorite is her newest one—*The Twelve Dancing Princesses*."

"Yes! That's her. I knew it was an unusual name. I'm looking for a baby gift for a friend whose daughter just had a little girl. They sound perfect," said the yellow-purse lady. "I'm a teacher too... do you have a discount for educators?"

"Absolutely," Jacqueline replied. She helped her find the books and was delighted when the customer bought one each of the four Darby Wright titles she had on hand.

As she was being rung up, the lady put her purse on the counter and stood there, waiting to pay. "Oh, hi there, Denise!" she said as another woman came into the shop. "Good to see you. How are things?"

"Hi, Judy! Everything's all good, but you know how busy it is. School's almost out, and the ballet recital is next weekend—I'll be really glad when that's over," said Denise, coming over to stand by the counter. Jacqueline noticed she was wearing a t-shirt that said *D-M-A Dance Studio*. "Love the girls, but they're teenagers, and they're not as cute and cuddly as they are when they're toddlers or grade school age." Then she leaned closer to her friend Judy. "It's the *moms* who are the worst, you know," she said in a low voice. "Cheerleading moms ain't got nothing on dance moms! But I'm sure you've had your share of manipulating moms too, in your classroom."

Judy shook her head and heaved a sigh. "I'm counting the minutes until school is over. There are days I'd love to stab one of those know-it-all moms with a freaking *fork*!"

Jacqueline was pretending not to listen, even though of course she was, and she smothered a smile. She knew the feeling—she'd worked in a library for twenty years. "You can insert your card here," she told Judy, moving the credit card reader toward the customer.

Judy opened her purse to retrieve her wallet and gave a funny little laugh. "Well, where did this come from?" She pulled out a fork, laughing—then, shaking her head, extracted her wallet. "So funny! And it's not even a plastic fork, or one of mine from home... I have no idea how it got in my purse."

"Well, you never know—it might come in handy if you run across one of those annoying moms," said Denise said in a conspiratorial voice.

"Seriously," said Judy, removing her credit card from the reader and sliding it back into her wallet. "Good seeing you, Denise. Good luck with the recital."

"I'm going to need it," said Denise, and gave a little wave as she made her way down the hall toward the genre fiction rooms.

Jacqueline, who was eyeing the fork a bemused Judy still held in her hand, handed over the bag of books. "I'm sure the mom and baby will love these," she said, wondering if it would be weird if she asked to see the fork. But before she could formulate a way to do so, the customer was already turning away.

"I know she will! Thank you—and thanks for the discount. I'll make sure the other teachers know." She stuck the fork back into her purse along with the wallet.

Jacqueline waved goodbye and went on to ring up the next customer. But she couldn't stop thinking about the weirdness of a fork appearing in the lady's purse. It had been right on top—wouldn't a metal fork fall to the bottom?

Strange.

And unsettling. Especially since the woman seemed to have no idea how it got in there.

Especially since she'd just mentioned stabbing someone with a fork...

That all made Jacqueline a little nervous. After all, it *was* an Egala bag.

Though she couldn't see her distant cousin's storefront from her current vantage point, Jacqueline glanced in that direction. Maybe she should go in there... just to see what was going on. Have a little conversation with Egala.

Ugh. Didn't she have enough to deal with?

As if the Universe had read her mind, there was a loud ruckus at the front door as the three ZAP Ladies poured into the shop.

"Good morning, Jacqueline!" sang Pietra.

The Universe was clearly laughing at her.

CHAPTER 5

"Good morning," Jacqueline said. Despite the sinking feeling of "what next," she didn't really mind seeing the crones.

Most of the time.

The trio could be amusing, interesting, and handy to have around. And no matter how much they might come across as a battering-ram-meets-Polish-Mothers, they meant well. After all, a couple weeks ago, Zwyla and her friends had helped Jacqueline move all of her furniture into the apartment—and get it arranged and set up—in one short afternoon, not to mention helping remove the curse from the handbag Egala had given Jacqueline's friend Wendy.

But despite Pietra's sunny greeting and her equally sunny dress of blue with orange poppies splashed all over it, Jacqueline could see that this wasn't a simple social call. For one, the sweet dumpling of a woman didn't have her ever-present basket filled with bakery items. (Darn!)

For another, Andromeda—whose hair was not sassy and spiky today, but simply combed back from her delicate face—hadn't immediately picked up Sebastian, who was sitting on the counter behind Jacqueline, watching with cool amber eyes. In fact, Andromeda hadn't even greeted the cat. Surprisingly, he didn't seem put out by her lack of attention as much as concerned and even a little wary.

And Zwyla, who towered over her friends and Jacqueline, wasn't wearing a head wrap today. Her smooth head had just the right amount of shine, and her earrings were large orange hoops that nearly touched her shoulders—and were the only color in her otherwise sober black ensemble.

"Presumably you've heard," Zwyla said in a low voice as she ducked her head slightly toward Jacqueline in confidence.

"If you mean about the dead woman, yes," Jacqueline replied. "Is it really... ?" She couldn't quite voice the words. "I heard about the... the puncture wounds." She kept her tone low too. "Is it possible it's... ? I can't even say it."

"TBD," said Andromeda. "*I* can't feel any sort of— you know—disruption in the energy that might indicate the presence of a vampire or some other kind of undead. But that doesn't mean there isn't one." Sebastian leaped gracefully from the rear counter to the one next to the computer in order to give his favorite crone proximity to his fluffy self. "You don't feel anything, do you, Z?"

"I feel something," replied Zwyla. "I'm just not sure what it portends. I thought you might have heard something from your *source*, Jacqueline."

Jacqueline was highly annoyed when her face flushed with heat. Why did her fair skin have to show off *every* single emotion ever? "If you mean Detective Massermey, no, I haven't heard anything from him. Yet."

Zwyla nodded grimly. "All right. You'll keep us apprised? Just in case? We've not had anything like that happen here before."

"Well, there was that time when Willy the werewolf showed up," Pietra piped in.

"Fifty years ago," Andromeda reminded her. "And he was just passing through. And he didn't *kill* anyone."

"That we know of," Pietra retorted primly. "No one ever did have a good explanation for where Tracy Hemington went."

"She ran off to Florida with the son of a cherry farmer," said Zwyla. "No mystery about that."

Pietra made a little huffing sound and jutted her chin forward, but didn't say anything else.

"So aside from the dead woman, there's something else we need to talk about," said Jacqueline. She glanced up as what appeared to be a family came in— mother, father, two children, boy and girl—all dressed in Sunday church finery.

"Excuse me, ma'am. Where's the chapter book section?" asked the little boy, whose face was covered with maple-syrup-colored freckles. He was also missing his two front teeth, so he lisped a little.

Jacqueline felt a sudden pang of adoration and smiled, exchanging a glance with the boy's mother. "It's upstairs by the tea room. There's a picture book section, but right next to it is all the chapter books. Are you looking for anything in particular?"

"Magic Tree House!" The little boy gave a fist pump. "*And* Captain Underpants!" He giggled, his cheeks turning pink.

"*I* want the mermaid books," said his sister, who was obviously older and—in her mind—wiser.

"They're up there too," replied Jacqueline. "Mrs.

Hudson is the very nice lady in the tea room. She can help you if you need help with the books or a snack, or I'll be up in a minute after I speak with these ladies here."

"I'm sure we'll find everything just fine," said the mother. "And I'll sit and have a cup of tea while they browse." She actually sounded enthusiastic about the idea of having tea. "And you can go look at business books, darling," she added with a smile at her husband.

Once the family trooped off in their respective directions, Jacqueline turned back to the ZAP Ladies. She spoke quickly and succinctly before something else interrupted them. "Mandrakes. In my garden. Did you put them there?"

"Mandrake? The plant?" Despite her sober mood, Andromeda had succumbed to the charm of Sebastian and scooped him into her arms. "No. No, I didn't." She exchanged glances with Zwyla and Pietra.

"Are you certain they're mandrakes?" asked Zwyla.

"Pretty certain, but why don't we go take a look?" Jacqueline gestured down the hall that bisected the shop. "You can tell me for sure."

The four of them trooped to the back door and outside.

"Oh, yes, those are mandrakes all right," said Andromeda immediately. She seemed both surprised and pleased. "I have several of them, and I can tell you for certain they're still in my garden."

"They just appeared here. Actually, *one* appeared yesterday, and when I came out this morning, the other two were here as well. Are they mating or something?" Jacqueline said.

Pietra giggled. "There are mandrakes that look like men and some that look like women, so it's possible."

"You're talking about the roots," Jacqueline said, giving the plants a stink-eye.

"Yes, that's correct," said Zwyla. She was watching Andromeda as she crouched next to the mandrakes to examine them. "When you pull them up—carefully— the roots often look like they form arms and legs and a head."

"And a penis," giggled Pietra. "Sometimes they have little, teeny roots right in that particular—"

"Right. I get it," Jacqueline said, smirking. "But you're not supposed to pull them up, right? Because they scream when they're uprooted, and the scream can kill you."

Zwyla gave her an amused look. "Been doing your research, have you?"

"Once a librarian, always a librarian."

"Anyway, that's all legend," said Zwyla dismissively. "Right, Andi? You pull up mandrake roots all the time. And you're still with us."

"I wouldn't say all the time, but yes, I have done and I haven't died yet. As far as you know, anyway," Andromeda added with a glimmer of mischief. Pietra giggled.

"So no tying a black dog to the plant in the moonlight and getting him to run away and pull it up?" Jacqueline said.

"Well, you *could* do that, I suppose, if you're worried about it," Andromeda said, looking up from where she still crouched by the plants. "The truth is, lots of times when a plant with large, thick roots is pulled out of the soil—carrots are a good example— they make a little squeaking sound when the dirt releases them. It's just natural, and doesn't mean anything."

"But that's where the legend comes from," said Zwyla.

"And one can assume that certain entities *liked* that element of the legend, which would keep people away from pulling up the mandrakes, and so they promoted it over the centuries in order to keep the mandrakes—and their mysterious efficacies—for themselves," Jacqueline said.

"Exactly." Andromeda pulled to her feet and dusted off her hands. "Mandrakes can be very dangerous if used incorrectly—they're part of the nightshade family, as I'm sure our resident librarian knows. But they're also very useful in herbology, so making certain only educated practitioners use them is important."

"Well, Andi, what do you think? How did they get there?" asked Zwyla. "Cuddy didn't have them growing there before, did she?"

"No," replied Andromeda. Her elfin features crinkled charmingly as she frowned. "I'm not certain where they came from. Obviously, they're not indigenous to Michigan."

"No. Europe and Asia, right?" replied Jacqueline. "The Mediterranean."

"Yes."

"But you have some plants, you said," Jacqueline reminded her. "That grow here? And overwinter?"

"Yes." Andromeda gave her an amused smile, as if daring her to ask the next question.

Which Jacqueline decided not to do, because she figured she pretty much knew the answer, and didn't really want the specifics. Sometimes, ignorance was bliss.

"I'm curious as to how you knew it was mandrake," said Zwyla. "It's not exactly a common plant."

Jacqueline explained her conversation with Lucy Frontera.

"So *she* had a mandrake plant as well. Where in the world did she get *that*?" Pietra said. "It's not like you can get one at Home Depot or even Bunek's Nursery."

"I don't know. And I don't know whether it's something to be concerned about," replied Andromeda. "Lucy does have a small specialty nursery—which is why she would have recognized the plant for what it was."

"Is there any connection between mandrakes and vampires?" Jacqueline asked. "I mean... it can't just be coincidence that we've got both showing up here within the last day."

Andromeda shook her head. "I don't know of any connection between those two entities, but that doesn't mean there isn't one. I could do some research."

"And so could I," replied Jacqueline.

"Excellent idea. And find out what you can from Massermey about what happened to the woman in the graveyard," said Zwyla. "If there is an undead making its way around Button Cove, we should take measures."

"Well, we've got Professor Van Helsing on hand if that's the case," Jacqueline told them, then went on to clarify that, yes, he'd come out of *Dracula*. "And he, unlike we modern-day people, writes 'Un-Dead' as a hyphenated word with the U and the D capitalized. Just in case you were wondering," Jacqueline went on, not even caring how pedantic she sounded. She was more than a little OCD when it came to grammar and literary references.

"Thank you for letting us know," Zwyla said

soberly. "That will make it easier in the event we have to send him written directives." But her dark eyes danced with humor, and in spite of the seriousness of the situation, Jacqueline smiled back. She appreciated it when people enjoyed her grammatical and literary trivia.

"I'd better get back to my customers. I'll see if I can find anything more about mandrakes. And I'll asked Professor Van Helsing whether he's aware of any connection between them and vampires," Jacqueline said. She started to go back inside the shop, but hesitated and turned back sharply.

When she did so, she found all three of the crones looking at her expectantly.

"I think Egala is selling bespelled purses," she said.

"And that surprises you?" said Pietra, who'd plucked a sprig of purple lilac and buried her face in the tiny flowers to inhale their essence.

"Well, not really... but what if something happens?" Jacqueline said, thinking of the fork that had suddenly appeared inside at the top of the yellow faux-crocodile purse.

"Something like what?" Pietra asked. "Surely it's nothing more than a simple charm to get people to buy them and carry them around and so on."

"With Egala, one can never be too sure," Jacqueline replied, and was gratified when Zwyla nodded in agreement.

However, none of the crones had anything else to add, leaving Jacqueline with no choice but to give a mental shrug. It wasn't her problem, was it?

She had more than enough things to worry about. She didn't need to add anything else to the list.

◯

CHICKEN PICCATA WASN'T VERY difficult to put together as long as you had the ingredients. Jacqueline had discovered this several years ago, and ever since then, it was her go-to when she was making a Dinner to Impress.

You pounded boneless, skinless chicken breasts until they were very thin, then tossed them in a shallow dish with flour, salt and pepper to coat them, then sautéed the flour-covered fillets in a pan of butter and oil.

"No one said it was low-fat," Jacqueline told herself when she sliced the three pats of butter into the warming sauté pan. "But I mostly lunch. So *there*."

She had an open bottle of Sauvignon Blanc chilling in the fridge and had already poured a small serving into a stemmed glass for her to sip. It was crisp and had an essence of pear, and she loved it. Plus she'd measured out a cup of wine for adding to the piccata, which meant there was more than a dent in the contents of the bottle already.

She hadn't heard from Massermey since their text exchange earlier, but after she'd closed up the shop at six—well, six ten, because of a flurry of five fifth-grader parents who'd come rushing in to buy the book their children were supposed to have read by the next day.

Fortunately, Jacqueline had been warned and had a good stock of Kate Messner's *All the Answers* on hand —which she was happy to sell to the frazzled parents as Mrs. Danvers looked on, silently exuding condescension.

Now, having had a busy and provoking day, she was playing the soundtrack from *Hamilton* while sipping white wine and sautéing chicken breasts.

Couldn't be more perfect... if she didn't have to worry about a vampire lurking in the town.

She sent a quick text to Massermey, *Swing by for a to-go container?* and snapped a pic of the chicken sizzling in the pan.

To her surprise, he responded right away. *I've got time to eat. In 15 min. Ok?*

She smiled, tamped down a little sizzle of interest in her belly, and topped off her wine a little more to take the edge off her nerves.

Perfect, she replied, then turned on the water-filled pot for boiling pasta. *I'll leave the back door unlocked. Come on up.*

By now, she'd finished sautéing the chicken fillets and moved them to a plate so she could make the sauce. Lemon juice, capers, butter, and white wine.

"What could be simpler?" she said aloud, dumping in a generous portion of capers because she happened to be particularly fond of them. She hoped Massermey didn't mind.

The water had begun to boil for the pasta, but she didn't add the angel hair quite yet because it only took a few minutes to cook.

When she heard the back door open and close below, she tamped down a little nervous flutter in her stomach and dumped two big handfuls of angel hair into the pot. The quiet creaks and thumps on the steps told her Massermey was on his way up, so she slid the chicken back into the pan with the sauce to reheat and become imbued with the flavors.

"Hello?" he called as he came down the hall from the back of the apartment.

"In the kitchen," she said, then came out from behind the half-wall counter into the living room to greet him.

"Hi," he said, and there was just enough of a warm note in his tone for her to feel... well, special. Noticed. That he was glad to see her.

She smiled at him and appreciated the little bump of heat she felt when their eyes met for an instant too long.

He was dressed in a simple button-down shirt with a light summer jacket over it and belted trousers. The pale blue shirt had pinprick-thin stripes of navy that made large squares on the fabric, and the colors made his blue eyes even more blue. She was pretty sure he'd trimmed his beard since she'd seen him yesterday. He looked good, but tired.

"Rough day," she said, not bothering to make it a question. "I'd offer you a glass of wine or a beer, but not sure if you're still on duty."

Massermey grimaced. "On duty for the foreseeable future, unfortunately. Iced tea or some of that demon bean brew would be great. Um... sorry about having to cancel," he said. "Especially since that smells out of this world." His attention wandered briefly to the kitchen, and she heard his sniff.

She shook her head. "There's nothing to be sorry about, Detective."

He gave her a funny look. "Not Miles?"

She felt her cheeks heat. "Sorry. I'm in the habit. So, *Miles*," she said with a smile, "I happen to have coffee already brewed in anticipation of your request. But I also have iced tea. Which one?"

He opted for coffee—he was a cop, after all—and at her urging sat at the four-seater dinette table situated in a little nook between the half-wall counter of the kitchen and the living room area with her beloved blue velvet sofa.

"It was nice to see you and Mandy yesterday," she said. "Cullen seems like a really nice, good boy."

"I have to admit, I wasn't too crazy about it when she brought him home—without checking first, might I add. I mean, the dog is as big as a horse," he said with a chuckle as she set the coffee in front of him. "But then she gave me those sad puppy-dog eyes of her own, and this whole sordid story about how no one wanted him and that she needed to have a dog if she was going to be a vet—which was a big stretch of an argument—and the next thing I knew, we had a furry, ninety-pound roommate. Who sheds. Like *crazy*." Despite his grimace, she read the wry humor in his eyes.

Thinking about Mandy's request that she help her father get used to the idea of her dating a man nearly his age, Jacqueline thought she might keep his daughter as a topic for another few minutes before she grilled him about the dead woman in the graveyard. "She doesn't live with you full-time, does she?"

"She does, except when she's away at school. She's lucky her landlord is letting her keep Cullen—or should I say, *I'm* lucky—because otherwise he'd be staying with me when she goes back to school in the fall," he said with a laugh.

"That is lucky," she agreed as she went back into the kitchen area. "Does she date much?"

He lifted a brow. "More than I'd like, but I'm her dad. You know?"

Jacqueline laughed, but felt uneasy. Yeah, he was going to be *pissed* when he found out about Luke Blackstone. "But she's an adult, so you don't really have much say."

"Yep. And she and her mother had a big blow-up about her dating an older man a while ago, so I just try to stay out of anything related to Mandy's social life. That doesn't mean I'm not going to take the opportunity to run anybody she's seeing though," he added with a steely look that reminded Jacqueline he was, in fact, a cop—and probably could be very dangerous if need be.

"It must be comforting to know you can check up on anyone she's dating," she said, looking out at him from between the half-wall and the cabinets above. "But she probably wouldn't be very happy if she knew."

He gave her a humorless smile. "I'm not going to tell her... unless there's a reason to do so."

"So an older man, huh?" she asked, just to test the waters—then wondered *why* she was getting involved. She didn't have a horse in this race!

"Yes. He was thirty." Massermey's voice was flat.

Jacqueline gulped. If he wasn't happy about Mandy dating someone seven or eight years older than her, he was really not going to be pleased about Luke.

Time to change the subject, because she was definitely not going there.

"So... is there anything you can tell me about the woman who died?" she asked, setting a plate with a simple green salad sprinkled with tomatoes, cucumbers, and green onions in front of him.

He didn't immediately respond. Instead, he thanked her for the salad, then sighed as he cranked a generous amount of black pepper onto the greens and added a good dollop of vinaigrette. Finally, he spoke. "Young woman—Cary Whitehall—age twenty-five. Local girl home from college for the summer. Was working at one of the fancy cocktail bars—you know, the ones where the twenty- and thirty-somethings hang out. Jilted, it's called. Kind of a new and trendy place, and not cheap. Fifteen dollars for one lousy drink!" He shook his head with a frown. "Anyway, she left after her shift—alone, as far as anyone knew—and never went home. Mrs. Kilmeade was the one who reported the body, of course—I'm sure by now you've heard Whitehall was found in the graveyard."

"The body was found in the same place as the possible vandalism," she said. "Any connection?"

"Doubtful," he replied. "But, of course, I'm not going to rule out any possibilities. The so-called vandalism wasn't really vandalism. Though it does mean we'll give things a closer look."

Jacqueline nodded as she set her own salad on the table across from him. "How was she killed?"

"Bled to death. Lots of lacerations, especially on the chest and throat," he said. "She'd only been dead a few hours when she was found."

"Do you think she was, um, killed there? In the graveyard?"

He gave her a sharp look. "I know you're a fan of mystery novels, but don't think you're going to be running around playing Phryne Fisher."

Absurdly pleased that he'd even heard of Phryne (who was not only the protagonist of a book series but also a television show), she grinned as she set the plated chicken piccata in front of him, then settled with her own serving at the small table.

"At least Jack Robinson doesn't mind if Phryne investigates," she teased, referencing the cop in the television series who usually worked in reluctant tandem with the amateur detective.

Ooh. What if Phryne showed up here at Three Tomes one day? Jacqueline would love that for a number of reasons—including the fact that Phryne wore stunning late 1920s fashion.

Massermey scoffed and shook his head. "I know you're a book lover, but it's called fiction for a reason. Seriously, Jacqueline... let the professionals handle it. I wouldn't want anything to happen to you." He gave her a meaningful look, then turned his attention to the pasta dish.

"I don't have any intention of investigating," she said truthfully. "I'm just curious. Can you at least tell me, were the lacerations from a knife? Or what?" Jacqueline figured she'd press as much as she could until he completely shut her down. And when he did, she wouldn't take it personally.

"Jesus, this is amazing," he said, looking at her with unadulterated delight as he sampled the chicken. "I wish I had more time to enjoy it... and other things."

She smiled, blushing a little. "Thank you. It's really an easy dish, and one of the few things I can cook well." Was that his way of ending the conversation about Cary Whitehall? She'd pry a little more and see what he said. "I heard... Well, I'm sure you're aware of the rumors. Puncture wounds, on the neck... is it true?"

His mustache twitched a little in a sort of grimace/frown. "I had hoped that information hadn't gotten out."

"So it's true. Puncture wounds on the neck." Jacqueline felt a shimmy of dread. "Like a vampire bite."

He gave her a quelling look as he swallowed. "A vampire bite. Come on, Jacqueline... you don't really think that's possible, do you?"

"I have an open mind," she replied. "And might I remind you that only a few weeks ago, we had a dead body in this very room who'd died from... what was it? His heart iced over, literally *froze*, and there was no explanation for it. What does the medical examiner think about the puncture wounds?"

"Look," he said in a mild voice, "I know it *sounds* possible, but two little wounds like that could be made by any number of things. Including someone trying to make it *look* like a vampire bite. And that's the tack we're taking at the moment."

"Because the other option isn't an option," she replied with a little grin.

"Exactly." His eyes gleamed with dark humor.

"You know, there *is* some historical and medical evidence for vampirism," she said in her librarian voice. "Although those individuals are not really like what we think of when we think of, say, Edward Cullen or Angel and Spike." She refused to mention Dracula for obvious reasons.

When he appeared confused, she said, "Don't tell me you haven't seen *Buffy*."

"Negative."

"Well, really the only thing you need to know about Angel and Spike is that they don't sparkle." She chuckled and sipped her wine, and their eyes connected across the table. "And I'm Team Angel—at least I was until the gossip about David Boreanaz being an ass got out, but I still am anyway—so... file that away for when and if you ever watch the show."

"I'm gonna queue it up on my Netflix as soon as possible," he said, the corners of his eyes crinkling. "Maybe you should come over and watch some with me."

"Maybe I should," she replied.

"Wish I didn't have to take off," he said, looking down at his empty plate.

"Me too," she replied. "But you do, and that's good. Cary Whitehall needs your help. Did you get enough to eat? There's more."

He made a groaning sound that caused her to smile, then shook his head. "Much as I want to, I can't. Gotta run—I'm hoping to get the PM results on Whitehall's body any time now. Rain check for a less rushed dinner sometime? And *Buffy*?"

"Absolutely," she said.

"I'll cook," he replied, standing to gather up his plates and flatware. "I do a pretty good slab of ribs on the grill."

"I'm in," she replied, following him into the kitchen, where he put his dishes on the counter. "You didn't have to do that, but thanks."

He turned, and they were right there, sort of crowded in the small space of the kitchen. Her breath hitched a little when their eyes met, and for a minute, she thought he was going to kiss her. Her throat went dry, and she gave a nervous little laugh then was mortified she'd done so.

Instead of leaning in to kiss her, though, he reached over and touched her cheek gently with the back of a hand. "Wonderful dinner. Even better company. Thank you. Looking forward to that rain check... and not being in a rush." His lips curved behind his mustache and beard.

She smiled and, miraculously, wasn't blushing this time. "Same. Good luck with everything."

"Yeah."

After he left, Jacqueline did a quick cleanup and then realized she had an unexpectedly free evening. It was just after seven thirty, and it wouldn't get dark for at least another hour.

She contemplated the options ahead of her, which

included finishing the bottle of wine while reading a good book or streaming something to watch (now she was sort of in the mood for *Buffy*)... or getting out of the house... and maybe going to the graveyard.

Even though she'd told Massermey she wasn't investigating, she felt obliged to at least... look into things. After all, she was probably the only person in Button Cove who could help if there *was* a vampire running loose.

With a sigh of frustration, she looked around the living room as if the answer to her dilemma would be there. The space was neat and cozy, with a fireplace on the wall directly in front of the plush blue velvet sofa, which happened to be perfect for napping.

Above the fireplace was a housewarming gift from the ZAP Ladies—a huge horizontal painting of a cedar tree in the middle of a forest. The image was one of all shades of blues, grays, and teals, with a little chocolate and forest green as well.

It was the most compelling painting she could ever remember seeing. It seemed to change, only slightly, just enough that she noticed, every day. In the morning, it was slightly lighter in color, as if the sun was rising in the painting over the dense forest, just as it was in real life. In the evening, it seemed to become darker, as if the sun was setting. And the little specks of yellow, gold, and white paint that represented fireflies became more pronounced and even seemed to glitter and dance.

Jacqueline had also noticed different shadows, silhouettes, and partially hidden creatures in the painting. It seemed like every time she looked at it, she saw something new. The picture was like a very complicated, very intriguing, and beautiful search-and-find image.

But tonight, the painting seemed sleepy. As if every living thing depicted in it—the butterflies, dragonflies, hedgehogs, stags, bumblebees, rabbits, and countless more—had burrowed away in their homes. Only the tree seemed alive, as it always did. Jacqueline swore she could see it moving, ever so slightly—as if it were shifting in a slight breeze... or breathing.

She looked at it for a moment—stared, more like —and let herself be lulled into the image... let herself become part of the image.

Floated. Absorbed. Drifted...

The next thing she knew, she became aware of herself—and that she was sitting on the sofa instead of standing. And that more than thirty minutes had gone by.

And that she knew she was going to end up going to the graveyard.

CHAPTER 6

Jacqueline had read plenty of books in her lifetime with what were known as TSTL characters—"too stupid to live."

Those were the ones who crept down into the basement, alone, with nothing but a flashlight or candle when everyone *knew* there was a murderer lurking about.

Or who went up to the attic, also alone, in a flowing white nightie like in those old 1970s gothic novels Jacqueline devoured as an eleven-year-old. Even back then she knew the heroine was dumb and deserved whatever happened.

Or who met with a murder suspect, alone, without backup or without notifying anyone.

Or who crept around spying on the villain—once more *alone*—without backup or a weapon or without notifying anyone.

Those were the characters that made Jacqueline want to scream at them... and sometimes even throw the book across the room. They were simply too stupid to live.

Jacqueline was anything *but* TSTL.

If anything, she was more of a shy, retiring, let-the-authorities-handle-it kind of woman than the brave and bold heroine who stuck her nose into places where it didn't belong—like Phryne Fisher and a host of other amateur detectives.

Which was why she talked very severely to herself about this crazy plan to go to the graveyard. There were any number of obvious reasons that she should just stay home and read or stream something... but she couldn't convince herself of that fact.

Before she knew it, she was putting on a light windbreaker and stuffing her fully charged phone into her pocket. She went into the kitchen and found a clove of garlic and tucked that into a different pocket. She considered a knife, but in most vampire mythology, a knife wouldn't do much to an undead. A sword, yes, if you could behead them—but Jacqueline knew there was absolutely no way she could behead a vampire (or anyone) even if she *did* have a sword handy. So that was out.

Obviously she should have a wooden stake, but she wasn't Anita Blake so she didn't have anything like that just sitting around. She wasn't keen on breaking her broom handle, and even if she was, she realized it was metal, so that was also out.

Maybe she could find a broken branch outside. Or a broken rake handle in the storage room.

Hmm. What else?

She looked around helplessly. Every vampire mythology was slightly different, so it was difficult to know what would work as a protection or a weapon. She didn't have any religious items like a crucifix, though she *did* have that New Age room behind the café. There were crosses and angel figurines and Buddha statues and other similar items.

With that in mind, she bounded silently down the interior set of stairs that led from behind her kitchen and its small laundry area to the rear of the second floor. But when she opened the door to the small service hallway in the back, she heard voices coming from the café... which was supposed to be closed.

A small pool of light spilled down the hall, and Jacqueline hurried past the New Age room toward the voices. Female, both of them, from what she could tell.

Mrs. Hudson was behind the counter, as usual. She wasn't alone, obviously, and the petite young woman energetically pacing the floor looked as if she was fired up and ready to take over the world.

The newcomer appeared to be about eighteen, with dusky olive skin and thick, dark hair pinned up in a Victorian style beneath her elegant feathered fascinator. Her clothing was similar to that of Mrs. Hudson's era... but not really, for the young woman was wearing a bronze-sheened *split* skirt that shivered and fluttered with her activity and wasn't quite long enough to reach the tops of her button-up, kitten-heeled shoes.

Victorian attire and a split skirt? Energetic and confident? Jacqueline caught her breath and her eyes widened.

Was she seeing the indomitable Amelia Peabody *in the flesh*? The very idea made her librarian heart go pitter-patter and whatever she might have said dry up with shock and awe.

For what did one say to their absolute favorite amateur detective character—who was also an archaeologist—when one actually met them in the flesh?

She had any number of questions—including whether Amelia's husband Emerson was as delicious in real life as the grumpy, passionate archaeologist seemed to be in the books, and whether Ramses (their grown-up son) was as well, and what had *really* happened when Amelia was alone with the tempting arch-criminal Sethos—but those questions faded away when Jacqueline realized two flaws in her assumption.

First, the young woman wasn't toting a parasol—and Amelia Peabody never went anywhere without her trusty parasol and its steel-reinforced handle.

Second, upon closer look, Jacqueline realized the woman looked like an escapee from a steampunk convention. The fabric of her skirt was a shimmery bronze, and her dress's design appeared more modern than anything Amelia Peabody might have worn.

And the young woman's fascinator that dipped over one eye was decorated with ostrich feathers as well as little copper cog works and delicate bronze chains. The most unique element of her attire was the supple coppery-brown leather corset she wore *over* her bodice—which was definitely not *de rigueur* Victorian wear. Her fingerless gloves extended past her elbows and had more little cogs and tiny mirrors attached to them, along with itty-bitty bronze buttons.

And then Jacqueline noticed there were a number of accoutrements dangling from little cog-work hooks on the bottom of the young woman's corset... including a wooden stake.

Well. Not Amelia Peabody. But who?

"What's all this?" Jacqueline asked, and both women turned to look at her.

Mrs. Hudson, to her credit, appeared chagrined when she discovered her supposed employer standing there with what Jacqueline was sure was a disapproving look on her face—at least, that was what she intended it to be, even as curiosity and apprehension warred inside her.

The younger woman had to be a vampire hunter, but she certainly wasn't Anita Blake or Victoria Gardella (her clothing was the wrong time period for either). She stopped her pacing and said, "Good evening, ma'am."

Before she could say anything further, Mrs. Hudson interrupted. "We were only talking, ma'am," she said to Jacqueline. "She might be able to help the situation."

"And 'she' is... ?" Jacqueline asked delicately.

As far as she knew, a book hadn't fallen from the shelf since *Dracula* the day before, but that didn't mean someone hadn't come loose from a set of pages. It had happened before. She gave Mrs. Hudson a meaningful look.

As if reading her mind, the landlady flushed and looked away.

"Evaline Stoker, ma'am," replied the young woman in a cultured British accent. She pronounced her name with a long i. The young woman gave a polite, abbreviated curtsy as she smiled at Jacqueline.

"Stoker? Any relationship to Bram?" asked Jacqueline, both mystified and fascinated. Now, where had she heard that name before... ? Evaline Stoker...

"He's my brother. Half-brother, in fact."

"And how did you, um, come to be here?" asked Jacqueline, giving Mrs. Hudson a cool look.

"Why, I—"

"I remembered her," said Mrs. Hudson before Evaline could continue and, possibly, spill the beans about how she'd been extracted from a book and brought here. Because Jacqueline suspected Sherlock's landlady had had a hand in this new arrival. "It took me a while to remember it all, but I did. She's a friend of Mr. Holmes's niece, you know."

That was when the light bulb went off in Jacqueline's brain and she remembered the book series. How could she have forgotten?

"Stoker and Holmes!" she said. "You and Sherlock's niece Mina, right? You were a team—reluctant to team up together at first, weren't you?—and you worked for Irene Adler?"

"That's quite correct," replied Evaline with a smile. "I understand you might have a problem with the undead." She curled her fingers around the stake hanging at her waist as her hazel eyes sparkled with enthusiasm. "I'm certain I can be of assistance."

"It's very possible," replied Jacqueline, still eyeing Mrs. Hudson coolly. The landlady didn't seem willing to meet her eyes, which strengthened Jacqueline's suspicions that the character had somehow instigated the arrival of Miss Evaline Stoker. "We aren't certain whether there is a vampire about or not."

"Quite. I'd be delighted to patrol the streets and see what I find," Evaline said, her eyes lighting eagerly as she slipped the stake from the small loop at her waist. "I can sense the undead, you know. It's a sort of eerie prickling that goes over the nape of my neck— it's a family trait, you know. Anyhow, I don't feel anything now, but only show me where to go."

"I—"

"Now vhat ees dis zhat ees happening here?" came a strident voice. Professor Van Helsing came into view as he tromped up the steps from the first floor.

"Oh," said Mrs. Hudson, looking as if she wanted to dissolve into the floor. "Oh dear, this is quite... awkward, isn't it?" She looked pleadingly at Jacqueline, who was fighting a smile. Mrs. Hudson would get no assistance from her.

"Good evening, sir," said Evaline. "We were just discussing the possibility of undead being in the area and what to do about it if they are."

As Van Helsing lumbered his way to the top of the flight, Jacqueline couldn't help but compare the two polar opposite vampire hunters.

A man in his early fifties—which would have been considered almost elderly in the late 1800s, when he was imagined by Stoker—with a solid, barrel-like body and a pedantic, scientific brain... and an energetic woman who was a foot shorter and three decades younger than he... and, if Jacqueline remembered the books correctly, with superhuman strength and speed.

And, to top it all off and make the situation even weirder, Professor Van Helsing was a literary creation of Evaline's brother Bram... while Evaline was a literary creation herself.

This made Jacqueline feel even more as if she was in the *Twilight Zone* (the old television show, not the vampire-in-high-school world... but either applied, she supposed).

"But uff course zhere are zee Un-Dead here," said Van Helsing. He was huffing just a bit from the climb, although his blue eyes were clear and sharp. "But zhat is nuffing about vhich a young voman should vorry herself."

Evaline glanced at Jacqueline, and the expression on her face clearly said, *What's up with him and the obnoxiously thick accent and the misogyny* (although Jacqueline didn't think the word misogyny was in use in 1890s England)?

"Does that mean you've confirmed the presence of

a vampire, Professor?" Jacqueline asked before Evaline could speak. From what she remembered from the books, Evaline was fast, strong, brave... and could be quite capricious in her actions and words.

Best not to have a conflict right out the door.

"Uff course not. I have been... restingk," he replied, rolling his r with great enthusiasm. "Frau Hudson has insisted I take zee rest. But now... now I am here, und now vee shall see about zese Un-Deads."

Evaline had been looking at him with a very jaundiced expression, but she remained polite as she introduced herself.

"I am Abraham Van Helsing, Miss—Stoker, you said?" He gave Evaline a perplexed look, which prompted Jacqueline to wonder...

Did Professor Van Helsing realize he was an imagined person... and did he have any knowledge or realization that his creator existed—and was named Stoker?

What a strange conundrum. Comprehending this literary-character-come-to-life muddle was worse than trying to understand string theory and time travel, she decided.

"Yes, Professor Van Helsing," replied Evaline, also giving him a strange look.

The fact that she'd known his title without being told implied to Jacqueline that Evaline (who was a fictional character as well) was fully aware of the characters in her brother's novel *Dracula*.

Fascinating, thought Jacqueline, her mind spinning. She wished she had more time to think about the implications of these two particular characters meeting and how it all worked, but there were other, more pressing problems to be dealt with.

But before she could speak, Evaline went on. "I'm a

vampire hunter, so you needn't worry about it all. I'm perfectly capable of taking care of the undead." She twirled her stake between two fingers like a baton and gave him a cocky smile.

"A vampire hunter? *You*?" Van Helsing didn't even bother to hide his skepticism and derision. "Vhy, that ees simply ridiculous. You are—vhy, you are nussing but a little girl! Zhey are very dangerous, and—"

"Indeed, you are quite correct—girls *can* be very dangerous," Evaline said pertly.

"No, no, *no*," replied a flustered Van Helsing. "Zee Un-Deads are very dangerous, und little girls are—"

"If I recall correctly—and I do," Jacqueline intervened a little more loudly than necessary, "Mina Harker was quite instrumental in the disposal of Count Dracula. You couldn't have done it without her."

"Bah!" Van Helsing flapped a hand at her. "She only did vhat I told her, and zee only reason she could help vas because she vas hypnotize by him. You—you are clearly not hypnotize," he said, giving Evaline a quelling look.

"I'll have you know I am perfectly capable of handling an undead—or an entire army of them," snapped Evaline. Her eyes flashed, and she held the stake at her side as if she were prepared to use it. "And I'm certainly not hypnotize—and it's hypnoti*zed*, as Mina would say."

"Mina? Do you mean Mina Harker? Vhen haff you spoke to her? Vhat ees zeese nonsense?"

"I am speaking of Mina Holmes—who, for your information, was my brother Bram's inspiration for Mina Harker," retorted Evaline. "She's far more organized and knowledgeable than I am, but I—"

"But zees—eet ees all *nonsense!*" Van Helsing's eyes

bulged from their sockets and his ruddy cheeks were turning dark red.

"Oh dear," murmured Mrs. Hudson. Her hands were flapping about helplessly and there were two red spots on her cheeks.

"Got yourself into quite a pickle, haven't you?" sneered a voice from behind Jacqueline.

She turned to see Mrs. Danvers standing there wearing an arch expression, her hands folded at her waist. A condescending smirk just touched her lips.

"I suppose that is only what one can expect when one interferes," Danvers continued.

Mrs. Hudson said something very unladylike under her breath, but she wasn't about to admit defeat to the likes of Mrs. Danvers. "It's none of your concern. Why don't you go off and—and set fire to something," she snapped, eliciting a gasp of horror from Jacqueline, who immediately responded.

"You don't need to give her any ideas—"

"Or croon over the photographs of your *precious* Rebecca," Mrs. Hudson continued. "Or moon over the frocks she'll never wear again or—"

"That's *enough*," Jacqueline said in a very loud, very angry voice.

She was shocked when all four of the characters stilled and looked at her as if she'd just tossed a hand grenade into the middle of the room.

"Everyone," she said in the same firm—but not as loud—voice, "will sit down and do as I say, or I swear I'll find your books and toss them into the fire. Even you," she said, fixing Van Helsing with a gimlet eye.

"But I am zee *only* man... " His voice trailed off under her glare.

"You might be the only man here," Jacqueline said in a frigid voice, "but you are certainly *not* in charge."

Evaline made a sound of agreement, and might have said something, but Jacqueline gave her a quelling look as well.

"Excellent," she said after a moment of silence. "Now. I am going to go to the graveyard where a woman's body was found with puncture wounds on her neck, among other lacerations. Who would like to join me?"

"I shall, of course," Evaline said.

"But uff course I vill come," said Van Helsing.

Jacqueline looked at Hudson and Danvers, the latter of whom still wore that supercilious expression. "The two of you can stay here."

Both women gave her thin-lipped looks, but prudently remained silent.

Without another word, Jacqueline started down the steps to the main floor. Admittedly, she felt far more comfortable going to the graveyard accompanied by not one but two vampire hunters, who trooped down behind her.

It wasn't until she opened the front door of the shop that it occurred to her to wonder whether Evaline and Professor Van Helsing would be *able* to leave the premises and go with her... but then she dismissed the worry.

Both Miss Gulch and the Artful Dodger, who'd previously erupted from books and invaded and disrupted her space, had gone outside of the bookshop: Miss Gulch rode on her bicycle, and Dodger had been doing his pickpocketing along the street.

Her two companions remained silent as Jacqueline stepped out onto the sidewalk and gestured for them to follow her. Neither seemed hesitant about exiting the building.

But as they reached the north end of the third

block of Camellia, well past Egala's shop, she noticed Evaline and Van Helsing lagging behind. Jacqueline stopped and waited for them.

"Is something the matter?" she asked.

"It's just that... I'm feeling a bit strange," said Evaline. "Rather... queasy."

"Und I am beginning to think zhat zee mutton pie I vas eating is not settling vell." Van Helsing rubbed his slightly protruding belly. "Or zomezing ees not quvite right."

Jacqueline frowned. "Mutton pie?" It didn't sound very appetizing to begin with.

"*Ja.*"

By now, the three of them had come to a halt in the middle of the sidewalk, just beneath the sign that said Camellia Court and Seventh Street. Three blocks from Three Tomes Bookshop. A little prickle went down Jacqueline's spine.

She knew Camellia Court was a unique location with supernatural energies. Perhaps the characters were limited to the vicinity of the energy field created by the crisscrossing of several ley lines. The further they went from the bookshop and the energy center, the weaker they became.

Which meant that Jacqueline was going to have to go to the graveyard on her own after all.

"Perhaps you had best return to the shop," she told them.

"But you can't go by yourself," said Evaline, clapping a hand to her stake as she straightened her shoulders. "It might be dangerous."

Jacqueline shook her head. "I don't see how I have any choice. I'm afraid if you go too far from my bookshop, you'll just continue to feel worse. I don't think you can go with me."

"Why, that's quite a problem then, isn't it?" Evaline said, her brow furrowing beneath the fascinator with its elegant bobbing feather. She looked down the street into the falling darkness.

"Zhat is not a güt zhing," said Van Helsing. "Just how am I going to help you if I can't go?"

"Ask Mrs. Hudson," Jacqueline said, irritated about the whole thing. "Maybe there's a solution I don't know about." That was surely true, since Jacqueline didn't know jack shit about this whole "literary characters coming out of books" business.

Evaline hesitated, then pulled a stake from its loop on her corset. "Take this, at least. And whatever you do, *don't* look an undead in the eye."

"Zhat ees right," agreed Van Helsing. "Zhey vill *hypnotize* you."

"Their eyes glow red," Evaline went on. "You can sometimes see them in the dark—since you can't sense them like I can." She gave Van Helsing a satisfied look.

"Zenze zhem? Bah," he said, shaking his head as his mouth twisted. "Nonzenze."

Evaline gave him an annoyed look and muttered to Jacqueline, "Is it only me, or is his accent getting worse?"

"It's not only you," Jacqueline replied.

Evaline tsked. "I'm going to have to speak to Bram about that. It's extremely irritating. It's rather a good thing Mina isn't here. She would have plenty to say to *him*."

Jacqueline could only imagine, as Mina Holmes took after her uncle Sherlock as well as her father Mycroft. "Thank you." She looked at the stake Evaline had given her, hefting it in her hands.

Van Helsing had already started back down the block to the bookshop.

Jacqueline was about to urge Evaline to follow him, but she had one more question. "They have red eyes?"

"They glow in the dark," Evaline reminded her. "And they'll enthrall you if they capture your gaze."

Jacqueline shook her head. She was no Buffy the Vampire Slayer, and even with the stake, she didn't think for one minute she'd be capable of stabbing a vampire with it.

As if reading her mind, Evaline said, "You can do it. Even *Mina*—Holmes, I mean, of course—has managed to kill a few vampires without injuring herself. Much, anyway. And if she can do it, you can." She ran her gaze over Jacqueline, likely noting her forty-eight-year-old body that carried an extra ten pounds. "Probably."

Jacqueline stifled a laugh, then pulled out the garlic she'd stuffed in her pocket. "Will this help?"

Evaline snorted. "Not likely. But this should." She pulled out a chain from beneath her bodice, revealing a large silver cross. "Wear this."

Jacqueline nodded. Silver and a holy object—that was a twofer when it came to vampire repelling. She tipped her head forward so Evaline could slide the necklace over her head.

The cross fell heavily over her breasts, and its weight and purpose gave her a little rush of confidence that she hoped wasn't misplaced.

"Good luck," said Evaline.

And Jacqueline walked off down the street in the growing darkness to find a vampire.

CHAPTER 7

The graveyard was silent and empty.

A chunk of moon hung in the dark blue sky. The trees, which were just beginning to bud out with leaves, looked naked and skeletal, their black shapes eerie against the sky. The tombstones, of all shapes and sizes but mostly thin, upright slabs of marble, rose in unsteady rows from the shadowy ground.

She'd decided not to use the flashlight on her mobile phone—at least not yet. There was no reason to advertise her presence.

At the thought, she looked over at the nearest house, which sat right next to the fence around the graveyard. The house had dark windows, and Jacqueline guessed it belonged to Mrs. Kilmeade. If so, she was probably watching out the window, even at this late hour. Jacqueline resisted the urge to wave, and, glad she'd kept her light off, turned away. Even with the part moon and swath of stars, there was enough light that she could make out their shapes and follow the natural pathways between them.

The heavy silver cross Evaline had given her

thumped comfortingly over her breasts as Jacqueline walked carefully among the graves. The stake felt foreign in her hand, and she wasn't confident it would do her much good. She was glad for the silver cross, at least.

The night remained silent except for the distant call of an owl and the gentle click-clatter of budding branches being brushed by the breeze. Even here, miles from Lake Michigan, the wind came in from the water, making its presence known.

She trudged up and down the rows of tombstones, feeling a lot like Buffy Summers on patrol when she should have been in her room doing homework—but far less confident. There were no open graves, but she did find the dirt that had been disturbed. She stopped in front of the stone.

Dorothy Renfield
b. 1827 d. 1874.

Jacqueline looked at it for a moment, relieved that this Renfield was a female and not a male, as in *Dracula*. But she noted there were no descriptive phrases, like "beloved wife and mother," or "gone too soon," or even "rest in peace." Just the name and dates. Probably didn't mean anything, but...

She heard a noise like a cracking twig and startled like a rabbit, turning to peer into the darkness before she remembered she had a phone with a flashlight on it. But she didn't turn it on, mainly because her fingers were suddenly shaking and her palms had gone damp. She'd probably drop the stupid thing.

Instead, she slipped behind a large maple tree and waited. Her heart thudded wildly in her chest, and that was when she realized that maybe she actually *was* too stupid to live.

What the hell was she thinking, coming to a grave-yard by herself when a vampire might be on the loose? What the hell was she thinking, coming to a graveyard by herself at night at *any* time?

Another crack of a twig and some rustling through overwintered leaves had her heart surging in her throat. Jacqueline needlessly reminded herself that she was forty-eight years old and pretty lax about doing any sort of cardio. Oh, and at this moment, she was having one hell of a hot flash... probably due to terror.

If someone was going to come after her, she didn't have much of a chance, stake or no stake.

Why on earth hadn't she made *herself* a protection amulet? Stupid, stupid, stupid...

If she got back to the bookshop alive, she would rectify that as soon as possible.

Jacqueline remained still as a mouse and listened as the person made their way through the graveyard. The sounds weren't coming any closer, as far as she could tell, which was good. She carefully, slooowly peeked from around the tree, gripping the stake in one hand and her phone in the other.

When she saw who it was, she jolted backward so quickly she scraped her cheek on the tree bark.

Luke Blackstone.

His tall, slender, militarily upright figure was immediately recognizable to her. His pale skin shined in the patchy moon- and streetlight, and his thick, dark hair fell over his forehead. He was wearing black from head to toe and moving through the cemetery like he was on a mission.

Jacqueline swallowed hard and felt a little faint.

She was remembering last night, when she'd encountered him and Mandy Massermey... how when he looked at her, she felt a little tug deep inside. And how, when he glanced back at her as they walked away, she'd seen a flash of red that might have been the light from Egala's shop window, but could also have been glowing from his irises.

And whatever you do, don't *look an undead in the eye...*

That was what Evaline had told her. That sizzle and tug from his gaze... had he been trying to hypnotize her? Or had it just been a warning?

Steadying her breathing, Jacqueline once more peeked from around the tree trunk. Luke was several rows of tombstones away from where she hid, but he seemed to be navigating his way in her general direction. She didn't want to move for fear of stepping on a twig and alerting him.

Could vampires sense the presence of a mortal? Could they scent them? Blood, definitely. But just the presence of a person?

Yet he didn't seem to be aware that anyone else was in the vicinity as he strode quickly between the graves, pausing on occasion as if to read the engraving on the stone, then moving on. He didn't have a flashlight—well, vampires could see in the dark, couldn't they?—but he seemed to be searching for something.

When he stopped in front of the Renfield tombstone, Jacqueline's heart began to beat faster. Surely it wasn't a coincidence.

He crouched next to it, right in front of the disturbed dirt, and she edged even further from around the tree so she could see. He appeared to be using his hand to scoop up some of the soil...

Just then, a light flashed on, cutting through the darkness.

"Who's there? What're you doing?" someone shouted.

Luke bolted upright and took off on his long legs. Jacqueline remained where she was—mainly because she wasn't certain her knees would hold her upright, for the sudden accusatory voice had nearly given her a heart attack.

It took only a moment for her to recognize the peremptory voice. It was Mrs. Kilmeade.

The old woman was moving through the graveyard with surprising speed, flashing her light around like a furniture dealer's Memorial Day Sale spotlight.

Jacqueline did not want to be discovered, so she kept the tree between herself and the light, and only breathed a sigh of relief after Mrs. Kilmeade and her spotlight passed by the Renfield marker and then on into other areas of the graveyard.

Luke Blackstone was long gone, and it was time for Jacqueline to do the same.

~

"THAT DOESN'T MEAN he's a *vampire*," Suzette said. "Just because he was there—after all, so were you, Jacqueline."

"But you have to admit, it does seem suspicious," Nadine replied.

"Why is that necessarily suspicious?" Suzette countered. "Lots of people find walking through a graveyard at night relaxing."

"They do?" Nadine gave her a major eye-roll. "Like who?"

"Well... I don't know. Some people do. I bet the ZAP Ladies do."

Jacqueline snorted. "Yeah, I'm not so sure about that. They don't need to go to the graveyard to do whatever it is they do over there." She glanced in the direction of the cul-de-sac where the three crones lived in their robin's-egg-blue Victorian, even though she was in the bookshop and couldn't see the multi-storied, filigree-trimmed house.

It was Monday morning, and since the store was closed today, she'd told her friends to come up to the apartment. She didn't want to run into Van Helsing or Evaline Stoker just yet because she didn't have answers... or the energy to deal with them.

And she wanted to be able to drink at least two cups of coffee without Mrs. Hudson noticing, because she'd gotten *zero* sleep last night... but nightmares and night sweats galore.

"Coffee?" she said, pouring two more cups without waiting for replies. She already knew their answers; it was barely seven a.m. Any sane person wanted coffee at that hour.

"Well, I'm just saying. There's no reason to conclude he's *definitely* a vampire. Here, I brought some of my latest cake effort," Suzette said, and set a little container with tiny muffins on the table. "I'm testing it for a wedding. Banana with chocolate cream cheese frosting. Let me know what you think. Anyway, we've got to give the man the benefit of the doubt."

"Fine. So we have to prove he's an undead," said Nadine, wasting no time in slicing a sliver of the cake. "Or is it Un-Dead—capital U, hyphen, capital D? How are *we* spelling it?"

Jacqueline giggled. She couldn't help it: not only had she survived the nighttime trip to the cemetery with only a bruised shin from where she'd bumped into a tombstone on her way out, but someone other than herself actually cared about spelling semantics.

"Or should we just stick with 'vampire'—though there are several ways to spell that too, aren't there?" Nadine said with a pained sigh. "I never expected to become friends with someone who was such a grammar queen. Do you know I even proofread my texts now? And the other day, my daughter texted me back and asked if I was being held hostage because I didn't type 'u-r' for the word 'your.'"

"Well, I'm certainly glad I've had some influence on you," Jacqueline said with a grin.

Nadine grimaced jokingly, then slid a forkful of cake into her mouth. "Zo-my-god." Her eyes went wide and dreamy. "Delicious. You're a goddess, Suzette. And they're even halfway good for you. You did say banana, right? It's fruit, so it's not all bad."

"I did. You're good. Anyway, Jacqueline's more of a pedant than a grammar queen," said Suzette, picking up a muffin. "Though she's probably that too. But I think Nadine's right. We have to find a way to prove whether Luke Blackstone is a vampire or not. Spelled with an 'i-r-e' not a 'y-r.'"

"Okay. So how do we do that?" Jacqueline said. "We could ask the crones—but when they were here yesterday, Zwyla said she hadn't sensed anything off quite yet... although maybe she has by now."

"We need to visit him," Suzette said firmly. "Get a vibe, you know? One of us needs to plan a funeral. I vote for Jacqueline. You've probably got someone in your family tree you can kill off."

"Geez. A little bloodthirsty, are we?" Nadine said with very little concern as she reached for another muffin.

"I'm just saying—don't you have a fictitious great-aunt or a nonexistent stepmother who is going to need to be funneled into an urn sometime in the near future?" Suzette said. "Don't worry, we'll go along with you for moral support."

And that was how Jacqueline ended up placing a call to Brittany Funeral Home that morning as soon as they opened at nine a.m. The answering service scheduled her for a two p.m. appointment.

~

SINCE MONDAY WAS her day off, so to speak, Jacqueline had things to do besides go to fake appointments at funeral parlors.

But it was with some trepidation that she went out the back door of the shop to the small courtyard. She'd intended to do some work on the garden in preparation for putting in annuals, but she was a little nervous about what she might find.

Wearing gloves and a pair of old sweatpants (apparently now they were called joggers, but Jacqueline wasn't quite that hip), she opened the gate and stepped down into the garden. Immediately, her attention went to what had been a trio of mandrakes yesterday, clustered unobtrusively in the corner.

One was gone.

There was a small hole in the ground where the third plant had been, confirming that Jacqueline wasn't hallucinating (although, as she'd learned, mandrakes were known for their hallucinogenic properties).

"What the hell," she said aloud. She happened to be facing the regal and sacred cedar tree. Perhaps she thought Jacqueline was speaking to her, for the branches swept together and then apart in a balletic sort of movement that she interpreted as *"Crazy, right?"*

She touched the cedar's rough trunk and felt a rush of something sparkling and warm...

"If only you could speak."

Another surge of energy, even stronger and more electric, barreled through her, and Jacqueline looked up into the complicated warren of branches and conifer needles. "If only I could *understand* you," she corrected herself.

Jacqueline had so much to learn about this new, "crone-ish" phase of her life. She just hoped she was up to the responsibility.

She returned her attention to the remaining pair of mandrakes, eyeing them mistrustfully. What would happen if she tried to pull them out—and in the middle of the day? Would they scream? Would she die?

Was she being crazy? They were just plants...

Still, she didn't feel brave enough to attempt it. Instead, she did an hour's worth of work around them, gathering up old branches and leaves. It was late enough in the season that any young insects had taken what they needed from their natural coverings, so it was safe to clear it all away.

Jacqueline was just about to call it a morning when she caught movement out of the corner of her eye.

"Egala." She straightened up abruptly, giving her distant cousin the same mistrustful look she'd been giving the mandrakes. And then in that instant, she knew. Or, at least, had a very strong suspicion. "Come to harvest more of your mandrakes?"

Egala was a woman of uncertain age with smooth,

unlined skin, but likely in her sixties. She wore her blond-going-gray hair like the big-screen version of Professor Umbridge, in the sort of weekly shampoo-and-set style popular with older women. Her eyebrows were penciled in in skinny, dark brown arches, and she wore jarringly bright pink lipstick and a tunic-like sweater over capri pants. She was carrying a very large leather tote with the stylized E on it. It was fashioned of coppery leather with a bronze and gold leopard-skin pattern on it.

Jacqueline's eyes fell on the bag, and she immediately felt a tug of covetousness. *Damn.*

"What?" said Egala.

"I'm assuming you planted those." Jacqueline gestured to the plants in question.

Egala went over and crouched next to them. It only took her a moment. "*Whoa.* Those are mandrakes. Real mandrakes! Where did you get them?"

"Someone planted them. I assumed it was you. For obvious reasons."

"No," said Egala, rising. Jacqueline swore she heard her knees cracking. "Wasn't me. Wish it had been," she added in a mutter that Jacqueline didn't think she was supposed to hear.

"Any idea who might have done, then?"

"Probably one of those nosy crones," Egala said.

"Of course it wasn't them. They have their own garden."

The reminder seemed to confound Egala. "True." She scratched her chin thoughtfully, and Jacqueline could see the trail where she removed a streak of foundation.

"There was one plant on Saturday," Jacqueline told her. She saw no reason to be reticent; after all, Egala was a witch of some sort, and any expert advice or opinion was useful. "It just appeared in my garden here. And then yesterday morning, there were three."

"One's missing," Egala pointed out.

"Yeah, I noticed," Jacqueline said dryly.

"Did you hear anyone scream last night?" Egala glanced up, and Jacqueline knew she was looking at the third-floor windows of her flat.

"No... but I wasn't home all night. I went to the graveyard." In for a penny, in for a pound, she figured. Might as well find out what Egala knew. "I was looking for a vampire."

Egala didn't seem surprised. "I heard about that. Did you find him? Or her?"

"No. Do you really think there's one here in Button Cove?"

"Yes."

That sounded far too certain. "What makes you think so?"

Egala shrugged. "Dead body. Bite marks. Blood drained. Disturbed graveyard soil. What else could it be?"

Damn. Jacqueline was hoping there'd be another explanation. "Right. So, what are you doing here, anyway?"

"Oh, yes. Well." Egala seemed uncomfortable all of a sudden. "I thought maybe we could do a trade."

"What sort of trade?" Jacqueline asked, not bothering to hide her extreme suspicion.

"Well... I wanted to give you this in exchange for a sprig from the cedar tree." Egala opened her massive tote and pulled out a large drawstring bag made from flannel. The now-familiar stylized E was stamped on it. Jacqueline recognized the sack as the sort of dust protector bag in which fine leather accessories would be stored, and that there was something inside of it.

She hesitated when Egala offered it to her, but curiosity won out. Pulling the drawstrings loose, Jacqueline peeked inside. Her heart fell.

"Oh," she said, unable to contain the breathless gasp as she caught sight of the stunning midnight-blue-emerald-amethyst tote. It was smaller than the massive one Egala was carrying, but still large enough to hold a computer tablet or even a smaller laptop, along with all of the other accoutrements a woman might stuff in her purse. The leather was buttery soft and somehow stamped with a faux-snakeskin texture, heavy on the rich, dark blue with green and purple subtleties. It seemed to shine and glow from inside its protective bag.

When she pulled it out, Jacqueline felt a sizzle of warmth and lust (on her end, for the bag) zip through her body. It was as if the tote had been made especially for her.

And it probably had been.

"What sort of curse did you put on it?" she said, giving Egala a skeptical look.

"No curse. On the heart of Mother Universe and our ancestors, I swear it. There might be a bit of a charm on it, though," Egala admitted. "Nothing that would cause any problem or harm to anyone," she added quickly when Jacqueline made to shove it back in its protective bag. "Truly. It's safe... for you, anyway."

"I'm going to take it to Zwyla and Andromeda," Jacqueline warned her. "And I'm going to tell them about your offer to trade. If they think it's all right—if there aren't any hidden curses or bad hexes on the bag, and if it's permissible for me to give you a branch from the cedar—then it's a deal."

Egala's tense expression eased slightly. "Do that.

You'll find that there's nothing wrong with the purse. I thought it might be a sort of... peace offering, maybe."

Jacqueline was still skeptical, but *the bag*. It was just perfect. It wasn't gaudy, but sleek and elegant and eye-catching. She suspected there was some sort of witchcraftery involved with the material—it was simply unlike anything she had ever seen or could imagine. Rather like the dress Cinderella had worn when Jacqueline found herself thrust into *Grimms' Fairy Tales*: something magically stunning and other-worldly.

"I'll get back to you," she said.

"The sooner the better," Egala replied.

"Why do you want the cedar branch, anyway?"

Egala's gaze darted away, then back to her. "All right. I'll tell you the truth."

Jacqueline braced herself.

"You know how in Chinese restaurants they put lucky bamboo near the front door in a vase? Well, sacred cedar is lucky and holy to—to the Stone family" —which meant Jacqueline's family, of course—"and I thought to do the same, using a branch from the family cedar. For luck and protection."

"That's all?" Jacqueline was still mightily skeptical.

"Honest."

"It seems your business is doing quite well as it is. Why would you need that?"

"There's never too much luck—or protection—in this world, is there? And besides... if there is a vampire romping about, one can't be too careful."

Jacqueline was still skeptical, but she'd given her word that if the ZAP Ladies found the leather tote safe for her to use, and that it was okay for her to give up a twig of the cedar, she'd hold up the deal. "All right. I'll talk to Zwyla and Andromeda and Pietra and see what they think."

When Egala left, Jacqueline wondered if this was a step toward some sort of truce.

You can't pick your family. You can only learn to live with them, she thought.

CHAPTER 8

"I don't see anything wrong with it," said Zwyla. "Or *feel* anything off."

She'd been looking over the dark blue bag Egala had given Jacqueline, sliding her hand over its supple exterior, then carefully around inside to feel around the dark blue suede interior. It looked like an exotic jewel-toned snake when she moved her hand from within, causing the leather to undulate gently.

"Andi? Want to check my work?" she asked, sliding the bag across the heavy wooden trestle table scarred with cuts, scrapes, and singes from decades—perhaps centuries—of use.

They—Jacqueline and the three ZAP Ladies— were in their workroom, a space Jacqueline had privately dubbed the "herbary," thinking of the tiny hut where Brother Cadfael had done his medicinal plant work.

There was everything a medieval—or twenty-first-century—herbologist needed in the long, narrow room: knives, scalpels, spoons, athames; bowls, flasks, funnels, vials; whisks, mortars and pestles; an electric spice or coffee bean grinder; and jars of all shapes and sizes with all sorts of ingredients, including dried toadstools and actual eye of newt, along with numerous other tools and vessels. And, of course, there was a stone fireplace with an opening six feet tall that used real logs. A large cauldron hung inside, but there was currently no fire burning.

"Why don't you ever ask *me* to check your work?" demanded Pietra, frowning from where she was cutting out some small, round pastries. Today she was wearing leggings over a pink tunic covered by an apron that said *Kitchen Witch*. Jacqueline didn't think the manufacturer had meant it literally, but if the shoe fit...

Zwyla faltered a little, then smiled and shoved the bag across the table. "I didn't ask because I thought you were busy."

Pietra gave her a skeptical look, but wiped her flour-dusted hands thoroughly on her apron then took up the bag. Jacqueline studiously did not look at Andromeda or Zwyla as their friend examined the faux-snakeskin tote. She suspected why Zwyla hadn't asked Pietra right away.

She was certain it wasn't that the enthusiastic Petey had a lack of competence for such a task, but perhaps it was that she tended to be more emotional, dramatic, and impulsive, while her friends (especially Zwyla) were, in contrast, calm and steady.

Besides, Pietra *had* been busy with whatever pastry she was making, and Jacqueline, for one, didn't want that process interrupted, for she was pretty certain they were mini versions of the divine blueberry cream scones she dreamt about on a regular basis.

"It's clean and safe," Pietra said after a thorough check. She gave Zwyla a meaningful look. "But it does have some minor charms on it—one that creates the shimmery color of the faux snakeskin, and another one that will keep it from getting lost or left behind. And there's one to keep it from getting scratched or stained. I sense something else—it's not a curse or a hex—but I can't quite put my finger on what it is... Andi?"

Andromeda took the bag with slender, beringed fingers. Today, her hair was back to its normal spiky style, but this time in a lemon yellow with a bit of glitter sparkling at the tips. Jacqueline resisted the urge to run a hand over and through her tangled mess of curls. She missed her sleek, no-nonsense French twist, but her hair would no longer cooperate for that style. Maybe she should ask Andromeda for some ideas on how to manage her own mop.

Pietra continued cutting out what was hopefully scones, while Zwyla rose and left the room, her color-ful, fringed caftan billowing around her ankles and her many bracelets jingling.

"No curses. Nothing with negative energy," Andromeda murmured. "Nothing at all." She had her eyes closed as her hands roamed over the exterior and then interior of the bag. "Nothing... Wait. No... " Her fine eyebrows knitted together. "There is something else here. It's a wish. There's a sort of wish attached to this bag." She opened her eyes and looked at Jacqueline.

"What—does she wish me dead so she can inherit the shop?" Jacqueline said with a nervous laugh.

"No, it's not that at all. There's no negative energy attached to this bag or anything about it that seems wrong. It's just a-a wish—for lack of a better descriptor—that it will give you what you need."

Jacqueline blinked. Interesting. "Like if I said I

wanted to stab someone with a fork, a fork would appear in the bag?"

Andromeda's brows rose. "Maybe."

"I think that's a trademark of Egala's handbags," Jacqueline said, then explained what had happened at the shop yesterday.

"Well, that could be a handy selling tool," Andromeda said, smiling. "After all, the bag is rather large. Difficult to find things down inside it."

"But a *fork?*" Jacqueline said. "That's not so bad, but what if I said I wanted to shoot someone? Then what would happen? Would a handgun appear inside?" She eyed the tote with distaste. "She's selling bags like this from her shop—and I'm pretty sure they've all got these sorts of charms on them. Or wishes. Whatever you want to call them."

"That is concerning. Still... I sense no negative energy from this particular bag," Andromeda said, once more closing her eyes. When she opened them after a prolonged moment, she shook her head. "No. Nothing. Petey? Z? What do you two think?"

"I think maybe we ought to visit Egala's shop and see for ourselves," replied Zwyla, who'd just come back into the room carrying a large, tattered book. "I'm in need of a new handbag anyway."

"But you think it's safe for me to use," Jacqueline said.

"As long as you don't want to kill anyone, dear," Pietra said brightly. Jacqueline gave her a dark look, and the other woman laughed, flashing an array of tiny dimples around her chin and mouth. "It's fine, Jacqueline. I was just teasing. There's no bad energy around it. I promise."

"All right." Jacqueline was relieved to hear this. After all, she did lust after that bag. And if there were protections on it to keep it from being lost or ruined, she could get down with that. She had a terrible habit of accidentally getting stray ink marks on her purses. The more expensive and luscious the leather, the more likely she'd mark it up.

"In exchange for the tote, Egala wants a sprig from the sacred cedar tree. Is there any reason I shouldn't give her one?"

Zwyla looked up from the book she'd brought with her back into the room. "That's what I was trying to find out," she said, gesturing to the open pages. They crinkled and were yellow with age. "I don't see anything in here that would suggest you shouldn't." She looked at her companions.

Andromeda shook her head. "No problem as far as I know. Cedar is sacred and holds great power, but a small branch shared willingly by you shouldn't be a problem. Although... I would ask the tree first, Jacqueline. She'll speak to you if you ask, and give you permission if it's all right."

Jacqueline nodded as a little shiver rushed over her body. She and the tree had already had a conversation of sorts. "All right."

"Petey, what do you think?" asked Andi.

"As long as she doesn't try to root it—or graft it? Isn't that what they do to fruit trees to make them grow—graft them to other trees?"

"Excellent point," said Andromeda, settling back in her chair with pursed lips. "I don't think it would be a good idea to let Egala propagate the cedar. Just in case."

"So what do I do? Tell her no?" Jacqueline looked sadly at the dark blue tote. She'd have to give it back after all.

"No... you can talk to it—the sprig, I mean—and

ask it not to root or allow itself to be grafted," Andromeda said.

Jacqueline nodded. "All right. Thank you." She rose, preparing to leave.

"Oh, Jacqueline, I made up a few tea bags with my new tea in it," said Andromeda. "For you. The purging tea with calendula and lemon balm."

"And the silver sage," Jacqueline said, trying not to sound too uninterested. "Like for smudging. Thank you so much." She tucked the tea bags into her purse, where she figured they'd stay until she cleaned out the bag.

"So did you find out anything at the graveyard last night?" asked Pietra. By now she'd finished cutting out the scones and was placing them delicately on a cookie sheet.

"Oh." Jacqueline sat back down. "How did you know about that?"

The three women merely looked at her and smiled sadly at her naïveté.

"Right," Jacqueline replied. "Silly of me to ask. But how can you know about that, but still not know whether there's a vampire loose in Button Cove?"

"Things are simply not always cut and dried, my dear," said Pietra, patting her arm with a floured hand. "So, what did you find out?"

"I don't know. Couldn't draw any conclusions," Jacqueline replied. "But I wasn't alone in the graveyard. The new mortician, Luke Blackstone, was also there. He didn't see me."

"Very interesting," said Andromeda. "He does seem the type, doesn't he?"

"I suppose so," replied Zwyla, still flipping carefully through the ancient tome.

"The fact that Professor Van Helsing has appeared

—along with another vampire hunter named Evaline Stoker—seems to be a clue that we do have an undead to deal with." *With which to deal,* Jacqueline silently corrected herself. It wasn't *technically* incorrect to end a sentence with a preposition, but she'd been taught back in Catholic grade school never to do it. It almost felt like she was bucking the system—or, at least, the nuns—when she did so.

"Van Helsing is here?" Pietra's head popped up. Her cheeks, always round and pink, were even rosier.

"He doesn't look anything like Hugh Jackman," Jacqueline told her. "Sadly."

"Oh," replied Pietra. But her cheeks remained pink. Or maybe it was because she was bending over to slide the scones into the hot oven.

"And who is this other vampire hunter?" asked Zwyla. "Stoker, did you say?"

Jacqueline explained, ending, "So... how does this work? With Evaline Stoker being the fictional sister of the man who actually created Van Helsing?"

"What do you mean, how does it work?" asked Andromeda. She gave her a kind smile. "It simply *is,* love."

So helpful. All of these people were so freaking helpful.

Jacqueline withheld her comments and tamped down the frustration. She supposed she should just stop asking why and deal with what was. There never was an answer for *why*, anyway, was there? Why had Josh Wenczel cheated on her? Why had her best friend Stacey died at forty-five?

Why did characters come out of books?

Why did one of them have to be Danvers?

"All right. Thank you. I'll ask the cedar if I can take

a sprig and then I'll bring it here for you to talk to," she said to Andromeda.

"We will visit Egala's shop," Zwyla said, closing the heavy book. "I hope your appointment at the funeral home goes well."

Jacqueline didn't even bother to ask how she knew about that. It just *was*.

∼

"I'M nervous and I don't know why," said Nadine as she and Jacqueline started up the walk to Brittany Funeral Home.

"You don't know why?" Jacqueline said with a laugh. "Maybe because we're about to beard a possible vampire in his den, so to speak? By the way, thanks for coming with me."

"Yeah." Nadine's voice was weak.

Before her friend could bail, Jacqueline took her by the arm and marched up to the door.

Brittany Funeral Home was, appropriately, in a homey sort of building with white-painted brick, a single-story ranch with a picket fence and pots of subdued white and green petunias at the side entrance.

"Hey, did you make a protection amulet for us?" Nadine said, stopping suddenly.

"Oh. No. Not yet." Jacqueline had completely forgotten about her plan to do so because of her visit from Egala. "But I have this." She pulled on the chain tucked beneath her long sweater and gave Nadine a glimpse of the large silver cross Evaline Stoker had given her.

"Me too," Nadine replied. "But mine is much smaller. I also stuffed garlic in my pockets."

"Good plan." Jacqueline chose not to tell her that

garlic didn't seem to work—at least, according to Evaline. She pushed open the door and stepped inside.

Immediately, she smelled lilies—common funeral décor—and beneath it, something very sterile and yet neutral.

"Good afternoon." Luke Blackstone himself was standing there. "Miss Finch, is it?"

"Ms. Finch," Jacqueline corrected him. "But you can call me Jacqueline, of course. This is my friend Nadine Bachmoto. She came along for... for moral support."

"Of course, of course," said Luke with a smile. Jacqueline couldn't help but look for fangs. She didn't see any, but that didn't mean anything. Oh, how she wished Evaline could have come with her. She would have sensed right off whether this man was an undead.

"That's very kind of you, Ms. Bachmoto," Luke went on. He was long and lean in his somber dark suit accessorized with a properly subdued navy and green paisley tie. His dark hair was combed into place without looking plastic or gelled, and his eyes were a vibrant blue. "This sort of thing is always difficult, and it's nice to have a friend for support. This way." He gestured them down a short hall that was studded with doors. All of them were open, and the rooms empty of people. "We haven't any viewings or services today, so we shouldn't be interrupted."

Jacqueline could feel Nadine practically quivering next to her, and she suspected it was because Luke was, in fact, ridiculously *hot*. Sexy, attractive, charming, and elegant equaled *hot*.

Like, Pierce Brosnan in *The Thomas Crown Affair* hot.

If he were a vampire, no one would have a chance against being enthralled.

"Stop drooling," Jacqueline hissed, and used an elbow to poke her friend in the side as they passed an empty room filled with rows of chairs and a smattering of sofas around the perimeter.

"Right in here, ladies," said Luke, seemingly unaware of their consternation.

Jacqueline and Nadine entered a small room. It was well lit with soft-glow lamps instead of overhead fluorescents, but the window blinds had been lowered and their slats slanted upward to keep any direct sunlight from coming through the windows. Jacqueline gave her friend a meaningful look as they took their seats at a small conference table. In the center was a small arrangement of flowers. Around the edges of the room were long tables filled with different types and styles of urns, small models of caskets, and wood, satin, and stain samples.

Caskets. Jacqueline shivered. Didn't a vampire sleep in his coffin? With the dirt from his grave?

Luke Blackstone would certainly have myriad choices amongst the caskets here...

She'd never realized that being a mortician would be the perfect job for a vampire.

"Please take a seat; make yourselves comfortable." He gave them a gentle smile, and Jacqueline was certain she felt a little frisson of... something... when he looked at her. Heat? A tug at her gaze? The beginning of an enthrallment? She averted her eyes quickly.

"Would you like some coffee? Tea? Water? Soda?" he asked.

"Water," replied Jacqueline, wanting to moisten her suddenly dry throat. She resisted the urge to touch the cross beneath her sweater.

"I'll be right back with that," he said after Nadine chimed in with the same request. "In the meantime, if you like, feel free to look about." He waved an elegant hand around the room.

"All right, now what?" Nadine whispered as he left. "How in the world are we going to go about this?"

Jacqueline was wondering the same thing. They were here, alone with Luke... but how to force him to reveal his true nature?

And get out alive?

"All right... we know vampires don't respond well to crosses and holy objects," she said in an undertone. She looked around the room and noticed there wasn't a cross anywhere, as often was in a funeral home. "I'll play with my necklace and pull out the cross pendant. You watch him and see if there's any reaction."

"Good plan," said Nadine. "Oh! Wouldn't a vampire respond to the scent of blood?" Her eyes sparkled.

"You mean like a shark?" Jacqueline said, choking on a nervous giggle.

"Well, I mean, my nose starts to quiver when I smell Suzette's baked goods," Nadine replied earnestly. "An undead might react similarly if he smelled blood. Maybe I can give myself a paper cut or something."

Jacqueline didn't have the chance to respond with anything other than a nod, for just then Luke came back into the room.

"And here we are, ladies." He set a silver tray on the table in front of them. On it were two highball crystal glasses and an unopened bottle of Fiji water. There was also a small plate of wafer-thin ginger snaps.

Nadine's nose quivered. Jacqueline stifled another nervous giggle.

"Now," said Luke, moving fluidly to take a seat at the table. He gave Jacqueline another somber smile. "I understand this is a very difficult time for you and your family... " He made a simple gesture with his long, pale fingers to encourage her to speak.

"Oh, yes... it's my aunt Esmeralda," she said, without the barest stumble on the name. She'd been practicing the story in her head all day, so the words came easily. "She's been in assisted living for three years now, but I know... well, the time is near. And so I wanted to start at least looking into... arrangements. It's only me who's left to... uh... take care of things. I have a sister in California, but she ran off with one of my cousins' husbands, and the divorce was pretty ugly, so she—uh... " Maybe that was a little too much fictional backstory.

Gathering her thoughts and studiously ignoring Nadine's poker face (which meant she was struggling not to laugh), Jacqueline glanced at the array of urns. "I think she'd like that mother-of-pearl one, trimmed with gold. Is that hand-painted?" As she spoke, Jacqueline began to fumble with the chain beneath her sweater, trying to make it seem like nerves.

"That's a lovely selection," he said. "A perennial favorite, in fact. Am I to assume you're looking at cremation, then? Not a graveyard plot?"

"Didn't you say your auntie wanted to be buried near the family?" Nadine said. "In the graveyard?"

Jacqueline immediately caught on to her friend's tactic. "She did mention that, but I'm not certain... Well, you know funds are limited. Still, that *is* what she wants... "

"Didn't you say there was a plot available?" Nadine pushed, giving her an insistent look.

"Oh... there might be. I'll have to check. Auntie Ez

can be a little confused sometimes, you know," she said to Luke with a sad smile. "She's ninety-six."

"Of course," he murmured. "What a long and robust life she must have led—er, is still leading, I mean."

"Yes," Jacqueline replied. "I think the family plot is right next to the Renfields—at the Rock Road Cemetery?" She watched him closely and saw his eyes widen just a bit.

"Isn't that where someone was digging up the dirt?" said Nadine, sounding horrified. "I heard about that."

"Terrible," said Luke.

"Why would anyone do such a thing?" Jacqueline said, still watching him closely.

"I mean... don't the undead need dirt from their gravesite?" said Nadine, still playing the horrified but gossipy friend. "And there was that woman they found... "

Jacqueline wanted to kill her, especially when there was an awkward silence for a moment.

Then Luke shrugged and said, "I don't have any idea why someone would deface a gravesite. Now, supposing your aunt—er, great-aunt?—does want to use the family plot, you'll need a casket. But don't worry—they're like cars: something in every price range." He gave what might have been a nervous laugh. Or not.

Jacqueline nodded and continued to play with the chain around her neck. "That's good to know. I just am not sure what sort of budget we'll have." She flipped the cross out in one smooth movement.

She *swore* Luke flinched. And did he ease a little bit away, settling back in his chair? Did his mouth seem a little tighter at the corners?

"Perhaps you'd like to... take a look at the wood

finishes we have available. Over there." He nodded toward the most distant table from where he was sitting.

Jacqueline exchanged glances with Nadine. It wasn't enough, but it was *something*.

"Ow!"

Jacqueline and Luke both looked at Nadine, who was holding up her finger. There was a line of blood glistening on it.

"What happened?" Jacqueline asked, on cue—even as she watched him closely. He seemed frozen in place.

"I don't know... I must have scraped it on something under the table." Nadine was still holding up her finger, and blood was still oozing from it. She made no effort to wipe it away or stanch the small cut.

"I'm so sorry," said Luke after an awkward moment. He rose stiffly. "I'll find a bandage for you, ma'am."

They both watched him go, and the minute he was out of earshot, Nadine leaned over to whisper, "He doesn't seem very comfortable. Did you see the way he got all weird as soon as I showed the blood?"

"Yes," Jacqueline hissed back. "And he wanted me to look at the urn samples—probably trying to get me to move farther away from him because of my necklace."

The two of them looked at each other with wide eyes. Jacqueline felt her heart thudding in her chest.

What would happen when he came back? Would he attack them? Lock them up somewhere?

"Should we leave now?" Nadine whispered, her eyes darting around the room. "Before he gets— Oh."

Luke came into the room, moving in a manner that Jacqueline would describe as stiff and formal. "If you'd like to wash up in the ladies' lounge... " he said. "It's down the hall to the left."

"Thank you." Nadine—the traitor—fled, snatching up the two Band-Aids he'd set on the table on her way past. And leaving Jacqueline alone with the possible vampire.

She played with the large cross, hoping it would be enough to keep him at his distance. "Should we look at price lists for the caskets?" she asked. He'd have to move nearer to do that, and if he made an excuse, that might be even more of an indication.

"Oh. Yes, of course," he replied, smiling. Turning away, he opened a drawer in a cabinet and flipped through files with his long, elegant fingers. "It was very nice to see you the other night, Jacqueline."

She froze for a moment, her heart lodging in her throat. Then, just as quickly, she realized he probably was referring to the evening she'd run into him with Mandy Massermey and not last night at the graveyard.

"It was a lovely night for a walk," she said, suddenly remembering that the young woman's body had been found the morning after she saw him with Mandy. "It's too bad Mandy had to go home early."

"She loves her job, so she doesn't mind," he replied, turning back from the filing cabinet. He held a manila folder labeled *PRICE LIST* as well as several glossy brochures featuring caskets of all colors and sizes. "Here you are... you can look at these at your leisure." He slid the brochures across the table to her, still keeping his distance.

"It must be difficult dating someone who has to go to bed early and get up with the sun, when you're on a completely different schedule," Jacqueline went on. "Hardly up before noon."

He paused and looked at her so suddenly that her belly dropped unpleasantly. "What do you mean?"

"I— Well, you mentioned h-how you like to stay up late and hardly rise unless you have an appointment," she said, curling her fingers tightly around the cross pendant.

"Oh, yes, of course," he said, his expression relaxing. "Well, we make it work."

"Have you met her father?" Jacqueline asked boldly. "Detective Massermey?"

He stilled. "Detective Massermey?"

"Yes. Mandy's father."

He was still looking at her as if he didn't quite comprehend her words. "No. No, I haven't met him."

Before Jacqueline could decide whether to press him further, Nadine burst back into the room. "I'm so sorry, Jacqueline, but we've got to go." She was brandishing her phone. "Mr.—uh—Blackstone, I'm sorry, we've got to go."

"What's wrong?" Jacqueline rose automatically, concerned by her friend's expression.

"Minor emergency back at the shop," Nadine said, taking her by the arm.

"All right," Jacqueline said with trepidation. What had Mrs. Hudson or Mrs. Danvers done now? She gave Luke an apologetic look. "All right if I take these?" She scooped up the brochures.

"Yes, of course. Thank you for coming. I do hope nothing's terribly wrong," Luke said, following them out of the conference room.

"It'll be all right," Nadine said, still gripping Jacqueline's arm firmly. "Once she gets back there. Uh —thanks again for your time."

Nadine didn't release Jacqueline until they were

outside and onto the sidewalk. "Oh thank goodness," she said.

"What's wrong? What happened at the shop?" Jacqueline asked as she rushed down the block toward Camellia Court.

"Oh, there's nothing wrong at the shop," Nadine said, a little out of breath. "I just said that to get us out of there."

"Why?"

"Because when I went to wash up, I took the opportunity to snoop around. I found his little kitchen, and guess what was in the refrigerator?"

"What?"

"*Blood*. Jars of *blood*."

CHAPTER 9

"Are you sure it was *blood*?" Suzette asked.

The three of them—Jacqueline, Nadine, and Suzette—were sitting in Jacqueline's apartment.

"It sure as hell wasn't tomato juice," Nadine said. "It was the wrong color, you know? It looked like... blood." She gagged a little, and was definitely green.

"Why would he leave it in the fridge where anyone could find it?" said Suzette, clearly skeptical. "And if he has a store of blood, why did he have to attack and kill that poor woman?"

"How would I know?" cried Nadine, exasperated. "I just found the stuff. I can't explain how it got there. But it was *there*." She looked like she was going to gag again.

"Well, if you think about it," Jacqueline said, "he probably could come by it quite easily. Being a mortician."

They looked at her. "Are you saying he—he drains the blood from the dead bodies when he's—you know, preparing them for burial? Formaldehyding them and all?" Suzette said. "And *saves* it?" Now she was looking green.

"It makes sense. Creepy, awful sense, but sense," Jacqueline replied. "I mean, he's just gonna throw it away otherwise—the blood I, mean—right?"

"So... if he has a plentiful supply of blood from dead bodies... why would he attack a person?" said Nadine. "And kill them? I mean, how much blood do these guys need?"

Jacqueline and Suzette shrugged.

"Maybe we ought to ask the experts," said Jacqueline. "Van Helsing and Evaline. They might be able to shed some light on the subject."

"I have a class in ten minutes," said Nadine with a sigh. "I've got to get over to the studio—and try to put all this out of my mind."

"Try meditating," said Suzette with a teasing grin. Nadine was always encouraging her to meditate, and Suzette liked to tease her back because she claimed she couldn't "turn off" her mind in order to meditate.

"Bite me," said Nadine, then her eyes widened comically. "Oh shit. I didn't mean to say that." She looked around for lurking vampires, then laughed. "All right. I'm off. I'll be done for the day around six —Brenda is doing my evening hot yoga class, thank goodness, because every freaking class is a hot yoga class for me; thank you, perimenopause—so keep me posted." She gave them a little "ta-ta" wave and left.

Suzette sighed. "I should go too. I've got to place a supplies order before four and—eek! It's three thirty. I'm sorry, I've got to go, Jacqueline. Keep me posted too,"

Jacqueline promised. Then, armed with a late-in-the-day cup of coffee (which she knew she shouldn't have, but these were extenuating circumstances), she took the stairs tucked inside her kitchen pantry down to the supply room on the second floor behind the café.

Mrs. Hudson was there like she nearly always was, even when the shop was closed, and Professor Van Helsing and Evaline Stoker were present as well. Not for the first time, Jacqueline wondered where they went when they weren't "there."

"Well, here you are, dearie," said Mrs. Hudson, giving her a smile. "How about a nice cuppa— Oh, I see you've already got one."

Jacqueline kept her mug of the demon bean brew close to her chest in case Mrs. Hudson caught a whiff and realized it wasn't tea.

"Did you have any luck last night?" asked Evaline. Her hazel eyes sparkled with impatience, and though she was sitting on one of the sofas, she was fiddling with a stake. She was obviously the type of person who couldn't sit still for long.

Van Helsing was sitting at the counter drinking his tea, but he slipped off the stool, standing as politely as any Victorian gentleman would at Jacqueline's arrival.

Jacqueline took a seat next to Evaline and explained what happened in the graveyard as Mrs. Hudson approached with a plate of tiny, unfrosted lemon cupcakes dusted with powdered sugar. Suzette's creations.

"I wish I could have been there too," Evaline said with great irritation. "I would have been able to tell for certain whether he was an undead."

Van Helsing snorted, and Evaline gave him a dagger look, muttering something under her breath.

Jacqueline interrupted what might have become a more animated discussion by describing her visit with Nadine to the funeral home. After explaining to both of them what a refrigerator was ("Oh! An *icebox*!" said

Evaline), she said, "Why do you think he would have
jars of blood if he just killed someone?"

"Zhere ees no reazon for it," said Van Helsing
firmly. "Zhey like zhe fresh blood, alvays. Zhey need it
to survife."

"That's not necessarily true," said Evaline. "There
are some vampires who have a conscience and don't
like to kill in order to live. Someone like that might
keep a store of blood."

"Zhere are *no* Un-Deads viss a conscience!" Van
Helsing said. "Never. No. *None!*"

"How would you know?" Evaline snapped. "How
many vampires have you killed? Or even *met?*"

"Vhy... vhy... *many*. Zhere vas Count Dracula, und
his sree witches—zhat vas four—"

"*Three* witches," said Evaline, her eyes bulging.
"Say it... thuh-*ree!*"

Van Helsing drew himself up, his gaze dark and
angry, but Evaline did not back down. "Do not be
rude, little gel," he said, shaking a finger at her.

"Rude? I believe you're the one being rude, ques-
tioning my skills and vocation. And calling me a little
girl. How many vampires *have* you killed, Professor
Van Helsing?" Evaline's cheeks were red.

"Vell, besides zhose, zhere vas Renfield and at least
vun ozzer." He folded his arms over his chest and
looked at her as if he'd just been pronounced the
winner of *The Great British Baking Show* after her
sponge cake fell.

"So you're saying you've killed six, maybe seven—
or, let's be generous, shall we—perhaps eight or nine
undead?" Evaline said. "Do you know how many vampires *I've* done away with? Over a hundred. So I think I
know a little more about the undead than *you* do."

"You are qvite zee vancyful little girl, aren't you?

Making up zeese stories." He laughed heartily while eyeing her with mistrust.

"And might I remind you that you needed *Mina Harker* to *help* you get rid of Count Dracula anyway. A *woman*." The way Evaline was looking at her stake and then at Van Helsing made Jacqueline more than a little nervous. "And Renfield wasn't even a vampire anyway, so he doesn't count."

"But remember, someone was attacked and killed the night before in the graveyard—and it looked like a vampire attack," Jacqueline said in a voice that was a little louder than necessary. "So the question is, how much do they eat? Or should I say, 'drink'? Do they have to feed every day? Multiple times a day? Would he have killed knowing he had blood in a storage?"

"I suppose it depends on the type of vampire," Evaline said, speaking over Van Helsing, who'd been blustering on about Renfield being a sort of vampirish-undead.

Even though he wasn't, even though he'd been sort of connected to Dracula... and ate living creatures for their blood...

Jacqueline held up a hand to him. "If you *please, Professor*." To her surprise, he stopped talking, though he did not cease glowering at his young rival. "You are correct. There are different types of vampires," Jacqueline said, giving Van Helsing a quelling look when he opened his mouth to speak (probably to argue). He closed it and settled back in his seat, sulking as he picked up several lemon cupcakes and began to stuff them into his mouth.

In fact, Evaline was correct—although how could she know there were different types of vampires when her brother had only written *Dracula*, and there'd only been the one kind of undead in her *own* books, the Stoker and Holmes series?

There were as many types of vampires as there were vampire books, movies, and television shows. Every one of their creators seemed to tweak vampire lore to make their own made-up world unique... which meant it would be all that much more difficult to find out how to get rid of Luke Blackstone if he was, in fact, a vampire.

Some vampires could only be staked through the heart with a wooden pike and exploded into dust. Some of them didn't, and then there was a staked body to deal with. Some could be beheaded. Some could fry to death in the sun. Some could even be shot...

"The only thing they all seem to have in common is that they drink blood and have fangs," Jacqueline mused.

"Most are sensitive to holy objects," Evaline said, slanting a look at Van Helsing as if to tempt him to challenge her.

"Mmph, *ja*," he said from around his third or fourth cupcake. The amount of powdered sugar sprinkles nestling in his beard was astonishing. "Und zhey do not like to go out in zee sunshine. Zhey loose zere powers."

"Yes, that is true," Evaline said, reaching for her own lemon cupcake. "They can fry to death."

"Well, that's not exactly true," replied Jacqueline, thinking of Edward Cullen sparkling in the sunshine.

Evaline looked at her in surprise as Van Helsing nodded. "*Ja, ja*... but zhey don't *like* zee sunshine."

"There are some vampires who can move about in the light, Evaline," Jacqueline said.

"Is that true? I suppose they have some sort of—

protection medallion?" the young woman said. She seemed fascinated by this idea. "I do remember hearing about my great-great-grandmother Victoria fighting off a daytime vampire who took a special potion to help go about in the daylight. So I suppose that could happen."

"Zo you mean to zay zhat zhere could be zee Un-Dead who valk about in zee daytime *viz* zere powers?" Van Helsing scoffed. "No, no. Zat ees impossible, I zay. Im*poss*ible."

"I am really going to have to speak with Bram about his ridiculous accent," Evaline muttered, giving the professor an exasperated look.

Mrs. Hudson seemed to have noticed the decimation of the treats, for she sailed over at that moment with another plate—this time bigger—laden with more treats: thumb-sized shortbreads, more miniature cupcakes—red velvet—and thin, crustless tea sandwiches of chicken salad. The last was a surprise to Jacqueline. When had tea sandwiches been added to the café menu?

She was just about to ask when Mrs. Hudson gave a startled shriek.

"What?" Jacqueline nearly upset her coffee as she jolted to look around.

"*That*," said the landlady, pointing with a shaking finger to that very cup, "uncivilized beverage does *not* belong in my tea room."

Damn. Her subterfuge revealed, Jacqueline snatched up the mug and guzzled the little bit of coffee that was left before Mrs. Hudson could exorcise it from "her" tea room. Fortunately, it had gone lukewarm by now, and Jacqueline didn't burn the crap out of her mouth. "All gone," she said, slamming down the empty cup.

Mrs. Hudson gave her a look of betrayal similar to what a Temperance woman might have given to her husband upon discovering his private stash of hooch. "I shall get you a strong cuppa straight away," she said, as if that would wash away the sin of ingesting the demon bean.

"Oh, er, well... thank you." Jacqueline decided it was easier to comply than to argue. Besides, she didn't really care at the moment. "Anyhow... the question we keep coming back to is how to tell for certain whether someone is a vampire. And it seems as if there's no real way unless we catch them in the act."

"I do *wish* I could have gone with you," Evaline said. "I can sense an undead when one is near."

Van Helsing scoffed, spraying scone crumbs over his beard. "Und how is zhat possible? You see zheir red eyes, is zhat it?"

"No," Evaline replied. "There is a chill that goes over the back of my neck and makes the hair prickle there."

Van Helsing's eyes bulged, and he began to laugh loudly and rudely. "Zhat is zhe most ree-diculous zhing I haff ever heard."

Jacqueline grabbed Evaline's arm before the girl could lunge at the professor, even though she knew from the books that Evaline had super strength and could throw her off easily.

"It is a shame," she said, giving the professor a dark look, "that the two of you can't agree to work together on this situation—much like you did, working with others, when you went after Count Dracula." This was accompanied by a penetrating look at Van Helsing.

He settled back into his seat, wearing a sulky expression once again. "Eet is nossingk but vancy," he muttered.

"Evaline, what if I was able to bring Luke Blackstone here, to the bookshop?" Jacqueline said before the young woman could respond to the misogynistic disregard.

"Oh, that would work perfectly!" cried Evaline. "I should be able to sense whether he is a vampire or not if he's here."

"Excellent. I'll figure out how to get him here, and you can—er—hang about and see what happens."

With that decided, Jacqueline took her leave of the tea room. She was certain Mrs. Hudson could keep the two vampire slayers from killing each other—after all, all indications were she'd been the one to bring Evaline here in order to protect Van Helsing from danger.

Jacqueline rolled her eyes. Her life was so freaking weird...

Downstairs in the front room of the shop, she found Sebastian lazing in the window among gardening books, the two flowering potted plants, and the tiny white stepstool she'd used in the display. He barely lifted his head to look at her, but it was a definite suggestion that she should pick him up for a cuddle.

She smiled—he was awfully difficult to resist—and went over to give him a few long strokes over his back and soft, fluffy fur.

"You're such a flirt," she said when he rolled onto his back and exposed his tummy for more attention. Nonetheless, she obliged while looking up and down the street as much as she could see from the window. No sign of the ZAP Ladies. Had they really gone to Egala's? If so, she wanted to find out what had happened.

Jacqueline also needed to ask the cedar if she'd be willing to share a branch with Egala. She should do that soon—and check on the mandrakes as well.

But... it was just after four o'clock, and for some reason, Detective Massermey popped into her head.

Maybe because it would be a really big problem if it turned out his daughter was dating a vampire.

Thinking of which... that might be the best way to get Luke Blackstone into Three Tomes for Evaline to assess his possible vampireness. Jacqueline could suggest that Mandy bring him by so she could get to know him better before advocating him to her father.

The only problem was... she didn't have Mandy's phone number.

Jacqueline smiled and felt her cheeks heat. That was an excellent excuse to reach out to Massermey, wasn't it?

She glanced up to find Max eyeing her with disdain from his usual perch on the highest shelf in the room.

"I want to talk to the guy. So sue me," she told him.

He lifted his chin and pointedly looked away.

Jacqueline picked up her phone. After a moment of thought, she texted Massermey.

Hey... how's it going with the investigation? Then, so he didn't just think she was being nosy, she added, *Hope you're not too stressed and are eating right. LMK if you need coffee.* ;-)

She didn't expect to hear from him right away, so she put her phone down and wandered over to the bookshelf built under the stairs leading to the tea room.

The shelves here were protected by custom glass doors that locked, and thankfully so. Most of the books in this cabinet were old. Not just vintage, but antiquarian. Some weren't worth much, but others—like first editions of *Jamaica Inn* and *Catch-22*—would fetch a tidy sum in an online auction. Jacqueline had sold several rare and vintage titles since she'd taken over the shop, and it always surprised her when she looked at the shelves and found other rare books she hadn't noticed before.

This time, her attention skimmed past the true first editions of Nancy Drew—in their smooth cobalt covers with orange embossing—and the signed copy of a first edition of *A Farewell to Arms* and settled on the lowest, smallest shelf tucked under the first few steps.

There, the books were so ancient that whatever might have been on their spines was illegible. They were old and brown and curling and tattered. One was very large—nearly the size and shape of a cinder block—and there were others of different heights and widths tucked in around it.

Jacqueline eyed the cinder-block book, whose title was long gone even inside, and hesitated. She'd used that book to create a protection amulet for a woman—and it had worked!—so she knew what to expect.

Her fingers tingled and the hair on her arms lifted as she considered whether to pull it out and flip through its crackling, yellowed pages. Would there be something in there about vampires that might be helpful?

What about mandrakes?

She stilled. Then, with some trepidation, she carefully worked the chunky book free from its moorings. As she did so, a tiny little booklet tumbled to the shelf, possibly having been freed by her moving the big book.

She picked up the pamphlet, which was very, very

old and its binding hand-sewn. One glance told her it was an old quarto: a book that had been printed or written out with four pages of text on each side of a single paper, then folded twice to create a small book. The binding was sewn with very old looping stitches of some heavy thread, and the paper was cut along the folds to make an eight-page pamphlet.

But aside from the definite *age* of the booklet, what caught Jacqueline's attention most definitively was the ink drawing on the front page.

It was a plant, and it looked an awful lot like a mandrake.

She was just rising to her feet when the front door rattled.

Jacqueline looked over and saw Detective Massermey peering through the glass.

CHAPTER 10

J acqueline's heart gave a happy little bump of pleasure, and she rose, groaning a little when her knees twinged.

"Detective Massermey," she said with a smile as she opened the door.

"Ms. Finch," he said with great irony as he stepped through.

"Sorry," she said. "Miles, I mean." She smiled up at him, and the look he gave her made her cheeks heat. *"Miles."*

"Much better. Jacqueline." The way he said her name with a soft J and a hint of French made her insides flutter. He touched her arm briefly then stepped aside as she closed and locked the door behind him.

"It's nice to see you," she said, feeling like a bumbling schoolgirl. Then her smile faded. "How are things? With the—the death?"

His smile disappeared behind his mustache and beard. "Slow going. As you know, Cary Whitehall was working at Jilted. After she finished her shift, she left as normal—alone, as far as anyone noticed—and her roommate didn't realize she hadn't come home until the next morning."

"That's awful. And sad," Jacqueline replied, setting the quarto on the counter by the register. "And no one has any idea where she might have gone after her shift?"

"No. But one of the bartenders said she'd been talking with a group of girls—er, women—who'd come in. Maybe flirting a little, you know?" He scrubbed a hand over his face. When he pulled his fingers away, he looked more haggard. "And everyone's buzzing about those puncture wounds. Makes things a lot more difficult when you've got people calling in with leads about vampires. Bunch of cranks."

"People have been calling in saying they've seen vampires?" Jacqueline said, feeling a little queasy. "What are they saying?"

"Oh, you know, the usual things—'I saw a big bat flying around.' 'There was a man with red eyes.' 'I saw someone wearing a cloak, hiding in the shadows.' Someone had fangs—or so they thought. Nothing substantive, but we have to follow up on everything... at least to some extent. Dory Kilmeade, of course, has been calling us hourly with a different complaint. She claims she saw someone in the graveyard last night."

Jacqueline made a sympathetic noise while sliding her gaze away. "That's not helpful, I'm sure." She began to straighten a display of books that didn't need straightening, then realized all of a sudden it was an arrangement she'd never seen before... of vampire novels. *What the hell?*

Danvers, of course. Had the woman read her mind? Or was she just being obstinate?

Massermey must have followed her attention, for he said, "Um... nothing like taking advantage of the situation, hmm?" The irony in his voice wasn't accusatory as much as it was resigned.

Jacqueline gave an uncomfortable little laugh. "Well... it's just that you and Mandy put me in mind of *Twilight* the other day when you came by with Cullen, and vampire novels *are* perennial favorites."

"Unfortunately, that seems to be the case." He picked up *Guilty Pleasures* and eyed its cover, then flipped it over to read the back before setting it next to *Interview with the Vampire*. "I'm not sure it's kosher to include vampire *hunter* books on a display with actual vampire books. Is it?" His mustache and beard twitched and his eyes crinkled at the corners.

Thank goodness he had a sense of humor.

"Oh, they all go together. Besides, Anita Blake falls for a vampire— Well, she falls for and, uh, well, hooks up with a number of otherworldly creatures, including vampires, weres, and more—so there's built-in conflict. If you ever watch *Buffy*, you'll see what I mean. Poor girl's got two different vampires fighting over her." She realized she was definitely flirting with Massermey... and that it felt good. And not too terribly awkward.

Hm. Maybe you *could* teach an old crone new tricks.

"When this case is put to rest, we've got a date to watch *Buffy*, don't forget," he replied. "Now... did you say something about coffee?"

"Oh, I see... " she said with a grin, still *totally* flirting. "You only stop in here for the forbidden coffee."

"Hey, it says right here 'let me know if you need coffee,'" he said, pointing to his phone screen and her text. "I'm just following directions." His blue eyes twinkled again.

"Mrs. Hudson is in the tea room. So we'll have to

go up to my apartment for the demon bean," she said, leading him toward the back of the shop and the rear stairs. She definitely did *not* want him going through the café and meeting Professor Van Helsing or, especially, Evaline Stoker with her wooden stake.

"Speaking of Mandy," she said as he followed her down the hall to the back of the shop. "Could you give me her phone num— What the... ?"

She'd happened to glance out the window of the shop's back door and now flung it open.

"What— Christ," Massermey said, shoving past her. "Call 911."

Jacqueline had already pulled out her phone as she rushed to the side of the crumpled figure on the sidewalk by the courtyard garden.

It was a woman dressed in a sweater vest and blue jeans, in her late fifties. It took Jacqueline a moment to recognize her. Lucy something. The woman she'd met on Saturday during the farmers' market who had the potted mandrake. What the hell was *she* doing here?

"I've got a pulse," said Massermey, coolly and calmly going about the business of laying Lucy flat, undoing the buttons on the sweater vest, then tilting her head back slightly.

By now, Jacqueline's 911 call had been connected and she quickly and succinctly gave the information. As she disconnected the call, Massermey was already pumping the woman's chest to the silent beat of "Stayin' Alive."

"Let me help," she said. She had been trained in CPR as well, having worked at the library for so long, and knew how to do it in tandem.

But before Jacqueline could get to her knees on the other side of her, Lucy's eyes fluttered and she coughed a little. Massermey moved back on his haunches and whipped off his suit jacket.

"Ma'am?" he said gently, settling his coat under her head like a pillow as she opened her eyes. "Ma'am, can you hear me?"

"Her name is Lucy," Jacqueline told him, kneeling next to them and ignoring the discomfort of the hard brick walkway beneath her knees. "Lucy, it's me, Jacqueline Finch."

The older woman's eyes were vague, then fluttered and focused. "Y-yes... " she managed to say, just as the sound of sirens blared into the parking lot. "I... w-was... " She moaned. Her head lolled to one side, and she lifted one arm ineffectually. It fell back to her side, her sweater sleeve bunched up.

Jacqueline was just about to haul to her feet when she noticed what the woman's lifted arm had revealed.

"*Miles,*" she said on a gasp, pulling the sleeve away from Lucy's wrist to expose two puncture marks on the front.

He swore, vehemently and earthily, when Jacqueline showed him the back of Lucy's wrist: two more puncture wounds there.

Exactly like a set of four fangs would leave.

CHAPTER 11

The paramedics took Lucy away as Massermey did his professional duty: calling in the incident and documenting the situation, along with speaking to the police officer who'd arrived along with the ambulance.

Jacqueline was still wondering what Lucy Frontera had been doing at the back door of her bookshop when she suddenly caught her breath with realization.

She fairly leaped from the back steps of the shop to the walkway for the courtyard garden and hurried over to where the mandrakes had been planted.

There were still two of them, as there had been this morning, with the small indentation of the missing third plant next to them. Nothing had changed. Her certainty deflated.

Frowning and still unconvinced, she looked around.

Could it be a coincidence that Lucy, who'd delightedly acquired a potted mandrake at the farmers' market, was here, where someone had planted three mandrakes in Jacqueline's courtyard?

No. She didn't believe for a minute that it was a co-incidence. Somehow it had to be connected. But how?

What the hell was going on?

Jacqueline poked around in the garden a little more, pulling up the few new weeds that had emerged since her work this morning and gathering up some of the old brush she hadn't finished removing earlier.

By this time, Massermey was finished with his professional duties.

"Did you still want that coffee?" she asked, walking over to him.

He looked down at her and quirked his eyebrow. His hands were on his hips. "Why do you always have dead or injured people showing up here? And other weird things happening?"

Jacqueline decided at that moment *not* to tell him about her sudden and unplanned acquisition of mandrake plants.

Instead, she shrugged and said with a wry smile, "Just lucky, I guess."

He gave her a close look, and Jacqueline figured he was probably remembering what Mrs. Kilmeade had said about strange things happening at the bookshop.

As if he hadn't already sort of known about some of it anyway.

Jacqueline assumed he never asked because he'd decided he'd rather not know. It was probably better that way.

"Yes, I'd love some coffee," he said, glancing at his watch. He swore under his breath. "Actually, I'll have to take a rain check. I didn't realize it was almost five. I've got to get back to the office." He gave her a woebegone look.

"Definite rain check. Do you mind sending me Mandy's phone number?" she asked, suddenly remembering that she needed it. Especially now that Lucy seemed to have been attacked by a vampire.

"Sure." He gave her a quizzical look, but tapped on his phone. A second later she heard the telltale chime of a text message arrival.

"Thanks. Um... do they think Lucy's going to be all right?"

He nodded. "The paramedics were optimistic. She'd lost a lot of blood— Don't *say* it, Jacqueline. Don't even *think* it, all right?" he said, holding up a hand as he grimaced.

She nodded. He could live in his fantasy world where vampires didn't exist—or date his daughter (yikes!)—for a little longer. Eventually he'd have to acknowledge it. "She'd lost a lot of blood, but... ?"

He scrubbed his face in a gesture that was becoming very familiar. "They replaced some of it and will infuse more at the hospital. Prognosis seems good."

"I don't suppose those marks on her wrist will remain a secret for long," she said, feeling a tug of sympathy for him. "That's just going to make your job all the more difficult."

"Yeah." He heaved a sigh and said, "I've got to get going. I'll see you later. Soon, I hope." He started to walk away, then froze and turned back slowly. His Nordic blue eyes had taken on that flat "I'm a cop" look. "Jacqueline, is there anything I should know about what's going on here?"

She felt her cheeks heat—damned redhead's skin. "The only thing that's weird going on here is that someone planted three mandrakes in my garden sometime between Saturday night and Sunday morning. And one of them was gone this morning."

He looked at her as if he was trying to determine whether she was punking him or not.

"And Lucy Frontera got a mandrake at the farmers' market on Saturday," she added with a rush. "If there's a connection, I don't know what it is. But that's all I know."

Except that I suspect your daughter might be dating a vampire...

"Mandrakes?" Massermey stared at her, his eyes narrowed. "Do you mean... the plants? The screaming plants?"

Before Jacqueline could respond, the back door of the bookshop opened and the ZAP Ladies burst out in a swirl of long skirts and arms akimbo.

Massermey muttered something under his breath.

"Detective Massermey!" cried Pietra, flowing toward them in a surge of hot-pink caftan. It was trimmed with sky-blue and silver beads dangling from the hem and the edges of the wide, bell-like sleeves. The beads clinked wildly like miniature maracas. She wore sandals on pudgy feet with fuchsia toenails. "What happened? We heard the sirens." The collection of tiny dimples around her mouth flashed with each syllable.

Jacqueline didn't bother to ask how the crones had managed to come through the front of the shop. Danvers or Hudson had probably let them in, the traitors.

"It's Lucy Frontera," Jacqueline told them, taking pity on Massermey. "She was injured. And the detective is just leaving, so I can answer your questions," she added, looking pointedly at the very large leather handbag Zwyla was carrying. It sported an ornate E on its clasp.

And the crones could answer hers.

Massermey tossed her a grateful look then slipped

into the bookshop through the back door. Jacqueline sighed. Apparently, her store was going to be a throughway whether she wanted it to be or not.

"Lucy Frontera? What happened to her?" said Andromeda. She hiked up the neckline of her *Flashdance*-style sweatshirt over the strap of a neon-blue sports bra. She was the only one of the trio not wearing a maxi dress. "I don't know her well, but I've bought some plants from her. She has a private little nursery at the base of SugarBread Mountain. Buys and sells a lot of unique plants... Oh." Her eyes widened with comprehension.

"We found her here on the walkway, unconscious." Jacqueline leaned closer to them even though no one else was around. "She had puncture wounds on her wrist. Four of them."

Zwyla hissed and swore under her breath.

"My sentiments exactly," said Jacqueline. "Shall we go inside?"

The four of them filed through the door then down the hall to the front of the shop. Jacqueline hesitated—she wasn't certain she wanted to mix the ZAP Ladies with the vampire hunters quite yet—but when Pietra led the way up the stairs to the tea room, Jacqueline had no choice but to follow.

To her relief, only Mrs. Hudson was there, fussing with cups, teapots, and tins of loose tea.

"Have a seat there, dearies," she told them needlessly, for the crones were already settling on the sofas in front of the fireplace. One of the couches was a comfy blue and green tweed that Jacqueline should have found ugly but for some reason didn't. "What's happened to give you all such long faces, then?"

"There's been another vampire attack," Jacqueline told her.

"Oh *dear*," said Mrs. Hudson, looking around as if to spot an undead—or a vampire hunter. Fortunately, none of either were in the vicinity. As one might expect, her next words were "I'll be setting the kettle on, then. We'll need a strong cuppa, won't we now, to get us through with this."

"And some cake," Pietra said. "Surely you have some cake on hand, Mrs. Hudson?"

"I certainly do," replied the landlady/housekeeper. "It's definitely cake we'll be needing for this, I can see."

"What I don't understand," Jacqueline said, diving in because if she didn't, conversation would surely center around tea, cakes, and teacakes for the next while, "is how Lucy ended up on my back porch. What I mean is, if she was attacked by a vampire and injured so badly, *how* did she manage to get there?"

"Well, the vampire might have broken into her house and attacked her last night," said Pietra, eyeing Mrs. Hudson as she bustled behind the counter. She was probably trying to see what sort of cake was on the way.

"And didn't call 911 but somehow got herself here, in town, hours later?" Jacqueline said. "That doesn't make sense. If she was that injured, she wouldn't have been able to get here."

"True. Unless she was attacked here in town," Andromeda said.

"But the same thing holds—why would she not call for help? Why come here? And hours later? Unless… " Jacqueline didn't like the other option.

"Unless she was attacked right outside your shop. And… during the day," Zwyla said, voicing what was probably the worst-case scenario.

"Yeah."

They were silent for a moment—even Pietra—for

they implicitly seemed to agree that a vampire attack during the day was not a good thing at all.

Jacqueline finally had to put it into words. "If the vampire is out and about in the sunlight, then all bets are off. It'll be even more impossible to figure out who it is—and to stop them. What if a stake won't do it? I mean, in *Dracula* they had to close off the coffin so he couldn't get back into it, cut off his head, stab him in the heart, *and* put garlic in his mouth... all that *plus* get rid of all the soil from his homeland in order to kill him."

"That's a lot more involved than what Buffy had to do," Pietra said sadly. "She just went *slam!* with the stake and they were gone. *Poof!*"

"No kidding. I need to read up on my *Dracula* and refresh my memory," Jacqueline said, "but I think he had a lot more powers than your basic *Twilight* or Sookie Stackhouse undead. He could shapeshift into different animals, I think."

"He could also turn into fog or mist," said Zwyla unhappily. "And slip through cracks."

Jacqueline shuddered. She'd forgotten that part.

"He might not be a Dracula-style vampire, though," Pietra said brightly as Mrs. Hudson brought over a tray of teapots, cups, cream, and sugar. There was also a three-layer sponge cake bursting with strawberries and creamy icing that would have made even Paul Hollywood swoon.

"But *Dracula* fell off the shelf," Jacqueline reminded Pietra as her friend took a healthy slice of cake.

Pietra's face fell as a strawberry did the same, plopping onto the plate. "True."

Jacqueline sighed. At least they had Van Helsing, the expert here, somewhere—along with Evaline, who was also extremely resourceful. Not to mention a glorious cake.

She decided things were Bad Enough (with deliberate capitals) that she, too, could indulge in a healthy slice of cake.

"But that doesn't necessarily mean it's a Dracula-type vampire," said Andromeda, taking a much smaller slice of the dessert. "And if I recall, even though Dracula *could* go about during the daytime, he didn't have his powers and didn't actually attack anyone."

"Wait... the first vampire attack happened *before* the book fell off the shelf," Jacqueline said. "I'd forgotten about that."

Zwyla looked at her sharply. "Is that so?" She exchanged glances with Andromeda, and Jacqueline did not like the expressions they were wearing.

"Could there be two different vampires?" Pietra asked, and everyone groaned.

"Let's hope not. I suppose it makes sense that the vampire could already have been here before *Dracula* fell off the shelf, because Van Helsing came out. Possibly because it *is* a Dracula-type of vampire we have to deal with," Jacqueline said. "That's why he came."

"That makes sense. Still... didn't one body have two puncture wounds and Lucy had four?" Zwyla said.

Jacqueline nodded unhappily. "Yes. Unless the rumors were wrong about the first body—Cary Whitehall's. The details, I mean. Maybe she did have four puncture wounds and we don't know it. Which is possible, because Massermey isn't sharing any details. Anyway, this puts us back to where we were: how did Lucy Frontera get here and when was she attacked?"

"Someone needs to talk to her and find out," said

Zwyla. "She's probably at the hospital." She looked pointedly at Andromeda.

Jacqueline watched in fascination as Andromeda's cheeks and the tips of her ears turned red.

"Come on, Z," she said with a groan. "Seriously?"

"It's the easiest way, and you know it." Zwyla gave her a smug look as Andromeda sighed and grimaced. Obviously aware of Jacqueline's ignorance, Zwyla turned to her and said, "Andromeda has a fan in the ER at Bolkens Hospital. She can find out nearly anything by asking him."

"Oh yeah, Stan will tell me anything... as long as I listen to him yodel," Andromeda said morosely. "You know, the last time I asked him for a favor, he made me go to an awards dinner with him after. He was being honored as a champion yodeler. It was the longest night of my life. And not in a good way, as there were no prophylactics involved."

Pietra choked off a laugh when Andromeda shot her a look that sparked. Literally.

"It couldn't have been that bad," Pietra said, trying to cover for her mistake as she forked up a strawberry that had fallen from the cake.

"Really? Being in a room with thirty people as they're all yodeling a version of 'Bohemian Rhapsody' was basically my idea of hell. I don't even know how there *are* thirty people around here who yodel." As she spoke, Andromeda grimly pulled out her phone and began to type a text. "You owe me for this, Z. And you too, Jacqueline." She gave Jacqueline a dark look with her green, catlike eyes.

"Me? Why do I owe you— Oh, never mind," Jacqueline said, shaking her head. "Just see what you can find out about Lucy. In the meantime, what did you learn from going to Egala's? I see you ended up with a nice bag of your own." Having no other choice, she took a sip of tea.

Zwyla lifted her nose as if to stave off any judgment Jacqueline might have sent her way. "Egala has excellent products. High quality, unique, and—"

"Yes. Products that have spells on them," Jacqueline said grimly. "That *normal* people are buying."

"Nonetheless, they seem to be perfectly harmless spells," Zwyla told her with a look that would have sent the Old Jacqueline shrinking back.

But the New Jacqueline—the one who had characters coming out of books every bloody day, and witches zapping curses at her, *and* who owned a thriving business—merely snorted.

"It is true, Jacqueline," Pietra put in. "We all examined the handbags and totes and found nothing of concern. The charms and spells are simply to keep the bags unblemished and to help the owner not misplace either the bag or any item they wanted out of the bag."

"And what if they want a *gun*?" Jacqueline said with a dark look. "Will the bag give them that too?"

"The charms aren't powerful enough for that," replied Zwyla. She glanced at Andromeda, who seemed to be in the midst of a furious text-message exchange. Hopefully she was getting information about Lucy.

"What do you mean, not powerful enough for that?"

"I mean that the charms only produce what could logically be in the bag. Little things."

"Like a *fork*?" Jacqueline said, rolling her eyes. Why were the crones taking Egala's side in this?

"Well, it's certainly not out of the realm of possibility that a fork might be in someone's purse," Pietra said primly, eyeing the strawberry cake for what would be her second piece.

"She's certainly right about that. Have you ever looked inside Petey's purse? Be careful if you do—you might never extricate yourself," Zwyla said with a laugh. "*She's* had not only a fork but an entire place setting—complete with seafood fork and glasses for both red and white wine—in her purse."

Jacqueline wasn't convinced, but at the same time, she knew she should defer to the elder and more experienced crones. If they weren't worried about Egala's purses, then she supposed she shouldn't be either.

"All right. So what about giving her the cedar branch? Any problems with that, assuming the cedar allows it?" Jacqueline hadn't had the time to ask the sacred tree, but she would.

"I think she really does want it for protection," said Andromeda, surfacing from her frenzied text conversation. "And as she is a Stone, I see no problem with it as long as the tree agrees."

"All right." Jacqueline was relieved that she would be able to keep her gorgeous leather bag. Maybe this would be the beginning of... if not a friendship, then at least an alliance of sorts between her and Egala.

She'd never trust the woman completely, but she might be able to find ways to work with her.

"Did you find out anything from Stan?" Zwyla asked, looking up. She'd been daintily eating a sliver of cake.

Andromeda nodded. "Yes. Here's the thing," she said, looking at Jacqueline. "Apparently, Lucy was coming here. To the shop. She was looking for a book —I guess she didn't know you were closed on Mondays. Anyway, she stopped at the garden there outside the back door."

"She must have seen the mandrakes," said Jacqueline.

"Most likely," Andromeda said. "I'm only getting bits and pieces from Stan via text. He's only verbose when it comes to yodeling, plus they've got a whole slew of kids in the ER who picked up a rash swimming in one of the inland lakes, so he's a little busy. Anyhow, Lucy was in the garden when someone came up from behind and caught her around the wrist. She didn't see them. She says she has no idea about who or what they were—except that they were strong. Very strong."

"Did they—did they bite her?" Pietra asked, her dimpled hands clasped together on the table.

"She only knew there was a sudden pain in her arm, and then she fainted. That's all she remembers."

Jacqueline shivered and glanced outside. It was nearly six p.m., and the sun was dropping close to the horizon. Soon it would be dark... but when Lucy had been attacked, it was daylight.

She didn't like that thought at all.

"Lucy doesn't remember anything about what their hands were like? Height? Anything?" Zwyla said.

"She might, but Stan doesn't have that information. Like I said—kids, rashes, and crazy parents have taken over the ER. And now I have to go to a yodeling demonstration with him next week," Andromeda said with a dark look at all of them. "I'm going to need some extremely strong herbs to get me through that."

Zwyla ignored her crony's bitter look and said what they were all thinking. "It seems pretty clear we have an undead on hand. At least one. And one that can apparently move about and attack during the daytime."

"And since the police either have no clue or don't

want to have a clue, we're going to have to take care of it ourselves," said Pietra.

Jacqueline nodded. "I have a plan." She told them about her idea to lure Luke Blackstone to the bookshop so Evaline could sense whether he was the undead.

"That's an excellent idea," Zwyla said. Then, to Jacqueline's surprise, she rose, and her midnight-blue maxi dress fell into a subtly sparkling column. "Let us know how it goes."

"But... " Jacqueline fumbled for words. They were just going to *leave*? Leave her here with vampires lurking about?

"It'll be all right, love," said Andromeda, giving her a little pat on the arm. "You've got everything you need right here."

Before Jacqueline could say another word, the three crones took off, vanishing down the stairs so quickly it was almost as if they'd apparated.

Perhaps they had. Jacqueline didn't care to know.

But one thing she *did* know was that a vampire had been lurking outside her bookshop. Her stomach lurched unpleasantly as she looked around.

She was alone. It was going to be dark soon. Night was coming. Why wasn't there a vampire hunter when she needed one?

Even Mrs. Hudson had vanished, she realized with another queasy lurch of her insides.

But undead couldn't enter without being invited, could they? That was one thing that seemed somewhat universal. She should be safe as long as she didn't go out of the building, because she sure as hell wasn't inviting anyone inside.

CHAPTER 12

J acqueline was heading up to her apartment, but on the way she raided the stock in what she called the New Age Room.

Located in the back of the second floor behind the café and the children's picture book section, the New Age Room had everything from tarot cards to singing bowls to crystals to incense to goddess figurines, angel statues, and any other tool for metaphysical connection one could imagine... including crosses, crucifixes, and candles with the Blessed Virgin Mary on them.

Jacqueline swept a bunch of spiritual objects into a basket. She went heavily for crosses and crucifixes, but also grabbed angelic items, as well as a small Buddha statue, a Shiva, and a Mother Goddess figurine for good measure. She figured she couldn't be too careful. Whether any of them were holy enough wasn't clear, but she would at least make the effort.

She'd just started to climb the steps to the third floor when she remembered the old quarto she'd found just before Massermey arrived.

Jacqueline hesitated. She did *not* want to go back

down to the shadowy, empty bookshop on the ground floor where a vampire could be lurking...

"That's silly," she told herself in a firm voice. Vampires could fly or climb walls, so it wasn't as if she were any safer up here than down there.

Not that that was a comforting thought either...

And where were Evaline and Van Helsing, anyway? Weren't they supposed to be waiting around for her to lure Luke Blackstone here? Not that she'd gotten around to that yet, but still.

She huffed a sigh, then turned back and ran lightly down the steps to the first floor.

The quarto was right where she'd left it on the counter, and so was the very large and ancient cinderblock tome that she'd removed from the shelf at the same time.

Jacqueline put both of them in her basket and was just about to go back upstairs when she saw a silhouette at the front door.

Her heart surged into her throat, then she swallowed it back and, recognizing the face, went to the door.

"Hi, Mandy," she said as she opened it. "Oh. Hello, Luke," she added, masking her shock when she saw that he was standing there with her.

"I'm sorry to bother you," Mandy said with a smile. "I know you're closed today, but we saw you through the window. Dad mentioned you were trying to get in touch with me."

"Oh, right, yes, I was," Jacqueline said, caught off guard. "Come on in," she went on, and then immediately realized what she'd done.

*Shit. Shit. **Shit.***

But it was too late.

Mandy and Luke stepped over the threshold into

the bookshop, having been duly and freely invited inside.

"I hope everything is all right," said Luke, looking around curiously.

It very well might not be, now.

"I hope nothing went too wrong," he went on.

It took Jacqueline a moment to remember that the last time she'd seen him—almost five hours ago—she cut their appointment short due to an "emergency" at the shop.

"Oh, yes, everything is fine," she said, glancing around and trying not to be nervous. Surely he wouldn't attempt anything with Mandy around.

But it didn't matter, did it? She'd already invited him in, which meant he could come back anytime.

Where was Evaline?

"So, what did you want to see me about?" asked Mandy.

Jacqueline pulled her attention from Luke, who'd picked up *Interview with the Vampire* from the display. He was looking at it with a funny smirk. Was he thinking how off-base it was? How wrong Anne Rice had been?

Should she be glad Lestat hadn't jumped out of a book?

"Oh, I... uh...just thought if you wanted me to... uh... pave the way with your dad, you know," Jacqueline said, giving a meaningful glance in Luke's direction, "it might be a good idea for us to, well, hang out a little bit. So I can, uh, get to know you."

"That's a wonderful idea," said Mandy enthusiastically. "Like a double date?"

"Uh." Jacqueline felt her cheeks heat. "N-not really. I was thinking just, maybe, the three of us. First, you know." She did *not* want to be the one who engineered Massermey meeting his daughter's boyfriend.

"Oh, sure, that's great too. When did you have in mind?" Mandy asked, sliding her hand through the crook of Luke's arm and leaning adoringly against him.

He was still perusing the display. Now he was flipping through *'Salem's Lot*, still with the same condescending smirk.

"Are you a fan of vampire novels, Luke?" Jacqueline asked, unable to help herself.

He looked up at her, that smile twitching into one of arrogance. "Not at all. I find them to be sappy and utterly unrealistic." He shoved the book back onto its stack in a careless gesture that made Jacqueline's hackles go up.

"Oh. Which ones have you read?" she asked innocently, knowing that most people who disparaged a particular genre of fiction often hadn't ever *read* any books of that type. "I know Mandy is a big fan of *Twilight*."

"Oh, Luke doesn't read fiction," Mandy said with a little laugh, hugging herself closer to him as he gave Jacqueline a look that made the hair on the back of her neck stand up.

It wasn't a glowing-red-eye look as she might have feared, but it was one filled with *knowing*.

"He prefers science journals and medical treatises," Mandy went proudly.

"I see," Jacqueline managed to say as she reached for the basket she'd filled with items from the New Age room—it was very heavy now with the book in it—and held it against her middle, like a shield between her and Luke.

And again: where the hell were Evaline and Van Helsing?

"Well, thanks so much for stopping by," Jacqueline said, watching the way Luke's eyes dropped to the basket then rose to her face.

His expression changed only slightly—from that arch, knowing look to a patronizing one. One corner of his mouth quirked in a terribly supercilious movement that made Jacqueline wish she had a stake at that very moment, because she'd drive it into his heart without a second thought.

"Oh, no problem," said Mandy, peeling herself from her companion. She was smiling with a giddiness that worried Jacqueline. "So, when do you want to get together? The three of us?" Her eyes sparkled with delight.

"How about lunch tomorrow? It's going to be a gorgeous day—we could grab a picnic and sit on the beach," Jacqueline said, bravely holding Luke's eyes with hers.

"What a lovely idea," he drawled. "Unfortunately, I've appointments throughout the day tomorrow. Perhaps a moonlit picnic would be a better idea, wouldn't it, darling?" He smiled down at Mandy, who fairly quivered with delight.

"That sounds *sooo* romantic," Mandy said.

"What time are you finished with your appointments, Luke?" Jacqueline pressed.

"They run from eleven in the morning until well into the late afternoon," he replied smoothly. "Apparently, there has been quite a rush of expirations in Button Cove over the last week. And I don't rise before ten," he added firmly.

I'll bet you don't, Jacqueline thought.

"Very well. I suppose we'll have to put some more

thought into it," she said, calling a truce—for now. He might have won the battle, but he wasn't going to win the war.

She hoped.

"Oh, that's such a bummer," said Mandy. "I really want Dad to meet Luke, but... I guess it'll have to wait. My goodness, what's that huge book?"

Jacqueline was still holding the basket to her middle, and Mandy had noticed the ancient tome. "Oh, it's just an old book I was going to—uh—take upstairs and try to repair," she said, hoping not to draw any more attention to it. But as she shifted it in the basket, the quarto fell out and tumbled to the floor.

"What's this?" Luke bent down and swooped it up with his long white fingers. "It looks very old." His eyes narrowed as he flipped through the crackling pages.

"It's mine," Jacqueline said in such a snippy tone that Mandy gave her a startled look. She made an effort to soften it as she continued, "It's very old and delicate, and I am taking it to an historian for dating and reference." She held out her hand for the pamphlet. Unfortunately, it was trembling slightly. She hoped Luke didn't notice.

"Of course," he said in the smooth voice that belied the glinting, knowing look he gave her. Taking care not to get too close to her and the basket she was holding, Luke dropped the quarto into her hand.

"I suppose we'd best let Miss Finch get back to whatever she was doing," he said. "Shall we, darling?"

"Yes, I suppose we should. I'm getting hungry. Have a good night, Jacqueline," Mandy said, sliding her hand around the crook of his elbow. "Let's try to get together soon, all right?"

"Definitely," Jacqueline replied.

She locked the door behind them, and watched with trepidation as they strolled up Camellia, away from the shop and the crones' house.

Should she let Mandy go off with him alone? How could she stop her?

Jacqueline's hands were clammy and her stomach in knots. Should she do something? Call Mandy and make some excuse to get her to come back? Call Massermey and tell him his daughter might be in danger? *Ha.* He'd think she was crazy if she did that.

And where in the hell were her two vampire hunters? Jacqueline was really ticked that they hadn't been around when she needed them.

"Well, that was most interesting."

Jacqueline whirled to see Mrs. Danvers standing there, her pale hands clasped at her waist, keys glinting on their ring next to them.

"What do you mean by that?" Jacqueline didn't care that her tone was still slightly snippy.

"That man." Mrs. Danvers sniffed and looked off into the distance. "I don't have a very good feeling about him."

Jacqueline gaped at her. This was the first time—ever—that she and Danvers had been in agreement on anything.

"Neither do I," replied Jacqueline. She was almost ready to confide in the housekeeper about her suspicions, but a sudden loud thump, followed by a series of thuds and thunks from above, cut her off. "What in the *world...*"

"Oh," said Mrs. Danvers with a more vehement sniff as she glanced upward. "It's that *person.*"

"Which per— Never mind," Jacqueline said, deciding it was best for her to find out herself. Still carrying the basket of possibly holy items, the quarto, and the big, ancient book, she hurried up the stairs to the café.

"Where on earth have you been?" she exclaimed when she came to the top and saw the source of the thumping and thunking.

Evaline Stoker was lunging and leaping, tumbling and spinning all about the room—over furniture, under tables, and across the space. She was battling either an invisible foe or simply blowing off steam, and she was wearing a completely different outfit from when Jacqueline had first seen her.

This time, the young woman was hatless, but her thick, dark hair was fashioned in a complicated style of braids and twists woven with beaded combs, cog-work pins, and several tiny bows. She wore a split skirt made from four different types of fabric—velvet, something glittery, something gauzy, and a shiny taffeta. Each was a different shade of bronze or copper, and each fabric was a different ruffle or layer in the skirt. It was a *glorious* piece of fashion.

Evaline's corset was black leather, and once again, it was worn over a white blouse shot through with gold threads. Her gloves were elbow-length and fingerless, lacing up along the wrists.

And, as before, several tools hung from her waist: a small dagger, a bejeweled cross, two different stakes, and a little device that resembled a flashlight but couldn't be, since there weren't flashlights in Victorian England.

Although... wasn't Evaline from an alternate Victorian England? Jacqueline thought she might have been, but that didn't matter at the moment, did it?

The swirl of luscious, glittery fashion came to an elegant, tumbling halt right in front of Jacqueline.

"What do you mean?" said Evaline, stake in hand,

every hair still in place. She wasn't even breathing heavily.

"The man I suspect of being a vampire was just here, downstairs, and you were nowhere to be found," Jacqueline told her.

"Drat," Evaline said, but she didn't sound terribly put out. She slipped the stake back into one of the loops on her corset. "Well, how long ago was he here? I didn't sense the presence of any undead."

Jacqueline shook her head, irritated. "I don't know. A while ago. A few minutes? Ten? How long have *you* been here?"

Evaline spread her hands. "I really don't know either."

Jacqueline gritted her teeth. She just *loved* dealing with teenagers. Especially ones who came out of books. "I don't know what to do, but I got the distinct impression he knows that *I* know he's a vampire. And he's not happy about it."

Evaline lifted a brow and cocked her hip. She looked ready to take down an entire army of undead. "I think we should hunt him down. Just go and hunt him down before he does something."

"Hunt down whom?"

She and Evaline turned to Professor Van Helsing, who was accompanied by a rosy-cheeked Mrs. Hudson. The landlady looked like a cat who'd just lapped up an entire dish of cream, and Jacqueline didn't really want to know why, especially when she noticed that one of Mrs. Hudson's blouse buttons wasn't quite fastened.

"It's none of your concern," said Evaline while Jacqueline replied at the same time, "The man who I believe is an undead." Jacqueline gave her younger companion a look meant to quell any further antagonism. Whether they liked it or not, the two vampire hunters were going to need to work together.

"Vhere ees this man?" said Van Helsing, standing upright. "I vill go."

"But... " Mrs. Hudson seemed horrified. "Abraham, you... you... *can't.*" She gripped his sleeve. "It's too *dangerous.*"

"Nagh," he said, waving off her fears but allowing her hand to remain. He even patted her fingers where they rested over his arm. "It vill be fine. I must go vith them. Zhey need zhe support and my expertise."

"Your expertise?" Evaline's eyes bulged. "Why—"

"Now, now, let us not get all vuzzled up, girl," he said.

"*Girl?*" Evaline sputtered.

"Vell, you are vun, aren't you?"

Jacqueline interjected loudly and firmly. "We will *all* go together, but *I* will be in charge. I will take guidance and advice from both of you, but *I* will make the strategic decisions. Is that understood?"

She didn't know whether taking such a stand would work, but it seemed to cow both of the vampire slayers—even the misogynistic professor—into a grumbling acquiescence.

"Very vell," said Van Helsing.

"Fine," said Evaline, a little snarkily.

Jacqueline leaned closer to Evaline and muttered, "Is it my imagination, or is his accent a little less obnoxious?"

"I mentioned something about it to Bram," Evaline murmured back. "Apparently, he listened."

Jacqueline blinked and turned that thought over in her mind, then decided not to pursue it.

Whatever worked.

At least the reader wouldn't be struggling to figure out what Van Helsing was saying in the book.

"So... vhen are ve leaving? Vere are ve going?"

"Not for a while. Don't you think we should wait until dark?" Jacqueline said. Then she shook her head. "Wait, wait, wait. You can't go very far from the book-shop. Either of you."

"Where does this man live?" asked Evaline. "Why don't we break into his house and look around?" Her eyes glittered with excitement, and Jacqueline was re-minded of how Evaline's partner in crime, Mina Holmes, was always struggling to keep her friend from going off on impetuous escapades.

Still... she thought Brittany Funeral Home might be close enough to the bookshop for Evaline and Van Helsing to be safe. It was only one block down and around the corner. If Luke was a vampire, surely he'd sleep in one of the caskets at the funeral home.

But... breaking in...

Jacqueline was a law-abiding citizen (well, except when she was breaking into zoos) who was also a busi-ness owner, *and* she was kind of seeing the town's po-lice detective. It would not be a good idea for her to get caught breaking and entering.

"Don't look so worried," Evaline said with a blithe wave of her hand. "I've done it a million times. We won't get caught. And if he *is* there and *is* an undead, I'll take care of him right away. And no one will be the wiser."

Jacqueline hesitated. Something had to be done, but...

"Let me think about it. Wouldn't it be best to break in early in the morning, when he's gone back to his bed—wherever it is—after being out all night?"

"*Ja*. Unless he kills somevone else tonight," Van Helsing pointed out.

Ugh. He had a point. But it wasn't as if Jacqueline could patrol the whole town, and the literary characters certainly couldn't go with her even if she could.

"We'll have to take that chance," she replied firmly, even as her insides did a little squiggle. "Hopefully he got what he needed for the day from Lucy Frontera."

"All right," said Evaline decisively as she faced the wall. She was holding her stake by the pointed end. "What time shall we go? Four o'clock in the morning? Five?"

Evaline punctuated her questions by winging the stake toward the wall in a spinning motion.

"Hey!" Jacqueline cried as the wooden point embedded itself with a *thump!* in the middle of her *The Great Gatsby* poster hanging next to the fireplace. "You're ruining my décor."

"Well, where else am I going to practice?" Evaline pouted. She already had a second stake in hand.

Jacqueline sighed. She'd never really liked *The Great Gatsby* anyway. "Fine. You can use that—and only that—poster as a target." She'd replace the ruined *The Great Gatsby* poster with one for *Dracula*. For obvious reasons.

Thwump!

The second stake had found its mark.

"All right. We leave at four thirty in the morning. That's... almost nine hours. You two stay here. Don't go *anywhere*," Jacqueline said, pointing a finger at each of the vampire hunters in turn. "All right?"

"I suppose. But that's a long time from now." Evaline flounced over to retrieve her stakes.

Then, as Jacqueline walked away, Evaline launched back into her athletic training sequences, while Mrs. Hudson spoke quietly and insistently to Van Helsing. Her eyes were flashing, and she even thumped him once on his barrel chest.

Jacqueline smothered a snicker as she stepped into the little elevator behind the café. If Mrs. Hudson had her way, the professor wouldn't be coming along with her and Evaline—which might be better anyway. The last thing she needed was the two of them scrapping with each other when she needed them to be focused.

Just as she stepped out of the elevator into her apartment, Jacqueline's phone chimed with a text.

It was from Suzette on the text thread with Jacqueline and Nadine.

I need to get out of the shop. And maybe have a cocktail. No, definitely have a cocktail. Anyone? Anyone? Bueller?

Jacqueline, who'd pretty much decided to go to bed early so she could get up in the wee hours of the morning to break into a funeral home, immediately did an about-face.

Me, she texted. *How do you feel about going to Jilted?*

Ooooh. It's so boogie! I'm in. Nadine?

I'm changing now, Jacqueline texted back. *What does one wear to a trendy cocktail bar?*

Nadine's text popped up: *No clue, but I'm in.*

That was how, thirty minutes later, Jacqueline and her two friends were walking into Jilted.

"By the way, it's boo-jee, not boogie—like *Saturday Night Fever,*" Nadine was saying to Suzette. "Not sure how it's spelled, but not b-o-o-g-i-e. Jacqueline?"

"Um... b-o-u-j-i-e, maybe?"

"All right, knock it off you two," Suzette said. "I'm not in the mood for your grammarian tendencies, and anyway, that was autocorrect. I need something stiff, and— That's *not* what I meant, Nadine!"

The three of them dissolved into giggles, standing in the doorway of the bar, and Jacqueline couldn't help but feel as if she were back in high school.

"All right, all right." Nadine said, flapping her hand. "Getting it under control right now. Sorry, ladies. I guess I've got sex on the mind."

"Speaking of sex, there's Gerry's hearse," said Suzette, looking out at the road.

Nadine's face turned bright red as she ducked inside the bar. "Good grief, keep it down. He might hear you."

"From across the street with his windows rolled up and us inside? I don't think so. All right, table for three, please," Jacqueline said as they turned to the hostess.

As the smiling young woman—who looked hardly any more substantial than a twig—led them to their table, Jacqueline looked around the place.

The basic structure was that of a deep, narrow space of brick with wide-planked oak flooring. Probably the original. The room boasted a high ceiling and a skinny, ornate brass handrail that led upstairs to half a second floor.

The interior was done in whitewashed brick walls with black accents. The exposed ceiling and all of its pipes, vents, and beams were black. The thick frames around the six life-size paintings—each depicting a bride or groom in various stages of shock and grief, each standing alone at an altar—were also black.

The paintings themselves were vibrant of color and just shy of being cartoonish or caricature-like. Instead, the two-dimensional images were bold and tasteful, with just a hint of irony or tongue-in-cheek snark. They were also hung crookedly on the walls, as if someone had just shoved them up there like a row of sticky notes.

A long bar lined one wall, fronted in shiny ebony subway tile with a gleaming white granite countertop. Its backdrop was floor-to-ceiling glass shelves, laden with every spirit or liqueur one could imagine. Three bartenders worked behind the space, measuring, pouring, shaking, and garnishing. One had even set something to smoking inside a glass.

Since it was a Monday evening, the place was busy and just about too loud, but not crowded.

"Thanks for letting me pick the place," Jacqueline said as they settled into their seats. "I wanted to come here for a reason."

"What reason is that— Oh, look at these drinks! They all have great names: Heartbreak Hotel, If You Leave Me Now, Don't Go Breakin' My Heart, and so on." Nadine was poring over the menu, which was nearly as large as a catalog and was bound in a book that resembled a wedding album. "Ooh! I'm going to have the You Don't Bring Me Flowers—it's got vodka, elderflower liqueur, lavender bitters, and some other stuff."

"It's gonna taste like laundry soap," said Suzette, looking at her menu. "Everything with lavender in it tastes like laundry soap."

"Not to me it doesn't," Nadine replied stoutly. "Why did you want to come here, Jacqueline?"

"Because this is where Cary Whitehall worked. She left after her shift, and no one saw her again until she was found in the graveyard. I just thought maybe someone might have noticed something." Even as she spoke, Jacqueline realized how silly that sounded. Of course Massermey would have interviewed everyone who worked here—or at least who'd been working here that night.

What did she think she was going to find out that he hadn't already learned?

When she said this to her friends, they waved her off.

"You never know," Suzette said, leaning closer in order to be heard over the low roar around them. "People don't like to talk to cops. And besides, sometimes people think of things later."

"Maybe," said Jacqueline, unconvinced. Now, instead of staying home and resting up before her breaking and entering, she was going to be buying an overpriced cocktail in a bar where she could hardly hear what the person sitting next to her was saying.

She decided on the All Too Well, which was a bourbon-based cocktail amped up with ginger liqueur, ginger beer, and something called Luxardo.

They'd just placed their orders when a movement caught Jacqueline's attention.

Someone was waving at her from a few tables away. It took her a moment to recognize the woman who'd been in Three Tomes the other day, along with her two companions. The three of them were sitting in a corner booth.

"Who's that?" Suzette, who was facing the same direction as Jacqueline, noticed them too. "Wow. They look like they just stepped out of Sundance Catalog. Super chic and expensive."

"I *know*! I thought the same thing. Oh, to be tall, slender, and willowy... " Jacqueline sighed. "Anyway, the three of them were in the café on Saturday, I think it was. They were talking about Luke Blackstone, and so I stopped to say hi," she explained. "This was right after Mandy Massermey asked me to help pave the way with her father about her dating an older man, and so I was trying to find out what they knew about him."

"Why do you look so weird about seeing them here?" asked Nadine.

"Because... they gave me the impression they were going to be coming back to the bookshop for something else. She said they'd just moved here—rented a house and would be here for the summer. The three of them."

"I'm confused... don't you want people in your store?" Suzette asked.

"I think they want... you know... the *other* stuff. The *specialty* stuff people think I do." Jacqueline had given a smile and little wave to the trio and turned her attention away, hoping they wouldn't approach the table.

"Well, you *have* been known to *do* some things. Like make protection amulets," Nadine said.

"I know, but I don't want to be doing that all the time—and definitely not for people I don't know. You saw how it turned out when I made the protection amulet!" Jacqueline hissed. Then she sat back from the table, for the server had arrived with their drinks.

"Well, well, well... look who the cat dragged in," said Nadine, looking up from her Flowers cocktail. "Don't gawk!" she added when Jacqueline and Suzette swiveled in their seats. "Sheesh. Didn't your mamas teach you any manners?"

But Jacqueline had already seen the new arrival at Jilted.

Luke Blackstone.

CHAPTER 13

"What is he doing here?" Jacqueline said, easing back a little to put herself out of Luke's eyesight as his gaze swept the room.

"Um... having a cocktail?" Suzette suggested. "Maybe some oysters?"

"He was with Mandy an hour or so ago. Maybe two hours," Jacqueline replied before taking a sip of her drink. "Ooh. Very good. Gingery. And a nice cherry flavor, too. How's yours, Nadine?"

"It certainly doesn't taste like laundry soap," replied her friend, giving Suzette an eye-roll. "It's really, really good, in fact. Anyway, Mandy gets up early for her job at the zoo."

"And we know that Luke is a night owl," Jacqueline said. When her friends looked at her, she replied, "He told me. And so did Mandy, as a matter of fact. She's a morning person."

"That's a match made in heaven," said Suzette dryly.

"What—or whom—is he looking for?" Nadine said.

Jacqueline pressed herself back as close to the wall behind her as possible. "Not me, I hope."

"Uh-oh. We've got company," said Suzette.

Jacqueline looked up just as the Sundance trio surged over to their table. Each was holding a drink, but seemed to have left their handbags and wraps at their table a few yards away. That was a good indication they didn't mean to stay long at Jacqueline's table.

"Hi again—Ms. Finch, is it?" said the one with *Daisy Jones and the Six* hair. She wore a long, flowy top with intricate embroidery and wide sleeves over jeans and dark red cowboy boots.

"Yes," Jacqueline said.

"We wanted to make sure you're open tomorrow," the newcomer went on. "We've got a whole list of books we want to get. And some other things, too," she said, her eyes gleaming. "If you know what I mean."

"Well, we've got a lovely selection of teas and baked goods," Jacqueline said. "Suzette's just begun to stock us with tiny cupcakes. And we have some other... um... decorative items."

"Right," replied the second of the trio. "That's what we've heard." She winked meaningfully.

Jacqueline squirmed, but she had been long trained to be polite, especially to customers and patrons. "Great, then. Hope to see you tomorrow."

"Oh, look, Staci—that guy's back," said the third member of the trio. She was speaking to the woman in red cowboy boots who'd initially approached Jacqueline.

"He sure is," said Staci, her eyes tracking to, and landing on, Luke.

"Do you know him?" Suzette asked.

"No. But he's been here almost every night. But then, so have we," said the second woman with an unapologetic laugh. "I'm *obsessed* with the Heartbreak Hotel cocktail. It's such a pretty pink color." She gestured with the drink, served in a faceted coupe glass with a fancy cherry impaled on a tiny sprig of thyme.

"You've seen him here before?" asked Jacqueline. "Was he here on Saturday night?"

The three Sundance women exchanged looks, then Staci said, "Pretty sure. It was super crowded that night, but I think he was here on Saturday."

"I don't remember seeing him for sure," said the second member of the trio.

"That's because you were too busy flirting with that cute server, Paige," said Staci, giving her pal a friendly nudge.

"She really had it going on," replied Paige a little wistfully, then took a sip from her drink. "Too bad what happened to her."

Jacqueline felt a little shiver go down her spine. "What do you mean, what happened to her?"

Again the trio exchanged looks.

"She—they found her. In the graveyard. She was... " Staci shook her head and clamped her lips together. "Didn't you hear about it?"

Jacqueline nodded. "Yes. It's very tragic. You saw her that night?"

"She was taking care of our table, and Paige wanted to take care of her," said the third woman with a grin.

"I was supposed to meet up with her when she got off shift at one, but she didn't show," said Paige. "I guess she met someone more interesting."

Jacqueline felt a warning prickle up and down her spine, and she looked over.

Luke was staring at her.

"Any chance she left with Hot Stuff over there?"

Nadine asked.

"I don't know. We left around midnight to get something to eat. We wanted bar food, not boujie tapas," said Staci with a laugh. "You can only eat so many oysters and hummus dips, you know?"

"True dat," said Nadine. "If I've been drinking, I always want something fried to sop it up. Or Mexican."

"Well, it was really nice seeing you again," Jacqueline said with a warm smile to the trio of women. "Looking forward to seeing you at the shop whenever you get a chance to come by." *Not,* she thought.

"Yes, we will," replied Paige. "Sorry to barge in— we just wanted to say hi."

"Oh, no worries. Have a great evening," Jacqueline replied in an unmistakable farewell.

"You do that really well," said Nadine after the Sundance trio wandered back to their table.

"What's that?" Jacqueline replied.

"Get rid of someone when the time is right. I can't seem to get out of conversations with people sometimes, and we just get stuck in them because neither of us can end it. The conversation just kind of goes in circles and dwindles, then picks up again. But you do a great job of telling someone you're done talking to them—I mean, in a *nice* way," she said quickly when Jacqueline looked stricken. "You're polite about it."

"Oh... kay," Jacqueline said. "I've never thought of that as one of my superpowers: telling people to go away."

Suzette and Nadine laughed, and Jacqueline couldn't help but join in. But soon enough her chuckles faded as she remembered all the crappy things she had to deal with.

For a moment, she considered telling Suzette and

Nadine about her plan to break into Brittany Funeral Home with Evaline and Van Helsing, but decided they'd find out soon enough when she called them to bail her out of jail. Might as well let them get some sleep.

Luke was still here at Jilted, sitting by himself at the bar, nursing what looked like a glass of whisky. He'd positioned himself so he could see the restaurant —including Jacqueline's table. By now he'd surely spotted her.

Maybe she ought to leave and get Evaline and Van Helsing to break into the funeral home *now* instead of later—now, when they knew where Luke was. Nadine and Suzette could keep watch and text her if he left.

But much as she liked the idea, for several reasons (including not getting up at four in the morning to commit a felony, and the likelihood of *not* encountering a vampire while snooping around his house), Jacqueline discarded it. The whole point of going with Evaline and Van Helsing was for them to tell whether Luke was an actual vampire—and to dispatch him if he was. And he had to actually be there for that to happen.

Jacqueline sighed and finished the last of her cocktail. "I've got to get going," she said. "I've got to get up really early tomorrow." Not a lie.

"Welcome to my world," said Suzette, waving over their server so they could pay.

When she left a few minutes later, Jacqueline passed by Luke. She gave him as warm and casual a smile as she could muster.

See you soon, bucko.

And then she shivered.

~

DESPITE HER BEST INTENTIONS, Jacqueline didn't sleep a wink. When she rolled out of bed at four a.m., she felt like a wired zombie.

She'd worried all night about whether she should have stayed at Jilted to keep an eye on Luke. Maybe he'd been scoping out his next victim.

Maybe she could have stopped him.

But it was too late now (and, realistically, how would she have stopped him anyway?). She dressed in black leggings and a black t-shirt with a light jacket (also black) over it. She pulled on a dark blue watch cap to cover her sproinging red hair and went down to corral her partners in crime.

She hoped they were still there in the tea shop.

She should have known.

Evaline was there, her eyes sparkling with excitement and anticipation. She had an entire arsenal laid out on the table: three stakes (one with a silver tip), a dagger, two necklaces with crosses on them, a small vial of holy water, and a broadsword.

A literal broadsword. Jacqueline probably couldn't even lift the thing herself, but Evaline scooped it up, swirling around and swooping and slashing with the blade in a lethal, easy arc.

Van Helsing was watching with an amused, condescending grin, but he too had his own tools laid out: a stake, a smaller sword, an entire bulb of garlic, and a Holy Bible.

Mrs. Hudson stood behind the tea counter, wringing her hands. "Now you'll be careful, won't you?"

She was, of course, speaking to Van Helsing. He seemed nonplussed by her fussing, and cast her an affectionate smile.

"I vill be fine," he said. "Now, are ve ready to go?"

Jacqueline swallowed hard then nodded. This had to be done. There was no one else in Button Cove equipped to identify and dispatch an undead.

"Remember," she said as she unlocked the front door of the bookshop and they stepped out into the waning night, "I'm the general. We work together, but you do as I say."

It was chilly and the moon was a sliver, giving off very little light. But the streetlights did a fine job of illuminating Camellia Court as she led the way up the block.

"We aren't going far from the store, but if you begin to feel strange or weak, tell me," she said.

"Oh, I think we're going to be all right," said Evaline. There was definite glee in her voice. "We have our books."

Jacqueline spun to look at them. "You have them with you? What if you lose them? Or they get destroyed?"

Good grief. *No.* That was the last thing she wanted: two feuding vampire hunters attached to her shop forever.

Or, worse, their stories would disappear if they couldn't go back into their books. What would the world be like without *Dracula* to pave the way for Anne Rice and Stephenie Meyer?

"We don't have them in our *hands*," Evaline told her in a persecuted teenager voice. "But they'll be close by. And— There she is. Mrs. Danvers said she'd bring them and watch over them whilst we're inside."

Jacqueline spun to see the wraithlike, gloomy figure of the housekeeper making her way along the street behind them. She was carrying a small satchel that, presumably, contained not only Evaline and Van Helsing's books but also her own *Rebecca*.

Jacqueline opened her mouth to ask several questions... then just decided not to. Why bother?

When they arrived at Brittany Funeral Home, Jacqueline hesitated... then forged on ahead. The windows were dark in the front, but as she and her companions made their way to the back of the building and its small parking lot, she noticed the pale glow from a single window. A night-light of some sort, she surmised, near the rear door that Luke might use to access his apartment.

Did that mean he wasn't home yet?

Did vampires need a night-light?

Jacqueline thrust away her persistent questions as they came to a halt near a large tree. It provided a shadow in which to hide, and also proximity to the building.

"We need to get inside," Jacqueline said to Evaline. "Want to take a stab—ha, ha—at it?"

Evaline gave her a strange look (maybe she didn't understand the slang, or maybe the shadows just made it look weird), then smiled. "I'll find a way in."

"Wait." Jacqueline grabbed her arm, and the young woman paused. "Do you sense any undead?"

"No," Evaline replied after the barest of hesitations. "But if he's too far away, or sleeping in a lead-lined coffin, I might not be able to sense his presence." Jacqueline looked at her in surprise, and Evaline explained, "The professor and I discussed that possibility. It was actually his suggestion," she added with a definite tone of disbelief. "And I *suppose* he could be right."

"Or else zee man might not even be here," said Van Helsing.

Jacqueline nodded, then looked at Evaline. "All right. In you go. Once you get inside, *you let us in*, all right? Don't go off hunting him down and leaving us out here."

She could tell by her expression that Evaline had intended to do just that, but to her credit, the young woman nodded.

"All right, then, yes," she said, then slipped off into the shadows.

Jacqueline hoped there wasn't an alarm system that Evaline would trip, but she pushed away that worry. There was nothing she could do about it if there was besides *run*.

She and Van Helsing watched for signs of life inside the building, while Mrs. Danvers plunked herself down on a bench and glowered into the darkness as she held the satchel close to her middle. The one time she caught Jacqueline looking at it, she gave her a warning sneer and clutched it closer to her, as if she expected Jacqueline to lunge and swipe it away from her.

Jacqueline rolled her eyes and looked away. She wondered who or what had convinced Mrs. Danvers to make herself so useful.

"*Pssst!*"

She looked over. Evaline was beckoning to them from an open window. It was on the ground floor, but Jacqueline thought it very unlikely that Van Helsing or herself could climb through it into the building. It was more than four feet off the ground.

"Let us in through the door," she hissed to Evaline when they got close. "Any sign of life? Or undeadness?" she added with a choked laugh.

Evaline rolled her eyes and ducked away from the window. A moment later, the side door opened and Jacqueline and Van Helsing crept inside.

"It's silent as a grave in here." Evaline's eyes glittered with delight, and Jacqueline saw that she was holding a stake in one hand. A large cross pendant rested on her bodice, which reminded Jacqueline to pull out the one she'd tucked under her own t-shirt.

"All right. Follow me," she told them.

Having been there only this afternoon, Jacqueline was familiar with much of the main floor, which helped, since the place was in near darkness except for the small night-light she'd noticed.

The meeting rooms were off to one side of the front of the building, while the spaces for services and visitations were larger ones on the other side.

But it was in the back of the building behind closed doors and in windowless rooms where the mortician did his (or her) work... the embalming and preparation of the body for viewing. That seemed a logical place to begin, so Jacqueline led the way down the hall past the meeting rooms and the gathering rooms until they reached a set of double doors.

"Locked," Jacqueline said.

"Allow me," said Van Helsing, pushing his way forward. "I haff a bit of zee experience, *ja*."

Evaline stood back, watching unhappily and with unconcealed impatience as he jiggled the doorknob. Then he pulled a long, slender tool from one of his overcoat pockets and crouched in front of the lock.

"We'd already be in there by now if you'd let me break down the dratted door," Evaline muttered, bouncing up and down on her toes.

"There's no need to announce our presence," Jacqueline told her. "Do you sense anything?"

"No. I'll tell you if I do. You don't have to keep asking," Evaline replied. "And if he doesn't hurry up—"

"A-ha!" Van Helsing stepped back from the door, pulling it open with a flourish.

The unmistakable scent of formaldehyde along with other chemicals and cleaning solutions filled Jacqueline's nose. The room was windowless and dark, but she could make out two long prep tables that resembled the ones she'd seen in the morgue on *CSI* and other crime shows.

Fortunately, the surfaces of both tables were flat, empty of dead bodies. The rest of the room was empty except for cabinets lining two of the four walls.

"Nothing in here," Evaline said in a voice that wasn't as low as Jacqueline thought it should be. She could feel the impatience sparking off the young woman and sympathized with Mina Holmes, who, in the books, spent a good portion of her energies trying to keep her companion from dashing headlong into danger.

"Are vee certain of zhat?" Van Helsing walked into the room, making his way between the two long tables. He looked beneath them as Jacqueline remembered her phone and pulled it out to use the flashlight. When she scanned the room with it, Van Helsing spun around. "Vhat! What is zhat? Oh, it's you. Very vell. Shine it here, if you please, Frau Finch." He squinted at the light, obviously unused to such technology, then gestured to the corner.

Jacqueline's heart seized up when she realized he was pointing to a coffin.

A closed coffin.

CHAPTER 14

E valine pushed past Jacqueline, stake in one hand, broadsword in the other, to stand next to the coffin.

"On the count of three," she said, exchanging looks with Van Helsing as he took up a position on the opposite side of the casket. He was holding a large handful of garlic and his own wooden stake.

Jacqueline's insides churned, and she curled her fingers around her cross pendant.

"Can't you open it for us?" hissed Evaline impatiently, looking at Jacqueline and gesturing with her full hands.

Uh.

Jacqueline braced herself and walked hesitantly to the coffin, debating whether she'd be safer at the foot or head as she opened it to a potentially murderous creature who could lunge out and entrap her with hypnotic eyes.

Evaline was fidgeting, impatience rolling off her as Jacqueline approached. Ignoring her, Jacqueline reached for the top of the coffin.

Holding her breath, praying, and ready to leap back the moment she flipped it up, she lifted the lid.

There was someone inside.

It took her a split second to see that it wasn't Luke Blackstone.

"Stop!" Jacqueline cried, just as Evaline's stake arced up to plunge down toward the still figure.

Somehow, the young woman managed to avert her thrust, slamming the point of the stake into the side of the coffin instead of the heart of whoever this was.

Jacqueline was shaking, and she felt sick to her stomach. What a near miss. How on earth would anyone explain that dear Auntie Caro or Uncle Buford suddenly had a big hole where their heart was?

"Bloody hell!" Evaline said, again in a far-too-loud voice. "What the devil was—"

"Zzzzzt! Such language vrom a young gell!" said Van Helsing, clearly worried more about verbal improprieties than misuse of a stake.

Evaline whirled on him, weapons in hand, eyes flashing. "I'm not a young girl!"

"Cool it, you two!" Jacqueline said, stepping between them on still-shaky knees. "I'm getting tired of your bickering. Each of you has a role to play, and both of you have experience with vampires. You need to learn to work together—just like *you* did with Mina Holmes," she reminded Evaline. "And *you*," she said, pointing a finger at Van Helsing and not caring that it was rude, "should stop judging a person by their age or sex. I don't care *what* time period you lived in—it's not an excuse."

Seething—partly because she was still shaky and upset from the near-miss of destroying someone's loved one—Jacqueline closed the casket with trembling fingers.

She was definitely not cut out for this sort of thing. It was fine to *read* about breaking and entering and hunting down evil and saving the world, but she didn't really like living it.

"Very well," said Evaline stiffly. She'd slipped the broadsword back into its sheath. "Apparently, *that* was not an undead. So what now? And before you ask, *no*, I don't sense anything."

"We need to find Luke's private apartment. It's in this building," Jacqueline said. "It might be on the second floor. The windows up there looked like they're covered with blackout curtains to keep out the sun."

"Right, then," Evaline said, still with a bit of a chill in her voice. "Let's go. It's getting close to dawn."

"Zhen he should be zleeping zoundly," said Van Helsing.

"If he's here," replied Jacqueline, who was beginning to wonder if he actually was. Because wouldn't he have heard them by now and come down to investigate?

They closed and locked the double doors behind them and started down the corridor, Jacqueline leading the way with Evaline fairly breathing down her neck and Van Helsing plodding behind.

It was dim and shadowy, and she'd tucked her phone away in a ludicrous attempt to remain unnoticed as they crept through the building. She wasn't certain where the stairs to the private second floor would be, but had a hunch they were near the side door where they'd come in.

Her suspicion was correct, and, becoming more nervous, Jacqueline began to climb the stairs. They creaked.

Up, up, up they went, as quietly as possible. At the top of the steps, Jacqueline motioned for her companions to stay together, even though it was obvious Eva-line was ready to march off down the hall in the opposite direction.

There were only three doors up here. One led to a lavatory, which was across from the top of the stairs and clearly empty of any undead. The others were at opposite ends of the hall. One door was ajar. One was closed.

Jacqueline opted to head for the ajar door first. She glanced at Evaline, who gave her an annoyed look and a shake of her head. No, she didn't sense any undead.

Feeling mildly more relieved, Jacqueline headed for the open door and peeked inside. There was a bed, and in the beginning light of dawn, she could make out that it was flat and unoccupied. The fact that cur-tains at the windows allowed light in from the edges indicated that if there was a vampire living here, he probably didn't sleep in this room.

She turned and nearly bumped into Van Helsing, but Evaline was gone.

Damn it.

Jacqueline moved quickly and started down the hall, where the other door had been opened. If Eva-line had ruined things—

A shadow emerged from the other room.

It was Evaline.

"Empty," she said in not a whisper. "No one is here."

Jacqueline felt a rush of relief followed by uncer-tainty. If Luke wasn't here, did that mean he was still out prowling the streets looking for his next victim?

Or did he have a different place he slept during the day?

But that didn't make sense, because he was *here*, at work, during the day, and that would require him to travel in the possible sunlight from his sleeping spot to the funeral home.

Nothing made sense at all.

"All right. There's one last thing we should check while we're here," Jacqueline said, leading the way to the stairs.

Her companions followed silently. Jacqueline could feel the disappointment and frustration rolling off Evaline.

She wasn't certain where Nadine had seen the refrigerator with the jars of blood in it, but she knew it wouldn't be difficult to find. And it wasn't. What was clearly a breakroom-slash-kitchenette was tucked next to an office. Its door was not locked (which elicited another sigh of disappointment from Evaline), and Jacqueline pushed it open.

"What's in here?" asked Evaline, suddenly interested. "Oh! Is that the icebox mechanism?" She and Van Helsing crowded much too close to Jacqueline as she opened the refrigerator door.

Just as Nadine said, there were jars—three pint-sized Mason jars—sitting in the fridge. They were filled with a dark red liquid.

"I want to make certain these are actually filled with blood," said Jacqueline, reaching for one.

Suddenly, Evaline stilled. "What was that?"

Van Helsing hurried to the window as Evaline rushed from the room.

"It zounded like a bird call," he said, giving Jacqueline a meaningful look. "It is Frau Danvers, giving us a varning. Somevone is coming."

Jacqueline snatched one of the jars and tucked it in the pocket of her jacket. It barely fit, but if she kept her hand on it, it should be okay.

Van Helsing had already rushed from the room,

leaving Jacqueline frowning in annoyance. What had happened to everyone listening to her instead of rushing off pell-mell to do whatever they wanted?

Ignoring the way her nerves skipped—after all, her two protectors had run off and left her alone—she made her way to the door and peered out into the hallway. It was dark and silent.

Where the *hell* had they gone? There was no sound of altercation or confrontation. Not even the sound of foot—

She saw and heard it too late. Something large, dark, and powerful flew out of the shadows, leaping toward her.

The next thing she knew, she was slammed up against the wall. The jar fell from her pocket, crashing to the floor.

And suddenly, there was a wooden stake pointing at her heart.

CHAPTER 15

Jacqueline looked into the eyes of Luke Blackstone.

"Wh-what are you doing?" she said, hardly daring to breathe. The stake hadn't pierced her skin yet, thank goodness, but she could definitely feel the sharpness of its point. There was probably already a hole in her tee.

"I *knew* it was you. All along," he said. One hand still held her by the shoulder, pushed against the wall, while the other kept the stake in position, ready to thrust home at any moment.

"Wh-what are you—what are you *talking* about?" But the fact that he had a stake practically drilling into her chest seemed like an obvious answer. "You don't actually think *I'm* a vampire."

If she wasn't so terrified, she would have laughed.

"I don't think it," replied Luke. "I *know* it. You've been taunting me all along. Don't think I didn't notice. It was as if you *wanted* me to figure it out. The vampire book display. The mandrakes in your back garden. The way you played with your cross necklace while you were here—and oh, what a *fool* I was, inviting you in here when I already suspected you!"

Now Jacqueline actually did laugh, but when her chest moved, the stake poked deeper, and it hurt. "*Ow!* Look, I'm *not* a vampire." She started to accuse *him* of being an undead, then thought better of it. After all, he *was* holding the stake.

And where the hell were her vampire slayers?

As if she'd summoned them, all at once there was the sound of running feet.

"Miss Finch!" cried Evaline as she rushed up then slid to a halt.

"Stand back," cried Luke, pushing the stake in a little harder. Jacqueline felt blood seeping into her shirt and swallowed.

Was this how she was going to die? Falsely accused of being an undead?

Could there be anything more ridiculous?

"Frau Finch— Güt Gott!" Van Helsing lumbered to a halt, his eyes wide. "But... Zhonathan? Vhat are you doing here? Vhy you hurting Frau Finch?"

It took Jacqueline a moment to realize Van Helsing was speaking to Luke... and that he'd just called him *Jonathan*.

As in... Harker?

No... *way*.

Luke barely gave him a glance. "My name is Luke. Who the hell are you?"

"Vhy, it is I... Abraham Van Helsing. Zhonathan, zurely you remember me." The professor stepped closer with some hesitance but also great earnestness, which Jacqueline hugely appreciated, having a stake nearly ready to ram through her breastbone should its wielder be startled or angered.

"Van Helsing? As in the vampire hunter? What

sort of fool do you think I am?" Luke glanced at the professor, and to Jacqueline's relief, she felt the stake's pressure relax a bit.

"Vhat? You don't recognize me? But how is zhat possible?"

"What in the bloody hell is going on here?" cried Evaline, clearly frustrated by her ignorance and, probably just as likely, the fact that a fiery battle had been avoided.

"Luke thinks I'm a vampire," Jacqueline told her, and was relieved when the stake eased up a bit more. "The amusing thing, Mr. Blackstone, is that *I* thought *you* were the vampire."

"You *what*?"

Now the stake completely fell away, and Jacqueline slammed a hand to her chest to make sure everything was still intact. She might be forty-eight, but the girls were still relatively perky, and she wanted to keep them that way.

"I thought *you* were the vampire," she said again, assuming he didn't mean his question rhetorically.

"Are you crazy?" Luke gaped at her. "Are all of you crazy? And who are *you* supposed to be? Buffy? No, Faith. Buffy was blond." This last was directed at Evaline.

"All right, just... let's just talk this through." At that moment, Jacqueline realized she was standing on the shattered jar of... whatever. "What is this?" she demanded, pointing to the mess on the floor. "Blood?"

Luke gaped at her. "*Blood?* You *are* crazy! It's beet juice."

"Beet juice?" Jacqueline gaped at him, then took a chance and crouched to swipe a finger through the puddle of dark red liquid.

"Yes, beet juice. I use it for my energy smoothies," Luke told her as she lifted her finger to her nose.

Yep. Beet juice.

Definitely not blood.

"Right. Great. Thanks for explaining," Jacqueline said, feeling that telltale heat washing over her cheeks.

"I ought to call the cops on all of you," Luke said, his eyes flashing... and not red.

"But... you are really not Zhonathan?" said Van Helsing, clearly just catching up to the conversation.

"Jonathan? No, my name is Luke— Wait, Van Helsing. Jonathan. You don't actually think I'm *Jonathan Harker*?" Luke's eyes were wide with what could only be described as serious apprehension.

And Jacqueline couldn't really blame him. He probably thought they were all stark raving mad.

She wasn't certain he wouldn't be correct.

"Are you *sure* you're not a vampire?" Evaline swept forward, stake in hand, obviously raring for a chance to use it.

"I'm most definitely not a vampire," snapped Luke. "Why on *earth* would you think I was?"

"B-because you never go out during the day," Jacqueline said. "And you had what we thought were jars of blood in your refrigerator. And you *live* at a funeral parlor, complete with dead bodies and coffins. And when I first met you and Mandy on the street that night, you gave me a really weird look... and your eyes seemed to glow red."

"*My* eyes? *Your* eyes seemed to glow red," Luke shot back at her. "That's what made me first suspect you."

"But... that's impossible! How... Oh... *Oh!* I get it. The lights in Egala's shop. There are some red ones," Jacqueline said. "They must have reflected in each of our eyes." She nodded. "All right, fine. We were both wrong. You're not a vampire and I'm not a vampire—"

"I'm not so certain about that," Evaline said, giving Luke a skeptical look. "Prove it. Prove you aren't an undead."

"You can't prove a negative," Luke shot back. "And of course I'm not an undead. I'm here *hunting* undead."

Evaline bared her teeth and pulled out her broadsword (Jacqueline still couldn't believe the petite young woman had managed to make her way around tonight without tripping over the stupid thing, or having its weight unbalance hers). "Like I said... prove it." With the gaze from her glittering, challenging eyes fixed on him, she sliced the palm of her hand with the tip of the blade.

Jacqueline gasped, but her attention went directly to Luke.

And although he looked shocked by the display of violence from Evaline, he didn't react to the sudden surge of blood from the cut on the young woman's hand.

No flare of red in the eyes. No fangs thrusting free. No claws or heavy breathing or lunging.

No, he didn't react... except to swivel and look right at *Jacqueline*. As if expecting *her* to bare a pair of fangs or lunge at Evaline.

"How could I be a vampire and be wearing a cross necklace?" Jacqueline said to Luke, lifting the chain so the pendant danced.

"Camouflage. Don't think I didn't notice you were playing with one today during our meeting," he replied, his eyes narrowing. "Crosses or other objects aren't a deterrent unless they're blessed or dipped in holy water. And it would make a great cover for you to wear an unblessed one."

"Fine. Well, since I'm not a vampire and you're not a vampire, then who *is* the vampire in Button Cove?" Jacqueline said.

"I don't know." He was still looking at her suspiciously. "I do know it's a woman. And I knew you were new in town, *and* you were always seen with two other women—which made you a trio. So I was suspicious from the beginning."

"Like Dracula's brides," Van Helsing said. "Zhe three of them at his castle. Are you qvite certain you aren't Zhonathan Harker?"

"For the last time... no. I am *not* Jonathan Harker."

"But you look just like him," said Van Helsing.

"I have no idea what Jonathan Harker looks like," Luke replied impatiently. "And it doesn't matter because I'm not him. He's a *character* in a book. Can't you see that I'm a real person?" He held up his arm and pinched an inch of skin.

"I am a real person too," huffed Van Helsing with a great roll of the R.

Jacqueline decided it was time to intervene before they continued to talk around in circles. "So you think there are *three* vampires here in Button Cove?" She didn't like the sound of that.

"Not necessarily," Luke said. "Yes, there were three female vampires in *Dracula*, but that doesn't mean there are three here. The only thing I know for certain is that whoever it is, they're new to the area—because I have been on her trail for over a year, always just missing her in whatever town she—or they—wreak havoc in." Once more he fixed her with that suspicious look.

"Yes I'm new. No I'm not an undead," she replied

with great patience. "But now that I know you're not either, we should try to work together on this and figure out who it is."

"That explains why I haven't sensed an undead since we arrived here," Evaline said belatedly and unnecessarily. "Maybe I should just go out and patrol the streets and see if I can feel any undead out there." Her eyes gleamed.

"And who are you, again?" Luke asked.

"Miss Evaline Stoker," she replied smartly.

Luke's eyes widened, then narrowed. Jacqueline could relate, but in the interest of not belaboring a subject that wasn't going to go anywhere, she spoke up. "So you've been tracking this female vampire for months and followed her here? And you don't know who it is?"

"As I said, I thought it was you," Luke replied. "Now I'm back to square one."

All of a sudden, Jacqueline had to yawn. It was a big, jaw-cracking yawn that reminded her she hadn't slept well last night *and* that she had to open her shop in—good heavens!—less than four hours.

It was time to go. There was nothing more that could be done right now.

But one more thought struck her. "So if you aren't the vampire, why don't you ever go out during the day? And where were you all night anyway?"

"Skin condition," he said. "Very sensitive to sunlight. *And* I was out... looking for you."

The way he eyed Jacqueline suggested he still wasn't quite certain she was innocent of immortality.

Well, the feeling was mutual. She narrowed her eyes back at him. What better way to throw off suspicion on himself than to direct it toward Jacqueline? Deflect and accuse?

Everything he'd accused her of—using a cross necklace as camouflage, being new to town, having "red" eyes—the same could also be said for him. He might have used the beet juice as camouflage. And a skin condition? *Right.*

As she said goodbye, Jacqueline gave him one last hard look, then marched out of the funeral parlor.

Even if he *wasn't* an undead, she certainly wasn't going to be defending his dating Mandy to Massermey.

~

THE NEXT MORNING—OR, rather, the latter part of the same morning—was *rough* for Jacqueline.

She'd slunk back to bed at about six (she could hardly believe that whole escapade had taken less than ninety minutes!) and crawled back out four hours later, but at least she'd slept a little bit. The only way to subdue her toss-and-turn hair was to fight it into a lumpy, straggly bun. She couldn't do much about the bags and dark half-moons under her eyes, but she did brush mascara over her lashes and swipe on a pale pink lipstick.

Unfortunately, when she dragged herself down to the tea room a few minutes after ten, she was greeted by two very disapproving glares.

"*What?*" she exclaimed grumpily, glaring right back at Danvers and Hudson.

"*That* was quite the useless kerfuffle," said Danvers. Someone else might have been surprised that a housekeeper from the nineteen-thirties used such a common, modern-sounding slang word, but Jacqueline was fully aware that "kerfuffle" had originated long before even Mrs. Hudson's time. "Last night." She sniffed.

"*And* the shop has been open for over an hour," added Mrs. Hudson. "Why, you look right batty-fanged, you do, dearie. Not at all the thing. Let's sit us down, now, and have us a strong cuppa—"

"Tea. Yes, I know," Jacqueline interrupted wearily. She'd downed a large mug of coffee upstairs in the privacy of her apartment, but even that hadn't taken the edge off her tiredness. Aside from that, she was in no mood to fight Mrs. Hudson and her "cuppas." "Lots of sugar and milk, if you please."

She ignored Mrs. Danvers's supercilious look. Yes, the woman had come with them last night and been helpful in her own silent, brooding, suspicious manner, but she could keep her opinions to herself.

"Someone's just come in downstairs," Jacqueline said, hearing the pleasant jangle of the bell hanging over the front door. "Perhaps you could help them, Danvers."

The housekeeper huffed, but despite her attitude, she knew her duty—and she liked to lord it over Jacqueline that she knew the workings of the shop better than the owner. Danvers spun as neatly as a soldier, then glided down the stairs and out of sight.

Jacqueline settled on the stool in front of the tea counter while Mrs. Hudson bustled about preparing her "cuppa."

But no sooner had the milky, sweet Assam tea been placed in front of Jacqueline than she heard the sound of footsteps on the tread.

"Well?" demanded Egala, appearing at the top of the stairs with her perfectly arranged hair. "Am I getting my cedar branch, or are you giving me back that bag?"

"Oh." Jacqueline slid off the stool. "I'd forgotten—I mean, I meant to take care of that yesterday but I got distracted."

Mrs. Hudson sniffed and muttered, "Hunting about for vampires. Should be leaving that sort of thing to the experts, now, shouldn't we, then."

Jacqueline rolled her eyes but didn't bother to respond to the snarking landlady. Instead, she beckoned for Egala to follow her.

"I have to ask the cedar if it's all right to give you a twig," she explained. "I'm certain you understand," she added in a firm tone in hopes of alleviating any argument or scoffing from Egala.

"Of course I do," replied Egala, surprising Jacqueline with her easy acquiescence. "I should hope you would do so. It wouldn't be right otherwise."

Jacqueline cast her a glance, but refrained from comment. Maybe her distant cousin wasn't as difficult as she'd thought.

"I don't understand why you haven't already done so," Egala added.

Maybe she was.

Jacqueline led Egala down the stairs and through the bookshop to the back door... and then she faltered a little.

How did she go about asking the cedar for permission to take a branch? How did she know which one? Or how big of a twig or branch she should take? Was it permissible to cut it herself, and if so, would it hurt the cedar?

She might not have had such a whirlpool of questions if her brain wasn't exhausted and murky from the cocktails at Jilted followed by no sleep, the stress of breaking and entering, and the terror of having a stake nearly shoved into her heart.

But as she let herself into the little courtyard garden where the sacred cedar flourished in one corner, the questions and worries seemed to slide away.

She held up a hand to keep Egala from following her, then went right up to the cedar and placed her palm flat on its beautiful, rough trunk.

Jacqueline stood there for a moment, just feeling the texture of the bark beneath her skin, the bumps and ridges against the pads of her fingertips. She swore she felt gentle waves of energy flowing from the tree into her palm.

"Thank you," she murmured, and looked up into the thick canopy of branches and fir leaves. Then she took a deep breath. "Egala wants a small twig or branch from you to provide protection and offer blessings in her shop. Will you allow me to give her one that won't take root?"

Two months ago, if someone had told Jacqueline she'd be asking a tree for permission to take a twig from it—and waiting for a response—she'd have laughed until she cried.

But things were so different now that she didn't even consider what the Old Jacqueline would have thought about this.

She just knew it was right.

No sooner had she finished asking than she felt a little surge of energy from the tree, and then the branches above clashed and danced quietly in a graceful choreography...

And a branch fell onto her head.

It wasn't a large branch; she barely felt the thud when it bumped her crown then tumbled to the ground.

But it was her answer.

"Thank you," she said, giving the trunk a gentle caress of gratitude. "She promises to use it well."

She bent to pick it up and noticed, at the same time, another thicker, shorter branch next to it. About the length of her hand and wrist, the circumference of a broomstick... and one end was very pointy.

Had the cedar tree just offered her a *wooden stake*?

Stunned, grateful, and a little nervous (what did the cedar know that she didn't?), Jacqueline picked up both branches and gave the smaller one to Egala.

"Thank you," said Egala, taking the branch reverently. It was no more than a foot long, but it branched out such that it resembled a small tree—almost like a bonsai. She thanked Jacqueline and was just about to leave when she said, "So what's the deal with the mandrakes? What exactly are you doing with them?"

"I'm not doing anyth—" Jacqueline gaped.

Yesterday there'd been two mandrakes left growing in her garden.

Now there was only one.

"I'm not doing anything with the mandrakes," she said slowly. "But someone is."

CHAPTER 16

The rest of the morning at the bookshop dragged on—an unusual situation for Jacqueline. Normally, she enjoyed every minute of running Three Tomes (well, maybe not the Danvers part), but today, things weren't quite as sunshiny.

Especially now that she realized: one, she had no idea who the vampire in Button Cove was, now that Luke Blackstone was off the list, and two, someone was obviously doing *something* with the mandrakes they'd planted in her garden, since they weren't leaving them to grow.

There was only one plant left, and Jacqueline was actually toying with the idea of pulling it up herself in order to stymie whatever the secret gardener's plan was. She didn't for a minute *truly* think that pulling up a simple plant would cause a fatal scream. Andromeda hadn't said so.

But Jacqueline hadn't done it yet because she wasn't one hundred percent sure it wouldn't happen to *her*. Just in case.

Despite her low energy and subdued mood, Jacqueline waited on customers with a cheery smile and helpful book advice. She was hoping things might slow down enough after two o'clock, when the lunch crowd had gone back to their offices or homes, and she could dash upstairs to the apartment and have lunch, a cup of coffee, and—most importantly—take a look at that old quarto.

She was a little disgusted with herself that she'd found the quarto—or, more accurately, that it had revealed itself to her—yesterday and she still hadn't taken the opportunity to look through it. With the drawing of a mandrake on the front, the pamphlet was obviously relevant to what was going on.

So why was she avoiding it?

What was she afraid was in it?

It didn't matter. The minute she had a break, she'd go upstairs to the apartment and look at it. And then maybe she'd be able to figure out what was going on with the appearing and disappearing mandrake plants.

Just as Jacqueline had hoped, by shortly after two, the steady stream of customers dwindled to one last person walking out the door with a bright blue Three Tomes bag, heavily laden with an entire set of Percy Jackson hardcovers as a middle school graduation gift.

Now, she could escape for a few minutes. Danvers was fussing with something in the romance room (Jacqueline wondered why the woman spent so much time in there; surely it wasn't because she was sneaking peeks at the erotica) and would be able to check out anyone who came in to buy.

The shop's telephone rang, and she answered it.

"Ms. Finch? This is Luke Blackstone."

Her brows rose in surprise. "Yes?"

"I need to talk to you. Can you come by in a little while?"

"Well... yes. I was just about to take a lunch break." Her heart was thudding for some reason. Should she trust him?

"I can't meet now. I have an appointment who should be arriving any minute now. But, say, three thirty? I should be done by then."

"All right." Jacqueline hoped he didn't correctly interpret the hesitation in her voice as one of wariness and suspicion. "Yes, I'll be there around three thirty, unless we get a big rush of customers."

He gave a little chuckle. "I'll understand if you do. Just come when you can, after three thirty. I'll be around. I think I might have figured something out."

"Okay." Thoughtful, she hung up the phone.

The door to the shop swept open, and she looked up as Nadine burst in.

"Well? How did it go last night? I've been waiting all morning to hear something from you besides 'all good, more later'—which, as dishy texts go, leaves *much* to be desired—and nada! Nothing!" Her eyes sparkled with enthusiasm. "Any vampire bites?" She leaned closer, peering at Jacqueline's neck.

Jacqueline laughed. Although she hadn't intended to tell her friends of the plan to break into the funeral home, the cocktail at Jilted—and her nerves—had loosened her tongue last night. "No vampire bites. Sorry for keeping you in suspense—I didn't get much sleep, and I've been sort of sleep-walking through the day, which was surprisingly busy for a Tuesday. I was just getting ready to go up-stairs and grab some lunch. I can tell you about it then."

"Well, let me text Suzette," said Nadine, already tapping on her phone. "She told me to let her know if you had stuff to spill, otherwise she was going to work on her bookkeeping. Obviously, she'd rather be here —yep, she's on her way over."

Jacqueline saw the door of Sweet Devotion swing open and Suzette's curly head and bright red tee as she bounded across the road.

And, not for the first time, she was struck by a wave of gratitude and surprised pleasure that she had two *really good* friends... two friends—at her age!— whom she hadn't known very long, but who supported her, accepted her for all of her quirks and oddities (and that of the shop), and truly cared about her... even so far as to be willing to risk their reputations and lives to support her.

Whoever it was who said life stopped at forty for women was a fool. For her, this was when life was just beginning.

A few minutes later, the three of them were ensconced in the third-floor flat, sitting on Jacqueline's velvet sofa. Suzette had brought over a bakery box filled with cake samples, over which Nadine was in raptures, as well as two pieces of quiche.

"We're trying out a daily quiche by the slice for the lunch crowd this week," Suzette explained. "It's been going over *really* well. I've already had special orders for two whole quiches for later this week, and it's only Tuesday."

"Zoh-my-god," Nadine said, her eyes gleaming as she bit into an orange-flavored sponge cake frosted with cream cheese. There were orange zest scrapings sprinkled on top, along with tiny pearlescent candy beads. "This is my favorite *ever*. Will you make this for my birthday?"

"Sure," Suzette said with an easy flap of her hand. "Now, Jacqueline, tell us what happened last night!"

Jacqueline told them. They listened silently, their

eyes widening as she went on. When she finished, Nadine and Suzette both burst out at the same time:

"He thought *you* were the vampire?"

"*Beet juice?*"

Jacqueline looked at them and said, "My sentiments exactly. To both of you."

"So now what?" said Nadine, who seemed miffed over her mistake regarding the contents of the Mason jars.

"Well, just before you got here, Luke called and said he needed to talk to me, and asked if I could come over."

"Whoa. Do you think that's safe?" said Suzette. "Maybe he still thinks you're the vampire and wants to stab you in the heart for good this time."

"Or maybe he really is the vampire and wants to get you alone," said Nadine.

"Exactly. So I'm going to take Van Helsing and Evaline with me," Jacqueline said. "Assuming I can find them. I'll *make* Danvers and Hudson find them for me."

"Are you *sure* it was beet juice?" Nadine said, slicing a tiny sliver of orange cake.

"It's all over my favorite black booties. You can check for yourself," Jacqueline replied, thumbing a gesture to the pair of shoes she'd left to dry on a towel. They, and her leggings, had been soaked from the shattered beet juice jar.

"So if it's not Luke, who *is* the vampire?" Suzette said.

"Well, if he's to be believed, it's a woman who's relatively new to the area. Which, considering we're moving into tourist season, could be a whole lot of people," Jacqueline replied. "But he made a point of mentioning that I was often seen with you two. I'm not sure how that figures, but maybe it has something to do with in *Dracula* there are the three female vampire seductresses that hang out together and wreak havoc."

"So is he implying there are three vampires, then? Or that one of them is camouflaging herself by hanging out with two other women?" mused Nadine. "And if he's been tracking her—or them—for a while, how does he not know who she is?"

"All of that is what I want to know. And, yes, of course I've thought about the Sundance Catalog women. They seem like good candidates," Jacqueline said. "New to town. Relatively attractive, which would make it easier for one of them to approach a victim. And they were at Jilted the night Cary Whitehall disappeared."

"One of them, Paige was her name, I think, was apparently flirting with Cary," Suzette said. "Seems maybe a little too obvious, but... " She shrugged.

"If this were a book, it'd be too obvious," Jacqueline said. "But since this is real life, we need to remember the basic tenet of Occam's razor: the most likely and simple explanation *is* the most likely explanation."

"Right. So... are you going to tell Massermey?" Nadine asked.

"Which part? That his daughter is not, in fact, dating a vampire? Or that one of three attractive women who've moved to town for the summer *is* a vampire?" Jacqueline said. "I'm not going to tell him anything until I find out what Luke has to say."

"Good plan," Suzette said.

"Agreed," replied Nadine. "And, damn, how am I going to lead a class after eating all that cake?" She moaned ruefully.

"You didn't eat all that much," Suzette assured her.

"There were only three tiny slices, and you just took a taste of each. You'll be fine."

"And that," said Nadine with a teary smile, "is why I love you so much! All right. Gotta run. Damn," she said, standing up, "running a business is hard work. So demanding. All these adult things I have to do *every single day.*"

"I hear you. I'm back off to do my books—and not the fun kind you sell here, Jacqueline," said Suzette with a laugh. "If you don't hear from me by tomorrow, send help."

"Thanks for letting me run all this stuff past you," Jacqueline said. "It helps to talk it out."

"We need a text after your meeting with Luke to let us know you're still alive," said Suzette.

"Unless you've been turned into a vampire by him," said Nadine with a grin. "Then we just want to know how to be vampiric seductresses."

Laughing, Jacqueline pushed them out the door. She had about thirty minutes to look over the quarto before her meeting with Luke.

The old pamphlet was sitting right where she'd left it—on top of the even older and more decrepit cinder-block book where Jacqueline had found the directions to make a protection amulet a few weeks ago.

Which reminded her that she should make one for herself, just in case. She hadn't been down to the cellar for a couple of days, but it was a very special place. Part of the cedar tree was actually exposed down there, with the brick wall having been built around it. A tiny channel of water wound through the floor of the cellar, and in the center was a circle of re-vealed earth—sacred and powerful soil, exposed at the juxtaposition of the many ley lines that connected there.

It was there, in the cellar, on the trunk of the cedar, that Jacqueline had made a handprint when she was a young girl—something she hadn't remembered until she came back here to Three Tomes. The mark was proof that this was *her* place, that she was connected to the location, to the earth, to the space by both family and spirit.

She'd used the sacred earth and the energetic flowing water when she made a protection amulet for a woman whose husband had been trying to kill her. And it had worked. She would make one for herself, in the same manner, and hope it worked as well.

For now, though, Jacqueline was going to give her overdue attention to the quarto with a drawing of a mandrake on its front.

But when she opened the booklet and got her first good look at the initial page, Jacqueline realized it wasn't going to be easy.

The contents weren't printed on a press. They were handwritten. The writing was in English, but not only was it old, faded, and spidery... it was also in Chaucer-like Old English, with Fs for Ss and a lot of unfamiliar serifs and connectors in the text... not to mention words that simply weren't in use nowadays.

Jacqueline curled her lip. She wasn't a huge fan of the Middle Ages, as far as historical time periods went. She'd futzed her way through Chaucer, *Beowulf*, and the like in every lit class she'd taken as an undergrad and a graduate student, preferring to focus on the latter part of the era with Richard the Lionheart, the legend of Robin Hood, and the Magna Carta, rather than the Dark Ages.

The only things she liked about the Middle Ages

and chivalry and fiefdoms and so on were Eleanor of
Aquitaine (badass warrior queen, wife of two kings,
and mother of two more, who was so powerful her
husband had to imprison her so she wouldn't over-
throw him) and the strong, chivalrous, and brave Ivan-
hoe. She still rewatched the TV movie with Anthony
Andrews in it. *Swoon.*

But neither of those aspects of medieval England
would help her make heads or tails of this quarto.

She could pore over it carefully with a magnifying
glass and an Old English dictionary and maybe make
some headway, but it would be slow-going and might
take too long.

The fact that it was old enough—or seemed old
enough—to have been written in Old English had initially escaped her notice. And when she did realize it
could be over a thousand years old, Jacqueline gasped
and nearly dropped the old packet.

But upon closer examination, she concluded the
quarto wasn't old enough to actually have been
written during the twelfth or thirteenth century; it was
merely a copy of a booklet. An old one, to be sure—
certainly several hundred years old—but not quite old
enough that she'd have to turn it over to a museum.

The other thing that made the hair on the back of
her neck stand up, besides all those Fs for Ss, were the
drawings she noticed. They did not look like they were
depicting nice or happy events. And she was pretty
sure one of the words she could make out was *darkness*
—or, in this case, *darkneff.*

Jacqueline shook her head and set the quarto
aside. Her hope that it would give her some information about mandrakes was definitely put on hold until
she could translate the script.

She was still as at sea about why those mandrakes had shown up and who was planting and taking them and why Lucy Frontera had come to her shop—

Suddenly, Jacqueline froze.

"Wait a minute," she said out loud, bolting to her feet. "Wait a *minute*."

What was it Luke had said? He'd been listing off all the reasons he'd suspected her being a vampire... and one of them was something about mandrakes.

The mandrakes in your back garden, he'd said.

Somehow the fact that she had mandrakes had made him suspicious that she was an undead. Why?

There was one way to find out.

Jacqueline gathered up her Egala purse and shoved her phone inside, along with a bulb of garlic she grabbed out of the kitchen, a good-sized chef's knife, and the stake the cedar had given her.

Two minutes later, she was bounding down the stairs to tell Danvers she was leaving and that the housekeeper was in charge—a situation the woman *lived* for, even though she bitched about it. Danvers loved telling people what to do, and this was evidenced by the gleam in her eye when she gave her characteristic sniff of condescension.

It was three twenty when Jacqueline started off down Camellia, away from the three crones' house at the end of the court. She realized she'd left the bookshop without Van Helsing and Evaline, and stopped short, spinning around and wondering if she ought to go back and find them.

But she didn't. It was the middle of the day, and she had weapons with her. Besides, if Luke thought she was a vampire because she had mandrakes growing in her garden, then *he* must not be a vampire himself, or why would he say that? Why would he draw attention to the fact that mandrakes were somehow related to undead-ness?

"Oh, excuse me," Jacqueline said as she spun to continue on her way and nearly trampled someone.

"Watch your step, missy!" snapped Mrs. Kilmeade, who'd been trundling along with her umbrella and a purse the size of Africa. Today she was wearing a Black Sabbath t-shirt that looked like it might have been from an '80s concert over a pair of baggy flare jeans. When Jacqueline would have kept going, the older woman stepped into the middle of her path and curled a pale white finger at her. "You. You're the one, aren't you?"

"Me? I'm the what?" Jacqueline said. She couldn't push past her and keep walking, even though it seemed she was about to get lambasted for some reason.

"You're the one with the bookshop. The strange one." Mrs. Kilmeade came closer. "Strange things happening there, I hear. Lights flashing. Books flying around. Oh, I hear all about it, missy." She squinted at Jacqueline, tapping the air with her curled finger. Her unpainted fingernail was dangerously long. "Don't think I don't know about it all. Don't think I don't know."

The woman was batty. Jacqueline felt a surge of sympathy for Massermey and his entire staff, having to deal with her constant complaints.

She only hoped Mrs. Kilmeade wouldn't start calling the police station to complain about Three Tomes as well as the damage in the graveyard.

"We sell books and tea at the bookshop," Jacqueline told her, forcing a polite smile. "Stop in anytime. I promise there won't be any flashing lights or flying books."

"Oh, I won't be doing that, missy," she said, clutching her handbag closer to her. "I won't be doing that."

"Have a nice day, Mrs. Kilmeade," said Jacqueline, and scooted past her as the woman continued to rail on about the bookshop and everything else on her shit list. Jacqueline hoped she never became that mean and judgy when she got older.

"Ms. Finch!" someone called just after she turned the corner onto Seventh Avenue, and she looked over.

"Lucy!" Jacqueline stopped and waved at the woman, who was crossing the street to talk to her. "I didn't realize you were out of the hospital."

"Oh, yes. They only kept me overnight." Despite her easy words, Lucy Frontera looked a little paler than Jacqueline remembered. "I don't like staying in the hospital anyway, you know. Anyhow, it looks like you're in a rush, but I wanted to thank you for helping me yesterday. You and Detective Massermey."

"Of course," Jacqueline replied. "I'm just so glad you're all right." She noticed the bandage around Lucy's wrist, hiding the puncture marks. "You were coming to the shop to look for a book?"

"Oh, yes. I was hoping you had a copy of *Culpeper's Complete Herbol*, but then I realized you were closed. I was just about to leave when I looked over into your courtyard. Nice little garden there." Lucy drew in a breath and hesitated, then said, "I could've sworn I saw some mandrake growing there."

"Oh. Well, there might be. I'm not certain," Jacqueline prevaricated. "It might be primrose."

Lucy looked at her. "You do know it is a very dangerous plant. You certainly don't want to simply let it grow where anyone might pull it up."

"Yes, I do know that. I'm... trying to decide what to do with it," Jacqueline said. "If it really is mandrake."

"I was looking at it when I was attacked." Lucy's voice was a little thready. "As if someone didn't want me to notice it was there."

Hmm. "You don't have any idea who it might have been?"

"No. I was crouching down a little, and they came up behind me." Lucy shivered. "They put their arm around my throat and cut off my air... I couldn't breathe... And the next thing I knew, I felt this pain on my arm, and then everything went wavery... and then I was in the ambulance."

"I hope they find out who did it," Jacqueline said with great feeling. "Whoever it was left some strange marks."

Lucy looked at her. "People are saying vampire bites."

"I've heard that too."

"I don't believe it, though," Lucy said. "Whoever heard of a vampire out in the daylight? And it *was* daytime."

"I don't know what to think. You're the second person to have been attacked with those sorts of markings," Jacqueline said. "I'm so glad you weren't badly injured."

"That makes both of us." Lucy shrugged, but her expression was taut as she looked away, as if staring into the past. "Anyhow, thank you again for helping me, Ms. Finch."

"Jacqueline. And anytime. I'm so glad we were there and found you before you... before it got worse. Have a nice day."

"Thank you."

"Oh, and I can check to see if we have that book," said Jacqueline.

"I would be very grateful. Thank you."

Lucy gave a little wave and walked off. Jacqueline glanced at her phone. She'd been delayed twice now, and it was nearly quarter to four. She didn't want to be gone from the shop for too long or Danvers would get all snarky and persecuted about doing what she liked doing: being in charge.

Brittany Funeral Home was halfway down the block, and she passed several people on her way there: dog walkers, a couple of women in their forties window-shopping, a passel of teens out of school for the day, and two women pushing strollers. It was a glorious spring afternoon—a fact that had escaped her until now, due to all of the craziness going on—and Jacqueline took a moment to inhale the fresh, lake-scented air.

She arrived at Brittany Funeral Home refreshed and a little nervous. Her Egala bag hung over her shoulder, and she felt the comforting weight of the stake and chef's knife inside.

The side door was open, and she walked in as she had done yesterday for her appointment. As before, the hall was empty and there was no sign of Luke. Everything was quiet and still. The sign that would normally list names of the deceased was empty, indicating there were no viewings or services on the schedule for the day.

Jacqueline felt weird calling out; for some reason, being in a funeral home made her want to act like she would in a church, quiet and respectful. But after she wandered down the hall to the room where they'd met yesterday and saw no sign of Luke, she did call out.

"Hello? Anyone here?"

She heard a faint noise. A quiet thud. It was coming from behind the double doors that, she knew from last night, led into the back room where the mortician did the preparation of the bodies.

Jacqueline shivered. Funeral homes were eerie, strange places.

"Luke?" she called, and heard another quiet sound that pulled her attention back to the double doors.

Something felt wrong. She wished she'd brought Van Helsing or Evaline with her. Or at least someone else.

"Luke, it's Jacqueline Finch," she said, moving on to the double doors as she pulled out her phone to have it at the ready. "I'm here for our—uh—meeting."

Now she saw that one of the double doors was slightly ajar. Feeling an overwhelming sense of trepidation, she reached a hand into her gorgeous leather tote, murmuring, "I need the stake."

And there it was, just inside the top of the tote. She didn't even pause to wonder how it was there—suspended somehow? Her fingers closed over the smooth wooden pike, and Jacqueline had a moment of gratitude for Egala's charm.

Stake in hand, tote over her shoulder, phone in her other hand, Jacqueline nudged the door open.

The same scents of formaldehyde and cleaning products assaulted her nose, but there was something else... some other smell.

Something she was very much afraid she recognized.

Something like blood. A *lot* of blood.

Heart in her throat, stake at the ready, phone clutched in a sweaty palm, Jacqueline stepped into the workroom. There were a few lights on, keeping the windowless space from being dim and shadowy but still leaving dark corners.

"Luke?" she called.

She heard the blood first. Heard it *plop, plop, plopping...* then smelled it even more strongly.

Then she saw him. Luke.

He wasn't dead. Not yet.

She fumbled with her phone and stabbed 911 even as she rushed closer.

The operator answered immediately, and Jacqueline managed to give the details quickly and succinctly as she approached Luke.

He was sprawled on a table as if he'd been laid out by the mortician. One arm lay flung out to the side. Blood dripped from wounds—puncture wounds, scratch marks, and other lacerations—on his arm and chest.

"Luke!" she cried, nearly slipping in the blood pooled on the floor. Her stomach heaved alarmingly, and she gripped the wet edge of the table, fighting not to lose the meager lunch and coffee she'd downed.

She disconnected the call, knowing the operator had all the information she could give, and tried to determine if there was anything she could do for Luke.

When he managed to grip her arm with surprising strength, she shrieked, then realized he was trying to tell her something.

His lips formed words; she wasn't certain what he was saying over the roaring in her ears and the smells and sights assaulting her other senses.

"Kill... " he breathed with extreme effort, his gaze boring into hers, "...me...v...am...pi...re..."

"No, no, no, Luke, hold on, hold on!" she cried, looking for something to stanch the blood. "Help is on the way! Hold on, please... "

But it was too late. He gave a great, shuddering breath. His eyes went blank. His body, tense with the last bit of effort, stilled, sagged, stopped.

He was right.

The vampire had killed him.

CHAPTER 17

"He was alive—just barely—when I got here," Jacqueline said. "He said... he said the vampire killed him."

Massermey, who'd of course been called in, gave her a look.

"That's what he *said*," she told him. "And look at him!" She gestured wildly toward the room where the body remained, even though neither of them could see it at the moment, shrouded and out of sight as it was.

"I can't deny there isn't some evidence that supports it, but... " Massermey replied. He wasn't brushing her off; she knew that. He simply couldn't wrap his head around what she was telling him. Couldn't or didn't want to believe it. "I'll put it in the report."

"Miles... you might have to open your mind a little wider in this case." She put a hand on his arm and looked up at him earnestly. "I know it seems... impossible. But sometimes the impossible happens. Just remember what happened a few weeks ago with the woman at the winery. Remember how you mysteriously couldn't get near her? And then suddenly you could?"

He nodded, but she could see the stubbornness in his expression. But, notably, he didn't ask for more information about why she thought what she did. He wasn't ready to believe.

"Also," she said, stepping a little closer, still touching his muscular arm and dropping her voice low, "not to complicate matters, but you should know that Mandy and Luke had been seeing each other. So... "

Massermey's eyes bolted wide. "What? Like... *dating*?"

Jacqueline nodded. Hoo boy, he smelled good. "So you're going to have to be sensitive to her reaction to—"

A feminine cry from down the hall drew their attention. Apparently, Massermey was going to have to deal with his daughter's grief sooner rather than later.

"Dad! Dad! What happened?" Tears were streaming down Mandy's face as she ran down the corridor. "Is he all right? Is Luke all right?"

Jacqueline gave him one last squeeze of the arm, then stepped away so he could comfort his daughter.

She hovered for a minute, wondering if there was something she might be able to do to help, but Mandy clung to her dad, and then one of the other police officers led her away solicitously. Likely he'd need to take Mandy's statement as well, since she probably knew Luke better than anyone else in Button Cove.

When Jacqueline finally stepped outside, it was almost six. It had been a long and horrible two hours inside a building filled with death, and the fresh air was a relief.

But she didn't have time to dawdle. She needed to

talk to the crones and the vampire hunters, and they had to figure out a plan.

There was no doubt a vampire was on the loose here in Button Cove, and it wasn't Luke Blackstone.

When Jacqueline got back to the bookshop, she found Danvers managing a long line at the register. The housekeeper gave Jacqueline a dark look, for she'd been gone for over two hours.

Jacqueline hurried to assist with the customers, stowing her Egala bag behind the counter. One of those waiting was Harriet Wellburg, with the straw handbag from Egala's and the "Bad to the Bone" ringtone. She was back to buy more container-gardening books.

"I found some very unique plants that will fit just perfectly on my patio," she said enthusiastically. "But I need more ideas for how to care for them. This is my first season here in the northern Midwest, and I'm still not sure of everything that can be grown in this zone."

Jacqueline didn't mind in the least that the woman was buying out her entire stock of Midwest planting guides and container-gardening books. Most of them were hardcovers, too. She happily tucked them all into a double bag and handed it to her over the counter with a warm thank you.

"Did you hear all the sirens?" asked the next person in line as Harriet turned away. "Any idea what was happening? They've got Seventh Street closed off."

"Oh dear," said Harriet, pausing. "And I've got to go that way back home."

"Someone died," Jacqueline said. "Over on Seventh. At the—uh—funeral home."

"They died *at* the funeral home?" said Harriet.

"How awful," said the customer, placing her books

—two World War II historical fictions and a Manda Collins historical romance—on the counter. "What happened?"

Jacqueline wasn't about to say, but Harriet spoke. "It was probably some sort of accident. I hope it wasn't another of those horrible attacks like in the cemetery the other day."

"I *heard* about that. Someone said there was a *vampire* bite on the body," said the customer in a hushed voice.

"A *vampire* bite?" cried a new voice that Jacqueline recognized. It was Staci, of the Sundance Catalog trio, near the end of the line. She and her friends were standing there in a cluster, all holding go-cups of coffee and several shopping bags.

This topic stirred up the entire cluster of customers, and suddenly everyone was talking about vampires, vampire bites, and all of the elements that went with it.

"That's ridiculous," said Harriet. "It's just some crazy person trying to make it look something like that. Vampire bites! Ridiculous." She scoffed and marched out of the shop, the heavy bag of books banging against her side.

Jacqueline didn't add anything to the conjecturing that was going on around her. Instead, she focused on ringing up customers and helping them find books. She was relieved when the Sundance Catalog women didn't try to corner her, asking for "special" things. Maybe she'd misunderstood their previous comments, because all they bought were erotic novels and cookbooks.

Finally, after another twenty minutes, the shop was quiet and empty of customers.

"Nice of you to return," said Danvers with a sniff. "Ma'am."

Jacqueline ignored her. Instead, she made a snap decision and flipped the sign to CLOSED on the front door. She didn't like to have to change the shop's hours unexpectedly, but desperate times called for desperate measures.

She'd only just returned from changing the sign at the back door when her phone began to blow up with texts from her friends.

Jacqueline, what happened? That was from Suzette on the text thread the three of them shared.

Why is the shop closed early!?!?!? came the follow-up from Nadine.

Good grief. Were they watching her front door from their shops? She laughed a little—because what else was she going to do?—and sent back a series of super-short texts.

Luke is dead. Found him myself. BITE MARKS. Come over when you can.

Then she hurried upstairs to the tea shop. Mrs. Hudson was there, alone.

"Why, what on earth are you thinking, dearie? It's too early to close up shop today—"

"Where are Evaline and Van Helsing?" Jacqueline demanded. "Why are they never here when I need them?"

"Why, I don't know," replied Mrs. Hudson, stiffening. "And I don't take kindly to that sort of tone, now, do I? So you mind your manners, dearie."

"I need to see them. As soon as possible."

"Well, I'm not sure why you're telling *me*, now, dearie—"

"Oh, cut the innocent crap," Jacqueline exploded. She *felt* her eyes bulging. "I know very well that you brought Evaline Stoker here, and if you knew how to do that, then you know how to get her here right now! So, please, before someone else dies, could you do it?"

Mrs. Hudson drew herself up like a ruffled chicken and appeared just about to launch into some sort of tirade when a smooth-as-a-cat-in-the-cream voice said, "*I'd* be happy to assist, ma'am."

Jacqueline turned to see Danvers at the top of the stairs. There was an unholy gleam of delight in her eyes when she looked at Mrs. Hudson—a gleam that dimmed into something frighteningly demure when she returned her attention to Jacqueline.

Mrs. Hudson's face turned beet red. "Why, how dare you—"

"Well, if you're going to get into a snit every—"

"Quiet!" Jacqueline shouted. The room actually shook, and *OMG* did her fingertips just tingle with... sparks?

She shook her hands, staring at them. Her fingers felt strangely warm. She shook her hands, then huffed a breath and turned her attention back to the two women.

"*Please.* I'm sorry, but someone was just killed by a vampire. We need to figure out who it is before someone else dies. I need Van Helsing's and Evaline's help."

"Well now you're asking more politely, then," said Mrs. Hudson, studiously ignoring Mrs. Danvers.

Jacqueline rolled her eyes, but clamped her lips shut.

Just then, the door downstairs rattled violently in its frame. Someone pounded and the door rattled harder.

It had to be Suzette and Nadine.

Once again, Jacqueline felt the flush of warmth

that her two new friends were there when she needed them—although she wasn't exactly sure how they could help in this situation. Still, they were *there*. *For her.*

She dashed down the stairs (this was a good way to get cardio, she told herself) to let them in, but before she answered any of the questions they had, she led the way back upstairs (more cardio). She didn't want to take any chances of missing Van Helsing and Evaline.

To her shock, the tea room was empty of both Mrs. Hudson *and* Mrs. Danvers, not to mention there being no sign of vampire hunters.

She made a frustrated choking sound, then plunked onto the sofa in front of the fireplace.

"So Luke Blackstone is dead," Nadine was saying. "And he had bite marks too? What happened?"

Jacqueline explained, ending, "And now I have to wait until Danvers and Hudson show back up with Van Helsing and Evaline so we can figure out what to do next."

"What do you think Luke wanted to see you about?" said Suzette.

"I don't know. And I'm really pissed that he got himself killed before I had the chance to talk to him. Just like in every freaking cozy mystery ever! Someone has important information, and they end up dead before they can tell someone."

Jacqueline rolled her eyes and let her head rest on the back of the sofa. Then her head popped back up. "And here's another thing I remembered. Luke said something about my having mandrakes growing in my garden, and that was one reason he thought I was the vampire."

"All right. So what does a vampire want with a mandrake?" said Nadine.

"Have no clue. But I did find this old booklet." Jacqueline explained about the quarto with the mandrake drawing on the cover.

"So you haven't read any of it?" asked Suzette.

"I couldn't make out much of the script, and I had to go meet Luke," Jacqueline said. "Either of you want to give it a try?"

"Maybe one of the ZAP Ladies could take a look," suggested Suzette. "I could run it over to them while you wait for the vampire hunters. They might want to be brought up to date anyway."

Jacqueline nodded. It only now occurred to her that she didn't have any way to contact the ZAP Ladies other than walking down and knocking on their door. No phone numbers or anything like that. It had never seemed to matter before, because they always just showed up—whether she wanted them to or not.

"I'll run upstairs and get the quarto," she said. "If anyone comes back, *don't let them leave.*"

Nadine and Suzette agreed, and Jacqueline did a little more cardio by running up to her flat and grabbing the quarto.

"Here," she said, giving it to Suzette while trying not to sound out of breath. She'd only dashed up one flight of stairs and back down. She *shouldn't* be out of breath.

"Wow. This *is* old," said Suzette, flipping through the crinkling pages.

"So," said Nadine, "if the vampire isn't Luke, who is it? Are we thinking one of the Sundance ladies?"

"One of them seems like a good option," Jacqueline said, but something nagged at the back of her mind. Something someone said that had stuck in her thoughts that seemed important. "But there's really no reason to think it's one of those three except that they're new in town."

"Don't forget they were hanging out at Jilted, flirting with Cary Whitehall the night she died. They knew her, they were seen with her, and she was supposed to meet up with one of them," Nadine reminded her. "That all tracks with what we know."

"But most of what we know about who vampire's identity is based on what Luke said—that it's a woman and that she's new in town because he followed her here," Jacqueline pointed out. "What if he was wrong?"

"Or lying," said Nadine. "He might have been lying."

"Why would he lie?"

"Maybe he really *was* a vampire," said Suzette, looking up from the quarto. "And he tried to throw off suspicion by blaming you. And that's why he wanted to meet with you—alone, without the vampire hunters to put a stop to his plan to stake you."

"But Luke was killed by a vampire," Jacqueline said. "I don't want to believe there's more than one of them here in town." She scrubbed her forehead. "That would just be too much."

Where were the vampire hunters?

"This book is kind of dark," said Suzette. She was still looking at the quarto. "I've made out a few things, though. One heading says 'To Maketh a Permanent Sleep.' I hate it when they write Ss like Fs," she said, pushing her wiry hair away from her face. "And add Es on the end of words that don't need to be there. It makes it so much harder to read."

"Anything else interesting?" Jacqueline asked. "Is it all about mandrakes?"

"Yes. It seems to be. These illustrations aren't very nice, either. They're telling you how to use different parts of the plant. The roots and the berries... Ooh. Here's another one. 'To Turn One Mad'—'mad' spelled 'm-a-d-d-e.' Certainly not a very nice plant, is it?"

"No. And I have some growing in my garden that someone keeps pulling up."

"Oh, wow. Look at this one."

Suzette handed the quarto to Jacqueline, who slid on the reading glasses she kept around her neck while working at the shop and squinted at the page. It was the last one in the booklet, and its printing was a little less faded. The title of that page read:

To Raife the Demonf from their Tailles

"Yikes," she said, looking up. "That's creepy. Raise demons from their tails? I don't want to think about where they found demon tails." She shuddered. "Not that I really believe these recipes, or spells or whatever they are, actually work."

"We should definitely show this to the ZAP Ladies," said Suzette, rising. "I'll take it over to them."

Just then, Jacqueline's cell phone dinged and she looked at it.

"It's a message from Massermey," she said, scrolling to look at it.

We found this at the crime scene, said his text. There was an image attached.

"Ooh," said Nadine. "I love that the two of you keep bonding over dead bodies— *Wait.* That sounded bad. I'm not saying I like dead bodies or that it's good that you keep finding them because it's not, but it's such a cozy mystery meet-cute, you know, like in—"

"Oh my God," said Jacqueline, staring at the image —which Massermey probably shouldn't have sent her because it was a police investigation, but she understood why he did, because...

"It's a set of *fake fangs*." She showed her phone to Nadine and Suzette. "They found a set of *fake fangs* by Luke Blackstone's body. With blood on them."

Her friends stared at her, then looked at the picture, then looked up at her again.

"It looks like a miniature bear trap," said Nadine. "And just as deadly."

"Or like a metal version of those plastic Halloween fangs that never fit right," said Suzette. "But way more lethal."

They all looked at each other as Jacqueline said, "So... does this mean someone really *was* faking vampire attacks? Using these fangs to make marks on people?"

"Sure seems like it," replied Nadine.

"But what about the disturbed dirt in the graveyard?" Suzette said.

"Doesn't have anything to do with it," said Nadine. "Just some kids."

"So someone is faking vampire attacks," said Jacqueline. "Why?"

"Luke didn't think it was fake," Nadine reminded her. "And he said he'd been tracking the vampire for months."

"You two talk this out. I'm running this to the crones," said Suzette, holding up the quarto. "You might as well assume they'll be coming back with me."

"Right," said Jacqueline, then turned her attention back to the fake fang situation. "Okay... so what if all of the so-called vampire attacks were staged?"

"So we have a serial killer who wants everyone to think they're an undead," said Nadine. "To throw off suspicion, I guess? Or just to freak people out."

"Probably the latter. But remember, there've been three attacks, and only two people died. Lucy Frontera didn't die." Suddenly, a prickle zipped down her spine. "Lucy was looking at the mandrakes when she was attacked. And she wasn't bitten on the neck like the other two. She was bitten on the wrist."

"Is that why she didn't die? Or was it because it was during the day and the killer was interrupted?"

"Or... " Jacqueline's mind was working fast, darting through the warrens of her memory. "What if... Oh, this is really far-fetched... but what if Lucy *faked* the attack on herself?"

Nadine looked at her. "Why the heck would she do that?"

"I don't know. I *don't know*. It doesn't make sense. I'm just throwing out ideas—but... " Jacqueline sat up sharply. "I saw her today. Right as I was turning onto Seventh to get to the funeral home. She was coming from that direction."

"Didn't you say Luke had had an appointment so he couldn't meet with you until after it?"

"Yes, and I told that to Massermey. Hopefully he looked in Luke's appointment book to see who it was. Because I bet whomever Luke was meeting with was the person who killed him."

"And you're saying it could have been Lucy," said Nadine.

"I saw her there on that block. Plus she was interested in my mandrakes—*and* she wanted me to dig up a copy of an old medieval herbal called *Culpeper's*. She wants to use the mandrakes for something, I bet. And she's the only person who didn't die from the vampire attack. *Plus...* she's the only person who had bite marks on her *wrist*—which would be much easier to fake on herself than on her neck or shoulder."

Nadine's eyes were wide and she was nodding. "You need to tell all this to Massermey."

Jacqueline nodded. "Yes, I will, but I'm sure he's already putting these pieces together. I'll let him know I saw Lucy just before I got to the funeral home, and that he should call me when he can for more info." She pulled out her phone and sent a quick text to Massermey.

Nadine suddenly pulled out her phone, which had obviously been on silent. "Crap. It's Danny. She needs a jump—probably left her headlights on again." She sighed, shaking her head. "Daughters. They never leave a mom alone when she's hunting down vampires." She stood. "I won't be more than fifteen minutes."

"No worries. I'm not doing anything until the slayers get here," Jacqueline said. *If they ever do.*

"Well, if Lucy shows up, I wouldn't let her in the shop," said Nadine with a little chuckle as she started down the steps.

"Don't worry. I'm not letting anyone in," said Jacqueline.

But a little voice in her mind said, *Famous last words.*

CHAPTER 18

B ut Jacqueline didn't have to worry about *letting* a vampire in. Once they'd been invited across a threshold, they could just come in whenever they wanted.

So that didn't help her situation at all.

"But the vampire attacks were faked," she said aloud to herself, trying to ease her sudden rush of nerves. "So it's a non-issue."

But was it?

After all, Van Helsing had shown up out of *Dracula*. In her admittedly limited experience with characters coming out of books, Jacqueline had come to understand that they only spontaneously appeared when there was a need for them in the real world.

So why else would Van Helsing be here if not to kill a vampire? Was there anything else he could do or information he could provide that would alleviate the situation—namely, a serial killer pretending to be an undead?

Was the fact that he thought Luke Blackstone had been Jonathan Harker part of the reason for his appearance? But that didn't make any sense either, because Luke was dead and he *hadn't* been Jonathan Harker.

That whole thing was messed up. It was like the time the Wicked Witch of the West had shown up here and recognized one of Jacqueline's ancestors as Dorothy. There was no rhyme or reason to it; it just was.

And she supposed that made sense, in a way. After all, when a person read (or wrote) a book, they often had an image in their mind about what a character looked like. And everyone's mental image would be different. So Van Helsing—who, she supposed, had actually *known* Jonathan Harker—simply thought Luke looked like his friend.

Still... all of that conjecturing didn't solve the problem or mean anything.

Jacqueline heard a sound downstairs. Nadine was back already? It couldn't be Suzette and the ZAP Ladies, because they would be making a lot of noise. They simply couldn't help it.

But come to think of it, so would Nadine. She wasn't what one would call silent or subdued—unless she was meditating.

Jacqueline rose, her palms going clammy. Maybe it was one of the cats—who, by the way, she hadn't seen for a while.

There was another sound... one that was familiar to her.

The sound of a book falling to the floor.

No, no, no! Not again. Not again!

Jacqueline hurried to the stairs as she heard another thud. And another. And more, one after the other.

What the heck?

She came rushing down the stairs and stopped short just before the bottom.

"What... what is going on?" she said, then recognized the person standing there. She frowned in confusion. "Mrs. Kilmeade?"

Sure enough, it was the older woman. She was next to the vampire book display, and it appeared she was picking up each book and dropping it on the floor.

"How did you get in here? The door was lock— Oh, Nadine must've forgotten to—"

Jacqueline choked off her words when Mrs. Kilmeade looked over at her.

With eyes that burned *red.*

With fangs—real ones—that gleamed.

And she was holding a large jar of some dark greenish liquid... that she was about to pour on top of the books!

"What are you doing?" Jacqueline cried, rushing forward. At the moment she was more worried about the safety of the books than the fact that she was actually facing down a vampire.

What was wrong with her?

"I am about to raise the demons," replied Mrs. Kilmeade matter-of-factly.

Was it too much that she was still wearing her Black Sabbath t-shirt?

"Raise the demons?" Jacqueline heard herself parrot the words, but she couldn't help it. She was simply trying to wrap her head around what was happening. And it wasn't working.

"From these books. All of them." Mrs. Kilmeade's eyes burned brighter as she raised the bottle. "*All* of them!"

All at once, in spite of her murky brain, Jacqueline

did understand. Everything made sense, like a puzzle clicking into place.

The mandrakes.

The recipe in the quarto: To Raise Demons from their Tales.

Tales, as in stories... not *tails* as in rear-end appendages.

Mrs. Kilmeade was about to raise vampires—and probably some other sorts of demons too—from every vampire book Jacqueline had in the store.

That was going to be *really, really* bad. She and her shop were going to be overrun by the undead... and there wasn't a vampire hunter in sight.

"Wait, please—!" She launched herself at the old woman vampire, but Mrs. Kilmeade raised a hand, backhanding her with a blow across the chest that was far too powerful for an old woman. Jacqueline flew backward, literally airborne.

She slammed into the wall and fell to the floor. Her breath was knocked out of her and her knees were shaking, but she pulled to her feet.

But it was too late. Mrs. Kilmeade was pouring the contents of the jar over the jumble of books on the floor as she chanted what was surely a spell. A poof of some sort of malevolent energy... a *pop!*... the acrid smell of burning paper and something else... something ugly... filled the air.

Jacqueline had to do *something*.

She staggered her way behind the counter where she'd left her Egala purse and reached inside, and immediately the cedar stake found her hand.

Just as she came out from behind the counter, Mrs. Kilmeade turned to face her. Triumph gleamed in those horrific red eyes, and her fangs thrust free, erupting from her mouth.

"And now for you, you interfering little twit." Mrs. Kilmeade's eyes captured Jacqueline's gaze.

All at once, Jacqueline felt as if she'd been submerged into a murky gray pool. Everything turned sluggish and slow. She couldn't feel her appendages. She couldn't pull her gaze away. She couldn't speak or think... She was suspended in time...

She wavered there, trying to fight her way free, trying to yank her gaze from the trap of glowing red eyes...

She was stuck. Trapped. Time stopped...

Suddenly, from beyond the depths of the murky pool, she heard a sound. A loud noise.

There was a rush of activity around her, and the murkiness eased, then snapped as Mrs. Kilmeade's burning red connection to Jacqueline's eyes was severed.

Jacqueline blinked, realized she'd sagged against the counter, and now gripped it with her hand. When she came fully back to herself, she found herself in a horrific scene.

There were vampires. Everywhere.

Every *kind* of vampire from every kind of tale she could imagine.

She recognized Black Dagger Brotherhood vampires—not the sexy ones, but the evil ones. Vampires from Rice's Children of Darkness, from Sookie Stackhouse's Louisiana, from the Jane Austen-era Gardella series. There were Templar vampires from Philly, minions of Spike's from the Buffyverse, evil vampires from Pope's Watchers trilogy, and others from Reine's Artifact Hunters and *The Vampire Diaries*. There were some Jacqueline couldn't identify—and didn't want to.

And they were all in her bookshop.

All with fangs and glittering, evil eyes. Some

looked like they might sparkle in the sunlight... but the malevolence nevertheless gleamed from their expressions.

Just as she was certain her life was about to end, that this wonderful, crazy experiment of Three Tomes was over, there was a loud flash and explosion at the front door.

It slammed open, and amid the resultant burst of smoke, the three crones surged inside. At the same time, Jacqueline saw a figure hurtle over the railing of the tea room stairway and land in the midst of the throngs of undead.

Evaline Stoker had arrived.

And right behind her was Van Helsing, lumbering down the stairs, stake in hand.

But the vampire hunters were severely outnumbered. Despite Evaline's skill—she spun, twisted, leaped, and lunged—she was only one person. And Van Helsing wasn't nearly as athletic, although he certainly seemed as determined. There were dozens of vampires, dozens of different sorts of demonic creatures.

And they were all from different books, different worlds... different mythologies. How did you know *how* to kill any of them? One might die from a stake to the heart, while the other needed to be beheaded. Still another might need a metal weapon to be slain, and another—who knew?

They were all different. Each from a unique fictional world.

How would they fight them back? How?

All at once, something—someone?—slammed into Jacqueline. She tumbled to the floor and was followed by a heavy, strong creature that crushed her flat. Her scream was muffled as her face crashed into the ground. Powerful, clawed fingers curled around her shoulder, yanking back, bowing her spine so it arched up and back.

And then—the sharp, ugly plunge of fangs into her neck.

Jacqueline screamed again and tried to fight herself away, but she was trapped, and the sudden bursting of blood roaring free from her vein shocked and weakened her. She'd dropped the stake and had nothing to save herself.

Suddenly, the weight was gone, she was free, and a thick, heavy cloud of putrid-smelling ash rained over her. Coughing, sobbing a little, she rolled over and scrambled to her feet as Evaline somersaulted away to spin and face yet another undead.

Jacqueline staggered to the wall for stability, blood streaming down her neck as she looked out over the melee. It was terrifying the way more and more undead and demons appeared after each one poofed into ash or slumped to the ground as an undead corpse, depending on their particular mythology. There was a head that rolled across the floor, with eyes wide and tongue distended.

Some of the undead were even attacking each other, for those who'd been raised by Dory Kilmeade were simply rabid, feral, evil creatures who were bent on destruction.

Evaline was everywhere, a flurry of movement and skirts, wooden stake and slashing metal blade. Van Helsing worked methodically, employing a silver stake with precise movements but without the frenetic energy of his partner. He warded off the undead with a large silver cross and a braid of garlic. Jacqueline saw Zwyla, who towered over some but not all of the creatures, wielding a stake as well as shooting some sparks from her fingers.

Would sparks kill the undead? Jacqueline didn't know, didn't have the time to wonder.

Pietra stood on the stairway that led to the tea room, using her hands to create what looked like a barrier to the undead, for none of them seemed able to approach. Her face was set and shiny with perspiration.

Andromeda stood on a table, flinging stakes from across the room, one after the other, hitting some of the undead like the center of a target but missing just as many as she nailed. Jacqueline didn't know where the stakes were coming from, but Andromeda seemed to have an unending supply, even if her aim wasn't perfect.

Jacqueline wanted to do something—*needed* to do something to save her shop and save her town—but what? She wasn't fast or strong, and she certainly didn't have any way of shooting sparks from her fingertips, despite her little demonstration earlier. She saw her stake on the floor and swooped down to pick it up.

Was there something upstairs she could use from the New Age room that might help drive back the undead?

Holding her stake at the ready, mimicking the grip she'd seen on *Buffy*, Jacqueline started to ease along the edge of the melee in an effort to get to the stairs. She hoped she could get past Pietra.

Then suddenly a better thought struck her.

The cellar. The cellar, with its sacred earth and pure holy water... and where the cedar lived. The cedar that had given her the very stake she—

Jacqueline stifled a shriek as she came face to face

with a vampire; she had no idea what kind. She didn't have time to think—she just struck out.

The feel of her stake driving into the torso of another being was sickening and horribly satisfying at the same time. The world slowed to nearly a halt as her pike slammed through the bone of the vampire's chest. How could she be strong enough to do that? she thought murkily, gagging in the back of her mouth.

The vampire froze, just as the world did, and his face went into a shocked and bewildered expression... and then he was just *gone*. In a large, nasty poof of thick gray ash.

Jacqueline managed not to vomit as she staggered away, bumping into the sales counter. She was about to turn away when she caught sight of her Egala tote, still on the shelf beneath the computers. She snatched it up, then ducked and began to edge her way toward the hall that led to the back of the shop and the cellar.

There were undead back here as well, most of them fighting with each other, many of them in the genre rooms. She hurried along, hoping none of them would notice her as fresh blood, even though her neck was still bleeding. But there was so much blood scent in the air that it probably didn't matter...

What had Evaline said about treating vampire bites?

Ah yes... holy water. Salted holy water.

Downstairs. In the cellar. The water running through the stream.

Jacqueline didn't know how she made it down the hall through the ongoing battle without being noticed or stopped, but she didn't pause to think about it. She kept going, her bag bumping comfortingly against her side.

At last she got to the door that led to the cellar

stairs and quickly slipped through the opening, hoping none of the undead noticed. Closing the door behind her, she turned on the light and rushed down into the shadowy space.

The first time she'd come down here, the Wicked Witch of the West had brought her. It had been a terrifying moment in the creepy cellar, and at the time, Jacqueline believed there was a high likelihood she wasn't going to come back up. But it all turned out, and now she found the space welcoming and unique because she understood its purpose.

Even now, with the sounds of fighting above, she felt a frisson of energy sizzle over her shoulders and down to her fingertips and toes... and a sense of calm overtaking her as she went toward the tiny stream of water that wound through the floor.

She should have made the time to create her own protection amulet, here in this space. But it was too late, and now—

"Well, well, what have we here?"

Jacqueline spun.

Dory Kilmeade (Jacqueline couldn't really think of her as "Mrs." any longer) stood there at the bottom of the steps. Her eyes flamed an evil red, and her fangs were long and distended. Her slender nose seemed to quiver as her attention fell on the side of Jacqueline's neck that had been bitten.

Jacqueline was still holding her stake, and she tightened her grip on it. She clearly remembered the power behind the woman's blow. Dory might look like a harmless, skinny senior citizen that would blow away in a stiff wind, but she was powerful.

"What do you want?" Jacqueline said, not only wondering, but also trying to buy time so she could make a plan.

Being trapped down here with the most powerful vampire had *not* been the plan.

"Why, I want what everyone wants—power. Immortality. Pleasure." Dory smiled, running her tongue along the teeth between her jutting fangs.

"You've already got immortality—and by the way, not everyone wants to live forever," Jacqueline replied. "I certainly don't."

"Oh, yes, immortality I have. But a little more power wouldn't be out of order, now, would it?" replied the vampire. "And I did want to thank you for hosting my dear little mandrakes. It was kind of you to allow me to use your garden—the soil there is very powerful. Without it, I would never have been able to make my potions."

"The potion you poured all over the vampire books," Jacqueline said. "To bring them all out of the stories. But you didn't really think it through. Because once those vampires are destroyed—slain, staked, beheaded, whatever—and they don't go back into the books, their stories will disappear... and then what do you think will happen to the vampires who are left? If their stories disappear, then they could never have been created... and so they'll disappear as well. And you'll be right back to where you started."

It was too bad Dory wasn't from a book.

She was shaking her head, a sly smile on her face that was made even more unpleasant by the fangs jutting out. "Ah, you see, I know more about how these things work than you realize. I was telling you the truth when I said I knew about the strange things going on here at your little bookshop... and how powerful the place is. How powerful *you* are. Or could be.

"And that is why, when I raised those demons from their tales—such a quaint turn of phrase, don't you think?—I didn't pull any named characters from them. Just the nameless minions—the evil, irredeemable ones, of course—who won't matter if they don't return to the books because they don't play any specific role. In other words, the stories don't rely on them. They're as plentiful and anonymous as the orcs in *The Lord of the Rings*."

As Dory explained this, Jacqueline's heart sank. The woman was right. She made good sense. Jacqueline didn't know for *certain* that was how it worked, but it seemed logical. And it was true—she hadn't noticed any specific vampires coming out of the books. No Lestat, no Lilith the Dark, no Kurt Barlow—no Count Dracula, for that matter.

"So you're bringing all of these vampires to life, so to speak... to, what? Create an army of minions so you can— Please don't say rule the world." Jacqueline should have been more nervous, and later she would wonder why she hadn't been, but she simply wasn't. Perhaps it was the comforting grip of the stake in her hand and the heavy sag of her tote, or even the gentle trundle of running water that gave her confidence.

Even so, she was acutely aware of the battle raging above them that somehow she had to find a way to help.

Dory laughed. "I *like* you. You've got a bit of a snarky side, don't you? Anyway, ruling the world would take far too much effort—especially at my age. And you've always got to be watching your back for assassination attempts and coups and so on. No, I just want to be able to live comfortably and protected. Waited on and served—you know. The lap of luxury. Hence the undead minions who will all answer to me."

"How will you manage that?" asked Jacqueline,

still genuinely curious. "After all, they all came out of different books and they're all completely different—mythologies, worlds, powers, creators, and masters. That is... if there are any left after Evaline and Van Helsing are through with them."

"Why, I'll have their books, of course. In my permanent custody." Dory spread her spindly fingers. "They'll have no choice but to answer to me."

Jacqueline couldn't argue with that.

"And," Dory said, "I'll have the bookshop too and can continue to raise demons from their tales"—she smiled over the turn of phrase once more—"whenever I want and from any book I want, because you'll either join me—"

"Fat chance," Jacqueline scoffed.

"I can make you into a lovely undead, and there are many benefits aside from immortality, you know—"

"Nope," Jacqueline said. "No immortality and bloodsucking for me."

"Or you'll be dead."

CHAPTER 19

J acqueline knew that was the logical outcome—or at least, what Dory had intended—but even so, hearing it said so bluntly did send an ugly dart of fear to her middle.

Keep her talking so you can think.

That was what they always did in books, right?

"What about Lucy Frontera?" Jacqueline asked even as her mind scrabbled around for an escape. Oh *why* hadn't she made that protection amulet?

The spell was in that big, cinder-block book, way up in her—

Suddenly, her Egala tote felt *very* heavy.

"Lucy Frontera! Why, she *stole* one of my mandrakes," said Dory, her eyes flaming.

"She said she found it at the farmers' market," Jacqueline said, surreptitiously feeling the tote bag against her and, yes, holy crap, it felt like a brick had been shoved inside.

Not that that did much good for her now; she wasn't going to have the chance to open it up, find the spell—no, the *recipe*—and make a damned protection amulet right now while a stupid septuagenarian vampire had her in her sights.

Still, it was a little comforting knowing the book was here. Maybe she could swing the bag at Dory and knock her over with the brick-book.

"I had the mandrakes there with me. I was going to plant them in your courtyard while everyone was on the front side of the shop, walking down the street. One of them must have fallen out of my bag when I set it down," Dory said. "No one else would have noticed. Only Lucy. And I wanted my mandrake back! She had no right to take it. I saw her looking at the ones I'd planted in your garden."

"But you didn't kill her. You only attacked her," Jacqueline said.

"I was interrupted. Someone came by. It was the daytime, you know."

"It is interesting," Jacqueline went on conversationally, "that you were able to go about in the daytime. What sort of vampire *are* you?"

Dory gave her an unpleasant smile. "Wouldn't you like to know."

Another thought struck Jacqueline, and her whole body erupted with prickles. "You called and complained about the graveyard... about the dirt getting dug up. Was that camouflage for your own activity, or were you just being a busybody old lady in order to divert attention?"

Dory grinned, showing those freaky fangs. "Oh, you *are* a smart one, aren't you? Comes from reading all those books, I suppose. Surely you noticed the name on the gravestone."

Jacqueline remembered the name very well. "Renfield... Dorothy Renfield, I think it was... *Ohh*, that's *you*, isn't it? Dory is a nickname for Dorothy. But...

Kilmeade—did you marry or just change your name? Any relation to the Renfield in *Dracula*?"

Dory's satisfied grin told Jacqueline what she needed to know. That there was some connection to the character in Bram Stoker's book.

Which also gave her more information about what type of vampire Dory likely was. Able to go about in the day, but reduced powers... able to slip into buildings through locked doors... needing the soil from her own gravesite in order to sleep safely.

And to destroy her, Dory would probably have to be beheaded and staked and stuffed in the mouth with garlic.

That was a job for Van Helsing... so where was he?

"Very well... I can see you've figured it out. Renfield was my father."

Jacqueline shook her head. "But how is that possible? He's a literary character... He can't... couldn't... " Her voice trailed off.

Hell, she didn't know what was possible with literary characters coming out of books, did she? Maybe Renfield had, in fact, knocked up a real person here in Button Cove—or anywhere—sometime in the past during a visit from his book. After all, Jacqueline didn't think the characters-coming-out-of-books thing had started only with her. Surely Cuddy Stone, the original owner of the shop, had experienced it as well.

Dory was watching her with an amused expression. "I wouldn't worry too much about it, Jacqueline. You're not going to be around to wonder on it very much longer."

"So you think you're going to take over my bookshop when I'm gone," said Jacqueline, desperately trying to delay things to keep herself alive.

"Right. It makes a lot of sense. There's a lot of energy here," Dory said, spreading her arms around to encompass the space. "Only waiting to be harnessed. Not to mention enough horror novels to keep me staffed with countless minion servants for a long time, *and* it's the perfect place to grow my mandrakes. Now, enough talking. I do need to get back upstairs."

Her eyes glowed red, and Jacqueline felt a stab of real fear in her belly as, somehow, the vein in her neck leaped violently. What had slowed to a trickle of blood suddenly surged into more of a flow, as if Dory's gaze had pulled it free. Blood trailed along Jacqueline's collarbone and began to seep into the front of her shirt.

The stake she still held felt utterly useless.

"H-how did you get to Cary Whitehall?" Jacqueline asked desperately, backing up a little bit. Not that she had anywhere to go. The cellar had only the single entrance, and it was behind Dory.

"Oh, you know how it is—an old woman who needs help... who's going to think twice about it?" Dory shrugged. "Especially at two o'clock in the morning. It's the best thing about looking the way I do. The number of unsuspecting people I've fed on over the years because they were being good little citizens and helping an old lady... " She cackled.

"But why the fake fangs?" Jacqueline said, taking another step backward. She wondered how long it would be before she stepped in the little creek.

Then all at once it struck her.

Vampires—the Dracula type of vampires—*could not cross running water.*

She glanced behind her. The creek was right there. One more step...

Dory laughed again. "The fake fangs were simply a way to divert attention. I knew there was a lot of talk about vampires around. And so I created misdirection."

Jacqueline took a big step back, and her foot landed on the edge of the little creek, half in the water. She stumbled and fell, losing her grip on the stake... but she landed on the other side of the water with the heavy tote.

Her foot was wet and she didn't have her stake, but she was now separated from Dory by running water.

She hoped like hell it was enough running water to matter...

"Why, you... " Dory's eyes fired up red again as she looked down at the tidy little stream, then back up at her. "You little *sneak*."

Apparently it was enough. Jacqueline was still on the ground, and she scrabbled on the stone floor to get a grip and pull herself to her feet when she realized...

The water was special... filled with energy. Good energy—sacred energy, she knew, because she'd used it to make the protection amulet. Holy water! And so was the soil, exposed in a small circle in the middle of the floor. It, too, was sacred.

If only she had a vessel to pull up some of the water—

She reached in the tote bag, and there was a cup, right there on top. *Thank you, Egala.*

Without thinking, she scooped up a cupful of the running water and whipped it across the creek at Dory.

The vampire shrieked and held up her hands as the water splashed over her face and torso. Jacqueline did it again, quickly, before the woman could recover, tossing a second glass of water at her and wincing a little at the agonized cries.

Then, just as speedily, she turned and dragged the

cup through the dark, loamy soil as Dory continued to scream, holding her hands over her face.

Jacqueline flung the cup of dirt at Dory too, and was gratified when the vampire shrieked anew and sagged to the ground as if in mortal pain.

Wow.

Jacqueline felt a rush of lightheaded relief—or maybe it was from loss of blood. Holy crap, she was bleeding like a stuck pig.

Salted holy water, Evaline had told her. *To heal vampire bites.*

Jacqueline had holy water, but what about salt?

She reached into the bag and pulled out the cinder-block tome. With the big book came a small packet of salt. Still eyeing the collapsed, sobbing Dory, she quickly mixed some salt with a cup of holy water and dumped it over her wound.

Jacqueline barely held back her own shriek. It felt like she was on fire. Evaline hadn't told her it would feel like she'd freaking *branded* herself!

The bleeding stopped almost immediately, even as the wound throbbed with a searing pain.

All right, Jacqueline thought, panting a little. *Now what?*

She'd been down here for maybe ten minutes, though it had seemed like a lifetime. Everything was still crazy above—she could hear the pitched battle, and it had not waned.

Dory was still in agony on the floor, and Jacqueline eyed the stake. Could she ram it home right now, while the woman was incapacitated? What good would it do if she was a Dracula-type of vampire?

Jacqueline started to crawl to her feet for the stake and nudged the cinder-block book next to her.

It had appeared in her tote because she'd regretted

not making a protection amulet. Did that mean she should try to make one right now?

That didn't seem right, and she was certain she didn't have all the ingredients here—although, she thought, looking at the tote, they'd probably show up if she needed them.

But something nudged at her.

That wasn't it.

She didn't think.

Still eyeing Dory, Jacqueline opened up the big book. She was compelled to look in it for some reason.

Where was the recipe for the protection amulet that she'd used?

Aware—so aware—of the time flying by, of the horror happening upstairs, of the fact that she was hiding away and doing nothing to help, she flipped through the crackling, ancient pages—all the while keeping an eye on Dory, who was still holding her face and keening on the floor. The woman's sobs had lessened a little. Still, the vampire couldn't get to Jacqueline from the other side of the little stream, so she was safe for now.

She gritted her teeth, feeling a wave of guilt as she heard the sounds of thudding and thumping, cries of pain and triumph above her, and wondered if she should scoop up a large cup of holy water and go back upstairs to help.

But there were so many vampires and demons up there... so many of them that she didn't see how that would help.

The book.

Something told her to look in the book.

So she kept flipping through, her hands shaking, her ears tuned to the sounds above. Someone screamed—a woman—and Jacqueline felt a shiver. It sounded like Pietra.

Hurry, hurry... what do I do?

She found the recipe she'd used for the protection amulet, but when she paused there, something happened and the next page flipped over before she was ready. Apparently, that wasn't what she was meant to see.

She turned two more pages and then a title jumped out at her: *To Send Back Demons.*

Ohh.

That was it. She was meant to see this spell—no, recipe—that could... send demons back.

Put them back in their books?

Jacqueline squinted at the faded printing, wishing for her reading glasses, then remembered and reached into her tote. Along with the glasses came the tea bags Andromeda had given her the other day, their strings wrapped around the spectacles.

She put on the glasses and looked at the recipe.

Holy water

Sacred earth

Silver sage

Lemon Balm

Cinnamon

Combine with all pure intentions, stirring nine times to the left, nine to the right, then three to the left, all the while invoking the Good.

Then add five drops of Blood sacrificed willingly. Spill or sprinkle onto demon origins.

As Jacqueline stared at the list of ingredients, she felt the hair on the back of her neck lift and prickle, and she looked over at the tea bags Andromeda had given her.

She was pretty damned sure they contained lemon

balm because she remembered Andromeda listing off the ingredients. And sage too, because of the smudging.

But where was she going to get cinnamon? And blood sacrificed willingly?

Jacqueline picked up the tea bags and sniffed experimentally.

She smelled cinnamon.

She frowned at the bags of dried herbs, at the heavy tome, at the tote, at the world.

In a book or movie, this would be called a *deus ex machina*, or "the Hand of God," as the Greeks would call it: something that came from out of nowhere to save the day.

"It's not completely from out of nowhere," she said, looking up and around at an invisible audience. "Andi gave me the tea bags, and they *are* for purging— which makes sense, since I want to purge the shop, and the world, from those demons. And I don't have any idea where to get a willing blood sacrifice, so it's not like a done deal. And I don't have a spoon to stir with, either."

She looked back at the book and down at the spell. She did have everything she needed right here, except for the blood sacrifice...

She looked down at her hand. Could she just cut herself and use that blood? It would be willing, but how would it be a sacrifice?

As she wavered about what to do, she looked over. Dory had ceased moaning, and now she sat there, looking over at Jacqueline with a very, *very* malevolent expression.

"I'll fix you," she said, pulling herself to her feet. Her silver-white hair hung in straggles around her face. "Oh, I'll fix you good, you little bitch." Her eyes blazed red and her fangs were once more distended. "You'll wish you'd never been born."

She spun and started for the steps, rushing up them with surprising speed, leaving Jacqueline alone and safe... and terrified.

Dory was going back upstairs where the fight was going on, where Evaline and Van Helsing were hopefully still alive (Jacqueline didn't think about what it would mean if one or both of them had been killed) and battling with the demons.

What was Dory going to do? Bring down an army of demon vampires? Some of them *could* cross running water. It just depended on the type of vampire...

Or they could just sit there and wait her out. Blocking her exit.

Jacqueline surged to her feet. She had to get out of here *now*, before Dory came back and trapped her.

But first...

She quickly, quickly scooped up soil and water, haphazardly measuring them as well as she could into the cup. She dunked the tea bags in the concoction and felt around in her tote for the spoon that should be there...

But nothing came to her hand.

What the... ?

Fine.

Jacqueline could find something else to stir with— then she needed a willing blood sacrifice, and so she'd have to take it from herself.

But she had to get out of here first so she wasn't trapped.

As she stepped over the little stream, Jacqueline saw her cedar stake on the floor. She snatched it up and ran to the stairs, careful not to spill the cup with its concoction. If she was going to pour or sprinkle it over "the demon's origin"—which obviously were the books—she'd need quite a bit of it. She wished the cup was bigger, but...

She was nearly to the top of the stairs when she tripped.

The cup slipped, and she barely managed to hold on to it, though its contents sloshed and spilled. Panting, sweating, nearly sobbing with frustration and fear, Jacqueline looked into the cup. Two-thirds full. It would have to do.

Blood sacrificed willingly. It's got to be me. I've got to try.

She pushed open the door and came out of the basement stairwell into hell.

CHAPTER 20

Oh my God.

It was worse than she'd imagined.

There were vampires everywhere, battling in the hall, in the rooms, in the front of the shop. Screams filled the air. Jacqueline smelled blood—mortal blood as well as demon blood. She heard cries and screams and prayed to whoever might be listening that none of her friends were injured.

She huddled in the doorway, so far unnoticed. How would she ever manage this? What was she going to do?

Blood sacrificed willingly.

But first she had to stir. All right.

No spoon, but she had the stake given to her by a sacred cedar tree. That had to count for something. Maybe it would even help with the potency of the potion.

Jacqueline tried to clear her mind and make it pure and fill it with goodness (really hard to do when there were demons of death all around her), and she stirred—

Nine to the left.

Nine to the right.

Three to the left.

—all the while picturing white light because she couldn't think of any other way to imagine goodness and purity, and she was hella distracted.

When she'd finished it, she looked down at the concoction. It looked exactly the same.

But now, blood sacrificed willingly.

She edged away from the cellar door and stairway and ducked into a corner near the back entrance, still apparently unnoticed by the brawling demons. The cedar stake had a very sharp point, but the moment she punctured her skin, the smell of blood would draw attention from the undead.

Well, here goes nothing, she thought, and raked the tip of the cedar stake over her left palm.

It was so sharp it hardly hurt, but holy crap, suddenly there was *a lot* of blood.

It burst from her palm like an undammed river, and the shock of so much bright red lifeblood pouring out of her palm so suddenly was frightening.

Jacqueline held her hand over the cup and allowed the blood to flow into it.

Nothing happened.

Should she stir again? The directions hadn't said so, but...

She dipped the cedar stake inside and stirred. When she removed it, the stake dripped with a thick, viscous liquid.

That was good, she thought.

She hesitated, then used the stake tip to sprinkle a couple of droplets over her bleeding palm. Then, without waiting to see what would happen, she started to slink down the corridor, wondering how far she'd get before an undead noticed her.

Not far. Two steps before one of the red-eyed demons spun on her.

Before he could lunge, Jacqueline stifled a shriek and struck out with her stake. She wasn't even close to striking him in the heart—she got him in the arm—but nonetheless, the vampire cried out and spun away. The scent of smoke and burning flesh filled her nostrils. Well, the potion—or at least the holy water and sacred earth—had done *something*.

But still.

Jacqueline's heart thudded unpleasantly. There was no way she was going to get safely to the front of the bookshop by threading her way through the melee. But she could go around...

She flung herself out of the back door and breathed in the fresh spring air—so clean and welcoming after the horror inside.

Oh, yes. *Thank you. Thank you!*

She started to hurry to the side of the building, meaning to go around to the front where the pile of vampire books had been... and she stopped.

She could go.

She could *leave*.

She could just run and run and run... back to Chicago, back *somewhere...*

Away.

She could simply be away from all of this and never have to worry about Danvers and Hudson again. Or vampires, or any other horrible creatures writers had dreamt up over the years. Good grief, what if Dory brought Hannibal Lecter out of his book?

It was a split second of thought, of consideration, of *temptation*. She might have even taken a step toward the parking lot, toward her Subaru Outback parked there, waiting to take her to safety.

Then she shoved away the lure of freedom and security and, hand over the top of the cup, ran around to the front of the shop, stake stuck under her arm.

No. There was no way she was leaving her friends here in this battle, this melee of malevolence and evil.

And how long had she been gone? How was Evaline? Van Helsing? Were they all right?

The crones?

Heart in her throat, Jacqueline reached the shop and burst through the front door. The first thing she saw was the stack of vampire books still on the floor.

Then she saw Zwyla, bloodied and sagging against the wall, still fighting valiantly but with far less energy than before.

Andromeda was pinned against the wall by two undead, and just as Jacqueline would have flung some droplets of potion at them, Van Helsing staggered up and managed to shove his metal pike into the back of one of them. The undead screamed and sagged to his knees. Evaline swooped in with her blade and sliced it across his neck, then somersaulted away.

There were two men Jacqueline had never seen before in the melee, and they weren't vampires; they held stakes and were calmly and efficiently dispatching the undead, even as they were swamped and swarmed by them. One of them was dark-haired with cool eyes that for some reason reminded her of Max, the cat. And the other had amber-colored hair and eyes—exactly the same as Sebastian—and an insouciant manner to his fighting.

But she didn't have time to wonder about where they'd come from and who they were, for Pietra was nowhere to be seen. Jacqueline's heart fell. She tasted dust.

Not Pietra.

She was only feet away from the books. If she could pour some of the potion on them and see what happened...

"*Yaaaaaaah!*" came a deep, guttural cry.

It was Evaline, leaping from the sales counter onto a pile of undead on the floor.

That was when Jacqueline saw what they'd been piled on.

Pietra.

No, no, no...

But she didn't have time to think about that now...

Jacqueline ducked and dodged, somehow snaking her way to the pile of books. No one seemed to notice her, and her palm had stopped bleeding.

She knew the potion had repelled a vampire in the back hallway, but that might only have been because of the holy water and the sacred earth. It might not be enough to send the demons back, but she had to try.

She dropped her hand into the cup, then brought it out and used her fingers to sprinkle the water all over the books. They were tiny droplets, but they raised little puffs of smoke, giving Jacqueline some confidence.

She sprinkled more, taking care not to spill it all...

More puffs of smoke... were some of the vampires reacting? She looked around. The sounds of fighting seemed a little quieter... but nothing had changed. Nothing.

What had she done wrong? The ingredients were all there... the blood sacrificed willingly, right? That was the only thing she wasn't certain about...

Then, suddenly, she knew. She *realized...*

With a rush of certainty, she took the stake once more, and this time, she sliced it down her arm.

Her dark, rich lifeblood sprang free, and she held it over the cup again.

As her vital fluid dripped into the cup, Jacqueline felt the vessel heat. It became so hot she wanted to drop the cup, but she couldn't do that.

But at least she knew that she'd done it right this time.

Thinking pure white-light thoughts, she began to pour the very thick, dark liquid over the pile of books Dory had used to call forth the demonic undead.

As she poured, there was great sizzling and smoking—not only from the books themselves, but from the undead as well. It appeared they were simply evaporating, disappearing. *Poofing* into nothing like bubbles bursting.

The cup burned her fingers, but she held on, gritting her teeth against the pain, making certain to drip on every single book, and then, for good measure, she poured the last dregs over the few vampire novels Dory hadn't dropped on the floor.

At last, with a cry of relief, she allowed the empty cup to fall from her hand and tumble to the floor.

She'd done everything she could, and now—

Suddenly, the front door of the shop opened and Massermey burst inside, followed by Nadine, Suzette, and Gerry Dawdle, of all people.

"Jacqueline!" Massermey cried when he saw her.

She gaped at him, realized what he was seeing— vampires and demons everywhere, spontaneously disintegrating into the air with weird pops—and then, all at once, she lunged toward him.

It was a kiss of victory that she planted on his bearded and mustached lips, as well as a kiss of distraction. And pent-up curiosity and desire too, to be honest.

To her relief, his arms went around her automatically, and he met her lips without hesitation, even in the midst of the craziness.

That was part of what made that kiss *very, very* hot. It was so hot, Jacqueline thought she might disintegrate just as the vampires were doing. She could hear them popping away, beyond the roaring in her ears from the rush of heat and pleasure from soft, mobile lips and the sensual brush of facial hair.

But the kiss didn't last more than a few seconds, for he pulled his mouth away though he still held her close.

"What... Jacqueline... " He sounded rough and distracted, and yet he was obviously determined to put on his cop hat.

Pop! Pop!

"Just kiss me, Miles. It'll be a lot easier for you to handle if you don't have to see all this."

He looked around, then back down at her. His gaze was stunned and shocked—she certainly hoped part of it was from the kissing—and he gave a little groan. "I think you might be right."

CHAPTER 21

The only snafu with distracting Miles Massermey while all of the vampires were disappearing was that they didn't *all* disappear.

When she was vaguely aware that everything had gone quiet around them, Jacqueline gently, *reluctantly* extricated herself from Massermey's embrace and talented mouth.

The shop was silent. Everyone was gone—everyone except for Dory Kilmeade, who was lying on the floor.

The septuagenarian vampire had a metal stake through her heart, but she hadn't poofed into nothing. Her mouth was stuffed with garlic, and Jacqueline knew that in order for Dory to be completely and utterly destroyed, someone had to behead her...

Which really couldn't be done in front of a police detective, now, could it?

"Jacqueline... " Massermey said in a strange voice. He was looking around too, blinking slowly, his gaze soft and dazed as if he'd just awakened from some deep sleep.

She took his arm and squeezed (*very* nice!). He

looked at her, and she saw all sorts of warring expressions on his face. Shock, disbelief, bewilderment, even a little anger and... fear?

"Okay, so... where do I begin?" Her voice quavered.

But Massermey was already kneeling next to Dory, whose eyes were open and wheeling about. She didn't seem able to move, but she certainly wasn't dead.

"I can't get a pulse," he said in a voice that was hard and tight. "And I can't take this out"—he gestured to the stake— "or she'll bleed to death." He looked up at her, and there was something in his eyes that made her take a step back. "Jacqueline, I don't know what the *hell* is going on here, but this woman—"

She said it quickly: "Is a vampire, Miles. She's a vampire."

He scoffed, his blue eyes hardening to stony chips. "Jacqueline, I—"

"Look," she said, kneeling on the other side of Dory. She used her stake to carefully open the woman's mouth, demonstrating that there were fangs there. Real fangs. Fangs that still had traces of blood on them.

As she did so, Dory's eyes blazed bright, burning red, and she heaved helplessly beneath the stake that pinned her to the ground.

Massermey said something under his breath and fell back from his squat, landing on his butt.

"I know," Jacqueline said, truly sympathizing with him. "I *know*. But there's no denying it." She pointed to her neck. "See?" The bite marks there weren't technically from Dory, but it didn't matter.

"Jacqueline," he said again, seemingly unable to form any other words. "I don't... I don't know what to do about this." He was still sitting on the floor.

"Yeah. I get it. But she's got to be disposed of, you know. Completely, um... "

"But how am I going to write this up?" he said, *still* sitting there. "I don't even believe it myself."

She shook her head. "You don't have to write it up, Miles. Just... pretend it didn't happen."

"But we have a *body*, and I can't... "

"No, ve von't be haffing a body anymore," said a familiar voice.

Jacqueline looked up to see Van Helsing and Evaline making their way down the stairs from the coffee shop. To her relief, neither of them showed any signs of injury at all.

She didn't have the time to wonder how that had happened—for she'd seen Evaline with blood streaming over her face, and Van Helsing bloodied and bruised as well.

"Who are you?" Massermey rose, eyeing the big sword Evaline carried.

"Vhy, I am Professor Van—"

But Jacqueline quickly intervened. "They're vampire hunters. And they'll take care of Dory." She suspected there was only so much weird shit that Massermey could handle, and the simplest explanation was the best.

Massermey stared at Van Helsing and Evaline, then turned his attention to Jacqueline. That shocked, vacant, glazed look was back, and she couldn't take credit for any of it at the moment.

"Look, why don't we step outside for a minute. Get some fresh air," Jacqueline suggested, taking his arm.

For a minute, she thought he was going to be a stubborn, blockheaded policeman and resist, but then he heaved a great sigh and allowed her to gently tow him to the front door.

Once they were outside, she pulled him into her arms for a comforting embrace, keeping him facing the street instead of what was happening inside the shop.

"This isn't real," he said numbly, resting his head on top of hers. "Is it?"

"Which part?" she said with a little smile, pulling away to look up at him. "The part where we kiss again?"

His lips twitched in an almost-smile, then his eyes closed and he pulled her gently against his chest once more. "I'm definitely looking forward to more kissing, Jacqueline—and soon, but—"

"There's no explanation for it, Miles. I'm sorry. I don't have one. I've just given up on trying to figure out the why of—of what happened"—no need to imply there was anything else weird going on in Three Tomes—"and am just going with the flow."

He heaved another sigh, and she felt him relax a little more. "All right. I'll try."

After a few moments, she judged it was safe enough to go back inside the shop. She took him by the hand, and Massermey followed, trailing behind her like a dazed person.

The shop was empty. Dory was gone; Evaline and Van Helsing had disappeared.

Nothing was left except the old, yellow- and red-embossed copy of *Dracula*, sitting on top of the pile of vampire books—now neatly rearranged as they had been. The book was closed.

～

"OKAY, so... I get most everything that happened, except for a few questions," said Suzette.

"But first, before we do that, we really do have to applaud Jacqueline for the way she distracted Massermey," Nadine said with a grin. She was holding a *very* large glass of red wine, and had just finished pouring some for Suzette and Jacqueline, as well as the ZAP Ladies.

All six of them were settled in Jacqueline's flat above the bookshop, and whatever injuries Pietra and the others might have had, they were completely healed—perhaps the injuries had been "popped" right out of existence, along with the undead that inflicted them.

"Well, I couldn't think of anything else do to—the last thing I wanted Massermey to do was jump in and get himself attacked by a vampire," Jacqueline said. She felt her cheeks heating as Nadine and Suzette grinned at her and Pietra giggled.

"All I can say is, well done, my dear. *Well done.* And I assume it was delightful?" said Suzette.

"Of course it was delightful," said Pietra gleefully. Her wine glass needed to be topped off already, and she held it out for Nadine. "What else would one expect   from   Detective   Put-His-Massive-Hands-On-Me—"

"It was more than delightful," Jacqueline replied, loud enough to drown out Pietra's comment, "and that's *all* I'm saying about it. We're not high school girls."

"We sure aren't. We're old bitches who like and appreciate good sex, and we rejoice when our friends get to have it," said Nadine. "*However* they get to have it."

"*Exactly*," said Zwyla. She lifted her glass in a toast, and all of them joined her. "And may that never change."

"Hear, hear!"

"Speaking of sex and friends having it," Jacqueline said, looking at Nadine. "I noticed you had Gerry Dawdle with you when you burst into the shop."

"Oh," Nadine said. Her cheeks turned bright red. "Well, that was just an accident because Suzette and I went to track down Massermey when everything was going haywire inside the store, and we ran into Gerry's hearse on the way. He insisted on coming with us— and I swear, I saw him carrying a stake." Her eyes were wide and a little dreamy.

"Wouldn't surprise me," said Jacqueline. "After all, doesn't he ride around with ghosts in his hearse?"

"He does."

"Anyway, it looks like whatever bumps in the road the two of you had have evened out," said Suzette, giving Nadine a look.

"Well, we're just taking things really slowly because—"

"No, no, no, you don't need to give us an explanation. Just do what you do and I promise I'll stop teasing you," Suzette said. "All right, Jacqueline, let's hear it. I need some details and loose ends figured out."

"Like?" Jacqueline took a sip from her own very large glass of wine.

"Like the fact that you made a potion," said Andromeda. She was sitting in one of the chairs that had miraculously appeared near the fireplace when the six of them gathered. Sebastian was sprawled on her lap, enjoying her long, leisurely stroking.

"I did," Jacqueline replied, feeling a spark of something zip through her. "And it worked! But at first I had it wrong."

She explained how she'd had to cut herself twice to get the "blood willingly sacrificed."

"So... why did it work the second time?" asked Nadine.

"Because I had the chance to leave—to get away, to just be off from the bookshop and everything here, and I chose not to. So I guess it was sort of a sacrifice to stay, and then I cut myself as part of it?" Jacqueline was looking at Zwyla as she spoke. The woman nodded and lifted her glass in tacit agreement.

Jacqueline smiled. That was what she'd *thought* had happened, but it was good to know for certain.

"All right, that makes sense. I'm glad you didn't leave us," said Nadine.

"Me too," said Suzette. "Even though weird-ass shit keeps happening here." She looked around, pretending (or maybe she wasn't pretending!) to be nervous as everyone laughed.

"What happened to Dory?" said Pietra.

Jacqueline explained the requirements to destroy a Dracula-type vampire, then said, "When Massermey and I were outside, Evaline and Van Helsing did what had to be done and lopped off her head—which I'm glad I didn't have to see. And then, as I understand it from Mrs. Hudson, Van Helsing took the head and Evaline took the body, and they each went back into their own books. So there is no way Dory Kilmeade can be put back together again."

"That would certainly do it," said Andromeda. "Brilliant thinking on their part."

Jacqueline frowned, looking at the spiky-haired woman as she remembered something else. "I hadn't seen Sebastian or Max around for a while. But I could have *sworn* there were two men I'd never seen before, fighting off the undead and... well, this is going to sound weird, but they reminded me a little of Max and

Sebastian. I don't know why, but for some reason it just stuck in my head... "

Andromeda shrugged and gave her a very neutral, very innocent look. Pietra giggled. And Zwyla lifted her glass for another sip, her long, dark eyes gleaming as she looked at Jacqueline.

There would be no answers from them. And Jacqueline probably thought it was all right.

"So everything is good—here, and with you and Massermey?" said Suzette. "He's not going to arrest you or anything?

"Things are good, and no, he's not going to put me in handcuffs," Jacqueline said to Pietra, whose eyes had gone bright and giddy. "He seemed almost relieved when we went back inside the shop and Mrs. Kilmeade was gone. I didn't ask him how he was going to file his report—that's really up to him. But since Dory doesn't have any family around here, no one would report her missing or notice her not being here anymore."

"Except the police station won't be getting daily phone calls from her," said Suzette, laughing.

"True dat," replied Jacqueline. She sipped from her wine. "There is one thing he's holding over my head, though," she said with a little smile.

"And that is... ?" prompted Nadine.

"Well, he pointed out that I had Luke Blackstone's final words all wrong. *I* thought he said, 'killed me... the vampire,' but he was really saying 'Kilmeade... the vampire.' He was trying to warn me, and I didn't get it. And for some reason, Massermey has fixated on that." She was laughing, though, because it was rather funny that the detective was focused on her having the vampire's identity wrong. It must mean he accepted there was a vampire after all.

Plus, she was rather looking forward to seeing him again and "discussing" it further.

"Well, at least he believes what he saw," said Suzette, echoing her thoughts.

"Exactly."

"So what's going to happen now?" asked Nadine.

"I have no idea," replied Jacqueline, settling back into her seat with a sigh. "But I've got a lot of work to do to put things back together downstairs."

"Oh, that?" Zwyla made a "pish" sound. "That's all being taken care of. Danvers and Hudson will have it set to rights by tomorrow morning."

Jacqueline could hardly believe her ears. "Wow. That would be amazing. I guess I can't bitch about them anymore, can I?"

"Well, I don't think you have to get crazy about things," said Pietra. "You can still complain about Danvers. It's basically required."

"So now, I guess all I have to do is wait for the next book to fall," Jacqueline said, laughing. "Whatever it is."

They all grinned and raised their glasses for one last toast: crones and friends, women all, fully secure in their friendships and support.

What more could anyone want?

BEFORE YOU GO...

~

Don't miss any news from Colleen, plus get a *free* short novel,
exclusive only to newsletter subscribers.

Subscribe to her monthly newsletter for sneak peeks, news, freebies, and behind-the-scenes looks at her projects.

Click here: cgbks.com/news

Prefer not to get messages in your email?
Sign up for SMS/Text messages and help keep your
inbox clear!

Just type in 38470 for the phone number,
and then type COLLEEN in the message space!

ABOUT THE AUTHOR

 **Colleen Gleason** is an award-winning, New York Times and USA Today best-selling author. She's written more than forty novels in a variety of genres—truly, something for everyone!

She loves to hear from readers, so feel free to find her online.

∼

Get SMS/Text alerts for any
New Releases or **Promotions!**

Text: **COLLEEN** to **38470**

(You will only receive a single message when Colleen has a new release or title on sale. *We promise.*)

∼

If you would like SMS/Text alerts for any **Events** or book signings Colleen is attending,
Text: **MEET** to **38470**

∼

Subscribe to Colleen's non-spam newsletter for other
updates, news, sneak peeks, and special offers!
http://cgbks.com/news

Connect with Colleen online:
www.colleengleason.com
books@colleengleason.com

ALSO BY COLLEEN GLEASON

Abandon the Night

Night Beckons

Night Forbidden

Night Resurrected

Tempted by the Night (only available to newsletter subscribers; sign up here: http://cgbks.com/news)

~

The Lincoln's White House Mystery Series

(writing as C. M. Gleason)

Murder in the Lincoln White House

Murder in the Oval Library

Murder at the Capitol

The Marina Alexander Adventure Novels

(writing as C. M. Gleason)

Siberian Treasure

Amazon Roulette

Sanskrit Cipher

~

The Phyllida Bright Mysteries

(writing as Colleen Cambridge)

Murder at Mallowan Hall (Oct 2021)

9 781648 393723